INQUISITIVE

INQUISITIVE

Stephen DG Frame

The
Book
Guild

First published in Great Britain in 2025 by
The Book Guild Ltd
Unit E2 Airfield Business Park,
Harrison Road, Market Harborough,
Leicestershire. LE16 7UL
Tel: 0116 2792299
www.bookguild.co.uk
Email: info@bookguild.co.uk
X: @bookguild

The manufacturer's authorised representative in the EU
for product safety is Authorised Rep Compliance Ltd,
71 Lower Baggot Street, Dublin D02 P593 Ireland (www.arccompliance.com)

This work is entirely fictitious and bears no resemblance to any persons living or dead.

Typeset in 11pt Minion Pro

Printed and bound by CPI Group (UK) Ltd, Croydon, CR0 4YY

ISBN 978 1835742 365

British Library Cataloguing in Publication Data.
A catalogue record for this book is available from the British Library.

For M and J, always.

1

MR STEALS BOOKS

Lottie wasn't sure where she was going but that suited her fine. The afternoon surrendered to the evening as she crossed from the new town into the old. She strode on, turning one corner after another until she stood at the entrance to a narrow lane. No one walked this lane. The few shops, dotted between anonymous doorways, were all closed.

Digging in her pocket, she drew out the item she'd found on the doormat of her flat that morning. A cream-coloured postcard embossed with three lines of text. *Mr Steals Books*, it said. *Rare and unusual.* And an address: *Gallowgate Lane.* Lottie held the card up so she could compare it with the street sign above her. She gave it a satisfied smile. "Found you."

The bookshop, she supposed, was a lost cause. *Probably closed by now. But this lane should lead to the Grass Market. Eventually. Find a cafe there, have a hot chocolate, chill out for a bit, and watch the people go by.*

She glanced around as a flush crept up her cheeks. *Did anyone see me standing here like a dumpling? Get a grip, girl. Okay, supposing it doesn't take me to the Grass Market? Then I keep turning left. That'll take me west. I'll get there eventually. Or I can turn back.* She smiled to herself. *Yeah, like that's going to happen.*

Walking on, she noticed how dark it had become. No streetlights on yet. No lights of any kind. Except for one, some way ahead, a shop front with a hanging sign she couldn't make out. She hurried on, eager to see more.

The sign above the door read, "Mr Steals Books." Lottie wrinkled up her nose. *Not just the card then? Poor lost apostrophe. And you, a bookshop.*

There was nothing on display in the window. Beyond the glass, drapes the colour of dark wine blocked any view of the inside. No sign to say if the shop was open or closed. The brass door handle was cold to the touch. The door fought back with a judder when she pushed her way in. Dust floated in the air. The musty smell of old paper haunted the place. A single light bulb cast a meagre glow.

"Wow," she whispered.

A wall of books faced her. Thick tomes, a full hand-span broad. Thin volumes no wider than a fingernail. There was no order to them, no arrangement by subject or author. At the far ends of the shelves, to the left and right, archways offered up portals to further discovery.

"Okay, not your average bookshop but give it a chance."

The thick silence swallowed up her words. She wandered to the left, her gaze meandering up and down, picking out titles. *Notes on the Elder Races, The Lives of the*

Great Makers, Before Hydrogen – The Negative Elements, Fifty Uses for Bone.

Again and again, she reached out, eager to see what some of the books contained, but something stayed her hand – the feeling that the next one might be more intriguing. Until she found herself at the opening at the end of the row. Through it, the shelving arrangement was repeated, floor to ceiling and wall to wall, only here, the light was poorer still. At the far end, a narrow door was set into a recess. A vague worry gnawed at her. *Where's the shopkeeper?* She stepped through the archway and continued on.

Now she could reach out and touch the shelves on either side of her. The books seemed to lean over her, thick and solid and unrelenting. Some had neither title nor author on their spines, just anonymous slices of sleek leather, giving nothing away. The smell of paper was cloying. The silence, absolute. She walked with the studied care of a thief as her fingers traced along the ranks of books. Then she saw it – the light catching silver script on a scarlet binding. *Anatomy.* Below the title, the author was simply "Zachus."

"My subject," she said to herself.

Drawing the book out, she turned it over in her hands, enjoying the sensuous feel of the binding on her fingertips, opening it at a random page. And blinked at an illustration of a flayed torso with its skin peeled back and restrained by wires and hooks to show off the internal organs. The picture glistened, so realistic it begged to be touched, but she stared, confused. *The organs? Not quite right?* She let her fingers slide along the slick paper. *Too many ribs. Can't be human?*

"Medical student, are we?"

Lottie gave a yip of fright. The book snapped shut and tumbled to the floor.

The speaker was broad and thick-set, dressed in a shirt, tie, and waistcoat. Bald and olive-skinned, when he smiled at her, he showed teeth that were white and even and too sharp.

"Where did you…?"

"Not my cup of tea, *Anatomy*." The speaker kept his attention fixed on the fallen book. "All that cold flesh."

"Are you Mr Steal?"

"It's Mr Steals. No. Mr Steals is away on a buying trip. In the Low Countries. I'm Payge."

"Payge?" Lottie said. A half-smile stole onto her lips.

"That amuses you, does it?"

"Well, it's just, Payge as a bookseller's name? It's funny. Like a butcher who's Mister Lamb or a fishmonger called Herring. There's this thing called nominative determinism. I read about it in a science magazine one time…" She trailed off under his scrutiny. "No, I suppose it's not funny."

Payge ran his tongue along his teeth, under his lips. "It's not my name, it's what I've been named. I'm not a bookseller, I'm a bookkeeper."

"You do the accounts and stuff?"

"No. I keep these books. Are you sure you're a student?"

"You keep them for Mr Steals?" Lottie cringed at the stupidity of her own question.

"No. I keep them until their owners come for them. Or bring them back because they can't keep them any longer."

"I see," Lottie said, not seeing at all. She crouched down to retrieve the fallen book, keeping a watchful eye on Payge. A thought took hold in her head, irrational, but with a strength she couldn't deny. She didn't want him touching it. She didn't want his hands on her book. "You should have more light in here. So we can see what we're doing."

Payge seemed to consider this. "Some things thrive in the light. Others need the dark to get along. As I said, *Anatomy*. All that blood and bare flesh. Old Zachus there, he liked a drop of blood. A bit of bare flesh too, by all accounts. Not your kind though." He stopped talking and stared at her.

"I'll take this." Lottie held the book up. "How much is it?"

Payge moved with horrible speed, his big hand clamping around her wrist, pulling her towards him. "If you want it, take it from me."

"Get your hand off me." The grip on her wrist tightened to the point of pain. She tried to pull herself free. The calluses on his hand scraped at her skin.

"Good, Lottie," Payge said. "Very good."

Then she was free, let go, stumbling backwards, pivoting round, bumping and crashing into shelves in her haste to escape. She reached the door and hauled it open, sure a hand was about to fall on her shoulder and pull her back. On the street, pelting towards the end of Gallowgate Lane, skidding round the corner, running until she had nothing left to run with, walking the rest of the way to the Grass Market on trembling legs, the book cradled to her breast.

Once there, she pushed into the first busy bar she came to, immersing herself in its warmth and crowded humanity. Standing alone, jostled and shoved, feeling sick and shaky, it dawned on her she had run off without paying. Then she tried to remember when she had told Payge her name.

2

TIROCINIUM

L iz peered over Lottie's shoulder. "Eeuww! What is
that?"

"What? Oh, it's just some fantasy stuff." Lottie
closed the book in one quick motion. When Liz turned away
to cross the cramped kitchen, she slid a notepad on top of it.

Crockery rattled as Liz hunted through the huddle of
mugs crowded at the edge of the sink. "You guys must be
into some hard-core gaming if you're doing fantasy role-
play dissections. I think you're too much dungeon, not
enough dragon." Lifting two out, she peered inside each
one, grimaced, shrugged, and held them up. "Want one?"

"Please," Lottie said. "Tea would be lovely." She
stretched and checked the kitchen clock, following it
with a guilty look at her pile of textbooks. Another hour
of precious study time gone. But she still wanted to draw
Anatomy towards her, wanted to feel its leather binding
beneath her fingers.

Liz came back to the table. "It looks expensive."

Lottie bit at her lip as her friend pushed the notepad out of the way. "I know. It's fake but it looks the part."

"Kind of smells the part too, if you know what I mean."

"I, uh, got it second hand. You get that old paper smell all the time from those places."

"I was thinking it was more like the bins outside a butcher's shop on a warm day."

"Really?" Lottie watched Liz reach for the book, at the same time, fighting the urge to slap her friend's hand away. The kettle clicked off. Liz turned around, and Lottie slid the notepad over the book again. Then packed a heap of medical texts on top of it. "Have you seen Andrea?"

Liz looked up from stirring their tea. "She's been called away. The United Nations were on the phone earlier. Apparently, there's a world shortage of bitchiness and she's the only one who can resolve the crisis."

"Liz, that's an awful thing to say. Andrea's a nice person when you get to know her."

"You're right. She's not bitchy all the time. Sometimes she dials it down to insufferable."

Lottie smiled as Liz clunked a mug in front of her. "Who's being bitchy now?"

"At least when I do it, it's classy."

"Classy, as in staggering in at four in the morning with your heels in one hand and your knickers hanging out of your pocket?"

"Yep," Liz said. "That's me. Those knickers were expensive. I wasn't leaving them behind."

The two young women looked at each other. Lottie's

smile blossomed into a laugh. Liz gave her a calculating look. "You need to get out more. Get one of your cute role-play guys to buy all the drinks, then show him where the treasure's at."

"We're not like that. We're all just good mates."

"Says you. You're the closest thing to a date they're likely to get."

"You've got such a way of putting things."

"Sorry, I didn't mean…"

Lottie reached over to touch her hand. "I know what you meant."

Liz leant back in her rickety chair. "Anyway, what about you? Are you okay? You came back home yesterday looking upset and you've been quiet ever since. Not like you at all. Something bothering you?"

"No," Lottie said. "I'm fine." She rubbed at her wrist, at the marks Payge had left on her skin. "Just studying too much."

"You've been looking at nothing but that thing all day." Liz nodded at the book under its concealing pile.

Lottie scrabbled around the tabletop, herding up her papers and pens. "I know. I was thinking of going to the library. Get out of here for a while and try to get some work done." Standing up, she loaded her books into her backpack, checking that *Anatomy* was snug and secure. "I'll be back about eleven, okay?"

"Sure thing, kiddo. Be safe out there. By the way, were you looking for something in my room?"

"Liz, I wouldn't go into your room without asking." Lottie paused. "Is something wrong?"

"No. It's just, I could swear there's been some stuff moved around."

"Your room looks like a bomb site. I mean, when was the last time you saw the carpet? Or any other flat surface, come to it?"

"It's my mess and I like it. Must be my mistake. Maybe it was Andrea."

"She wouldn't go into your bedroom with a hazmat suit on."

Liz swung her feet up onto the sofa and made a shooing motion with her hand. "Get off to the library with you. I probably did it myself and forgot. Stop worrying. Go on, get on with what passes for your life."

Lottie pulled a face at her. "You're such a comfort. Have you ever thought about a career in the caring professions?"

"Be off with you, nerd."

"See you later, slapper."

☙

Almost midnight and the university library was deserted. She rubbed at eyes too weary to carry on reading as her hand strayed to the scarlet volume in her bag and her thoughts circled back to the question that nagged her most. *Who would go to that kind of trouble for a work of fiction?*

The book was handmade, she was sure of it. As she was sure some of the illustrations were hand-painted. Yet it was all utter fantasy, describing an anatomy that didn't exist. Which led her back to how it came to be in her bag.

Was it theft? I said I would take it. He never asked me for money. He offered me a deal, and I took it. That's not theft, is it?

Sitting back, she caught sight of a wall clock. It set her jumping to her feet, stuffing books into her bag, scurrying out of the library, breaking into a run when she reached the street, rounding a corner to see the taillights of her bus pulling away. She chased it for a few paces, then stopped and swore. The thought of a taxi flicked through her head. A thought driven away by the scant coins in her pocket.

Rain began to pat down. Walking to the next bus stop to keep the chill off, she wondered how much more miserable this night could become. By the time she reached the stop, her hair was plastered down, and water was leaking through her coat, dampening her clothes, making them clammy against her skin. The bus shelter was one wall and a roof, but it would keep the rain off, and for now, it was enough.

She shot an expectant look down the street, knowing it was pointless. Twenty minutes before the bus was due. Hunching up, starting to feel shivery, she leant back on the shelter to wait. And wait. And wait. She wiped at her nose and tried to conjure hot chocolate and cosy duvets in her head.

"It's a cold night to be out, isn't it?"

Lottie jerked around in surprise. She hadn't heard the questioner approach. He was big, tall, bundled up against the cold. "I suppose," she said.

"Been on a night out with your mates?"

"No… Yes." She bit her lip at her clumsy honesty. "I'm

waiting for them." A rustle of fabric and the scuff of shoes. He'd moved closer to her. His eyes were hidden behind glasses smeared with the yellow light from the streetlamps.

"Your mates better hurry up or they're going to miss it."

Staring at the street. Willing the bus to appear. "It'll only be a minute now."

He spoke with assurance. "More like ten. Maybe longer, at this time of night."

Now he was close enough to see out of the corner of her eye. Within touching distance. Lottie shuffled away until she stood at the very end of the shelter.

"Listen, I know a bar just around the corner. How about I buy you a drink?"

"No thanks. I don't drink. And I don't want to miss the bus."

Walk away. Walk away now. The thought flashed into her head. Another came after it. *And he might follow.*

He moved again, taking up a position opposite her. His smile was a gentle one of understanding. "Fair enough. It was just an idea. Rain's stopped." After looking upwards, he returned to his survey of her. "You look as if you're freezing. Why don't I walk you to the next stop? That way, we can keep warm. I wouldn't like you getting too cold."

Lottie gave her head a tiny shake. Her whole body, every muscle, was strung tight. She tried to tell herself it was the cold. The stranger took a step towards her.

"You don't say much, do you? Maybe you think someone like me isn't worth speaking to, is that it?"

"No, I don't think that at all."

"Then maybe we should—"

"Don't you speak to me," Lottie said, appalled at the high pitch of her voice.

"Sorry." The stranger stepped back; his palms held out in supplication. "I was only trying to be friendly. I'm afraid I'm not very good at this kind of thing."

"I—" Lottie closed her mouth, stopping up her apology.

"You think you've upset me," the stranger said. "It's okay. If you let me touch you."

"What?"

"You'll let me, won't you? Anywhere I want. To say sorry."

Lottie shook her head at him, while fear spiked in her guts. She reached out to grip the edge of the bus stop, ready to swing herself around and run. The rumble of the bus rounding the corner reached her first. Sweet relief swept through her as it ground to a halt at the stop. The doors hissed open, and she piled into the warmth and light of its interior, past the tired-looking driver who gave her travel pass a cursory glance. Collapsing into a seat halfway down the aisle, she stared at her reflection in the window, tension thrumming inside her.

The bus made its soothing diesel sound while the driver waited his allotted time at the stop. Lottie pawed at her damp hair and wished for the door to close. Finally, it slid to. Only, it halted and reversed itself. To let the stranger step on. He made a quick appraisal of the inside of the bus before smiling at the driver. "Sorry, mate, didn't realise you were the last one of the night." Then he was stalking past her, the thump of his footsteps mingling with the rising note of the bus's engine.

Lottie's fear receded as some warmth crept back into her and the bus carried her ever closer to home. The space her fear surrendered was taken up by rationalisation. *He hasn't actually done anything to me. Other than being unpleasant. No worse than some of the offers I've had at closing time on a Saturday night. And why didn't I pick up my bloody phone? Because I was going to the library and didn't need it, idiot.*

Sitting stiff-backed and miserable, trying to ignore the damp clothes sticking to her skin, she didn't hear him. He moved so quietly. But she felt the pull on the back of her seat when he grabbed it to lower himself into the seat behind her. Risking a glance at the window, she caught his reflection. He was leaning forward, staring at the back of her head. It felt like she could sense him, as though he was cutting through some invisible field around her. And then he touched her, stroking a lock of her wet hair, caressing it, slipping his finger through the slick curls the rain had made of it.

"So fine," he whispered. "So soft."

"Don't you dare." She spat her words into the air in front of her. "Don't you dare touch me." On her feet, moving before she realised it, rushing to the front of the bus. Outside, familiar territory passed by, shop fronts she knew, landmarks she passed every day. She was home.

Pressing the bell to signal a stop and then the bus was slowing. The urge to flee pushed her past the driver. The door folded back on itself, and she leapt. Hitting the ground, stumbling forward, flailing for balance. Finding it, catching herself, she hurried away.

A look back. The bus not moving, its engine idling. "Come on," she urged. "Please. Just go."

The stranger stepped out of the bus. The doors closed behind him with a rattle and the bus started away, its taillights washing the street with scarlet warning. They faced each other across perhaps thirty yards of pavement. Lottie felt a weariness and despair creep into her. *This isn't fair. What have I done to deserve this?* She had no answer for herself. The stranger took a step towards her. She turned away from him and began to run.

After a few strides, she glanced back. A whimper escaped from her lips. The distance between them had closed. Raw terror gripped her. *This is real. This is going to happen to me.*

Looking around threw her off balance. She clipped a streetlight, the impact making her stagger to a halt beside a pitch-black alleyway. He was bearing down on her, a feral grin plastered on his face. *The alley. That's where he'll take me.* Sadness tangled up with the fear inside her, and then a clear thought. *Only if I let him.*

She turned once more to run, then stopped when she heard the meaty smack of a blow landing, followed by an explosive exhalation. Looking back, astonished at the sight of the stranger being dragged into the alley by the bookkeeper, Payge, with his arm locked around the stranger's throat. The darkness swallowed them. A moment of silence. Cracking sounds, like dry kindling being snapped.

She fled, with no thought for what was behind her, sprinting for the safety of her block of flats, of her home.

Running through the small park that fronted her building, heedless of its deep shadows. At the door to her building. Fumbling keys from her pocket. *Don't drop them, don't drop them.* Holding the key with both hands, she slotted it into the lock, opened the door, slipped through, and pushed against it with all her weight. The door thunked home, locking with a metallic snick.

You're okay now, you're safe. Repeating the thought over and over as she climbed the stairs. She found she was crying and hadn't realised it and that made her cry all the harder. Fear still coiled inside her. And beneath it: *the bastard, the utter bastard. He would have done it. Done it to me. I could be in the alley right now, him on top of me.* A feeling surged up inside her like a wave rising on a hidden reef. Anger. Incandescent fury.

At the door to her flat, the key skittered and scratched around the lock. Her shaky, insubordinate fingers refused to co-operate. She swore at her ineptitude. When her free hand fell on the door handle to steady herself, the door swung open, leaving her key poised useless in mid-air.

What? We never leave the door open. Never.

She stepped inside, drawing in the familiar scent of the flat, the musty smell of old carpet and the homely aroma of pasta sauce lingering from their evening meal. The television was on, but it was a tiny sound, turned all the way down. She followed it to the front room, where the back of the sofa faced her. Dark hair was draped over the end of it and an arm, hanging at an odd angle. "Liz?" she said.

"Uh?" The sofa creaked, and Liz rose from it, pushing away locks of hair. "Lottie?" she said. Then, "Lottie! What's wrong? What's happened?" Liz struggled out of the sofa to pull Lottie into a hug, her vodka-scented breath filling the space around them.

Lottie started to cry, quiet tears that drained the tension from her. Liz held her out at arm's length and regarded her with bloodshot eyes. "You look terrible. And you're freezing. And wet. Here, let's get this bloody thing off you."

Her backpack thumped to the floor, and her coat followed it. Liz guided her to the sofa, gathering Lottie's hands in her own. "You're like ice. What happened?"

"There was a man. He followed me."

"Oh. Oh no. He didn't…?"

Lottie shook her head, squeezing her eyes shut, tears leaking out, as Liz drew her into an embrace. "No." She spoke into the soft fabric of Liz's sweater. "But he could have."

Liz gave her a final hug and then let go. "You look like you could use a drink. Here." Leaning over, she picked up an empty glass from the low table in front of her. "Hang on." Rooting around on the floor, she came up with an empty bottle of vodka. "Must have drunk more than I thought."

"It's okay," Lottie said. "I'd love some tea though."

"Sure thing." Liz stood, her knee banging the table, sending the empty glass clattering.

The living room door opened, and a bleary face poked through. "I'm trying to get some sleep. You two are making so much noise. Have you any idea of the time?"

Liz gave a negligent wave of her hand. "Hi, Andrea. Lottie nearly got attacked in the street. Sorry to have woken you for nothing and all."

Shock banished the irritation on Andrea's tired features. "Oh, Lottie." Brushing back tousled hair, she hurried over to the sofa, drawing Lottie to her. "I'm sorry." The fresh cotton scent from her pyjamas nearly brought Lottie to tears again.

"You're soaked through," Andrea said. "Come on, let's get you into some dry clothes." She stopped. "Do you want to call the police?"

Lottie thought about it. "He didn't do anything. He was talking to me at the bus stop, he wanted to go for a drink. Then he started getting all weird. Following me onto the bus and touching my hair."

"Ugh, creepy," Andrea said.

Liz set a steaming mug in front of Lottie, slopping tea over the rim, before settling in the ratty armchair beside the sofa. "Did he do anything else?"

"He got off at the same stop as me." Lottie thought for a moment. Her recollection, which she thought would be clear, was fuzzy and fragmented. "I mean, it might have been co-incidence. But I took off."

Andrea leant forward. "What happened then?"

"I bumped into something. He was coming towards me. Then, I think, he was pulled into an alley, or he went into an alley, and he was gone. I ran home." She finished with a helpless shrug. Here, in the warm flat, what happened to her on the street seemed diminished. "I think someone else was there. But I never really saw them."

Andrea gave her a quizzical look. "You should report it. Nobody should be scared to walk home."

"In the morning?" Lottie said. "Please?"

"Yeah, I think she's had enough for one night and whoever it is will be long gone." Liz gave a hiccup and a burp.

"I think I know someone who needs to go to bed as well," Andrea said.

Liz scowled at her.

"In the morning, then." She clasped Lottie's hand. "Promise me?"

"I promise," Lottie said, feeling she was about nine years old.

"Go on. Bed."

⁓

Lottie stared into the dark, sure she would never sleep. The sound of gentle snoring came from Liz's room. The creak of Andrea's bed when she turned in her sleep. The quiet sounds of the flat – the tick of a clock and the hum of the fridge in their kitchen. The bright numerals on her bedside clock wore away at the long minutes. She thought about getting up, maybe reading something. Not *Anatomy*. No. For the first time since she had fled from Mr Steals Books, she had no desire to open the scarlet book. With a heavy sigh, she rolled over, and somewhere in the next few minutes, drifted into a troubled sleep.

She woke knowing something was wrong. A glance at the clock. An hour had gone past. Lying still as she could, she listened. Nothing, save the silence. But there had been something. She was sure of it. *A noise in the flat? Get up, go for a look.* She couldn't bring herself to do it. The bed was warm, and weariness soaked through her. She told herself it was nothing. She froze again. There was a noise, low and stealthy.

Slipping out of bed, she flicked on a light and padded across to her bedroom door, pushing it open without a sound. Across the tiny hallway, the doors of Liz's and Andrea's rooms were closed. The light shining from behind her let her see into their living room. Nothing there.

The noise came from the only other door off the hallway. The door into their flat. It creaked. As if a weight was being pressed against it from the outside. To the accompaniment of what felt like every hair on her body prickling up, Lottie watched as the door handle pivoted downwards. Again, the door creaked with strain. Slowly, so slowly, the handle returned to its raised position. A moment's silence. Metal scratched and clicked in the lock.

Her anger was a bright spike inside her. She wasn't alone. Her two friends were here. She ran at the door, hammered on it, shrieked at it. "Go away!" Given voice, her anger flared, fed by the hurt she felt, burning away all caution. Her fingers fought with the lock. She pulled the door open, ready to scream in the face of whoever was there.

She was staring at an empty corridor. She looked both ways down the length of it. Nothing. *How? No one could move so fast.*

Liz and Andrea were pulling her back inside, soothing her, saying she must have had a nightmare. It was her imagination. She was still in shock. Lottie didn't argue. She went along with being tucked up in bed and watched as Liz and Andrea retreated to their rooms, darting worried looks back at her as they did. And as she tried to get back to sleep, as her heartbeat slowed to a steady rhythm, Lottie knew her friends were wrong.

3

LOTTIE MEETS PAYGE (AND CERTAIN ISSUES ARE DISCUSSED)

Tapping her pen against her notebook, the policewoman then looked up from her words. "Are you sure you can't give me any more details?"

Lottie huffed out her frustration. "I thought I would be able to but when I think back, it's all pretty vague."

"It's not unusual." The policewoman gave her a sympathetic look. "Many people find the same after being in a stressful situation. But you've reported it. That's important. We can increase patrols in the area. You should look at your personal security as well. Think about when and where you're going. Always try to go with someone. Perhaps buy an alarm."

"Give in to him, you mean? Change my life because of what he did to me?" Lottie glared across the table at a woman not much older than she was.

The woman looked back at her, her face neutral, her voice mild. "It's advice, nothing more. And I'm sorry for what happened to you. Unfortunately, it's all too common. For all of us."

Lottie dropped her gaze to the tabletop. "Being afraid every time I leave my home is no way to live, is it?"

The policewoman didn't have an answer and the interview was over. Lottie dawdled home, thinking over what had been said. At her flat, she found the door partway open. She touched her fingers to it, images of the previous evening flashing up in her mind. "Hello? Hi, anyone?"

"I'm in here."

"Andrea?" Lottie made her way inside, locking the door behind her. "What's going on?"

Andrea was hunched on the sofa, clutching a sodden tissue, her eyes red-rimmed, cheeks flushed, a glisten of mucus at her nose.

The thought rose unbidden in Lottie's head. That she didn't look so pretty anymore. She dismissed it with a pang of guilt, then sat down, clasping her hand over Andrea's bunched fists. "Are you okay?"

"It was Liz. We had a huge fight. I didn't mean to, it just happened. I don't know how. I think Liz had been drinking. Who drinks at eleven in the morning?"

"I don't know. Students like us, I suppose. How did it start?"

"I... I asked Liz, I asked her if... I left some money on my bedside table, and I couldn't find it and I asked her if she had seen it, and she blew up at me. She said I was a rich, stuck-up bitch and I had no right to accuse her of

23

stealing. I never did. I never said she did. Only…" Andrea drew her shoulders up, then let them slump down. "I'm sure someone's been in my room. You know how you know where everything is and when it's been moved. Not by much, but not where you left it. You and Liz wouldn't do that. But who else could? Who else could have been in here?" She looked away. "Sorry, I know how that sounded and I didn't mean it that way. I don't know what to think right now."

"I know how you feel," Lottie said.

Realisation dawned on Andrea's face, her tearful expression becoming fraught. "After what happened to you. I'm laying this on you. You must think I'm a total shit."

"No." Lottie smiled, pleased when her friend lit up a small smile in return. "Never." A moment of silence passed between them before she spoke again. "So where did Liz go?"

"Don't know. She didn't say."

"She'll come back when she comes back. You know what she's like."

"I suppose." Andrea pressed her lips into a thin line. "I worry about her."

"Me too. But Liz can look after herself. I'm sure of it." Lottie stood, not feeling sure at all. "I'll put the kettle on?"

Busying herself with the distraction of mugs and tea bags, caught up in her thoughts, she said nothing more. Though she listened when Andrea spoke again.

"I'm worried about my course as well. My dad's hassling me about it. He's always on at me to work harder. He was furious at my exam results last year. I mean seriously mad. I'm trying so hard this year but there's so much of it I don't get."

"You told us you did well in your exams."

Andrea offered up a weak smile. "I was fibbing. Just trying to fool myself and please him. I'm sorry I lied to you and Liz about it. Lying to your friends is the worst thing."

Lottie tried to shrug it away, but it didn't want to go. "You thought it was the right thing to do at the time."

"I was wrong." Andrea scrunched her tissue. "It's my dad. He so wants to get on. To achieve. Not just himself. Me. My sisters. Our whole family."

Lottie stared, wondering where this was going.

"He's talking about maybe standing for parliament at the next election."

"Really? I thought he was already high up in the city council?"

"Yes, he is. He's deputy chief executive."

"And now he wants to be a member of parliament?"

"He's joked to us about how he'll get a government minister's post and be on TV. Only I don't think he's joking. He believes in himself so much. And he wants us all to be like him. I didn't want to do this bloody course. It was dad's idea. Parents, eh? They're a nightmare."

Lottie kept her gaze on the tea things. "I wouldn't know."

Andrea covered her horrified expression with one hand. "Lottie, I'm sorry. I didn't think. That was an awful thing to say."

"It's okay. It's the way it is. You know, Liz said she thought someone had been in her room as well. I'm sure she did. Maybe we should speak to the landlord."

"Maybe it is the landlord."

"She doesn't seem the type." Lottie trailed off as a thought struck her. The book. The book Payge offered her. The book she took. She could picture it on the table beside her bed, the scarlet binding almost luminous in the dimness of the room. It was at the centre of this. Everything had happened since she picked up the book.

With a start, she realised the kettle had boiled and Andrea was looking at her with an expectant expression on her face. She shook away her daft notion. "Listen, I think I'll go take a walk around, see if I can find Liz. I promise I'll calm her down before I bring her home."

"Thanks," Andrea said. "I'll phone you if she gets back before you do. And I will say sorry to her."

"Make sure the door's locked behind me." She stopped by her room and scooped up *Anatomy*. The leather felt slick against her hand, greasy even. The smell in her room wasn't pleasant. It had the smell of an airless place shut up for too long. Dropping the book into her backpack, she left the flat and started for Gallowgate Lane.

As she walked through streets fresh with autumn sunshine, the idea of there being no Mr Steals Books in Gallowgate Lane crossed her mind. Just a dusty, empty shell in its place. She smiled at her flight of fancy, the heft of the book in her bag dispelling any such idea.

The lane presented itself with mundane drabness. Outside the bookshop was a wooden chair and in it sat Payge. He was as broad and heavy-built as she remembered. He looked to be asleep, his clasped hands resting on his stomach, his chin on his chest. Just a middle-aged bookseller enjoying the afternoon sun. She slowed her pace the closer she drew to the slumbering figure. When she was some ten yards away, Payge spoke without opening his eyes, without stirring from his repose.

"Hello, Lottie. You're back. Good for you."

She stopped; her brow furrowed in puzzlement. "How did you even know it was me?"

"Your scent."

"No way. You saw me, didn't you?"

Payge breathed in deep. "No," he said. He opened his eyes. "But you don't have to believe me." Straightening up in his chair, which gave a warning creak, he pulled at the hem of his waistcoat. "How can I help you?"

"I wanted to ask you about the book."

"Is that all?"

"Maybe not."

"But you don't want to say. For reasons that are probably complicated. To you, at least." His stare was both placid and unwavering. She had to look away.

"Yes, the book. I wanted to bring it back. It feels like I stole it."

"You didn't steal it. You can't steal something that belongs to you."

"It doesn't belong to me."

"Are you sure?"

The question stopped her hand going to the zip-top of her backpack. "Yes, I think I'm sure."

"You think you're sure? So, you're not sure?"

"I don't like the feel of it. When I touch it."

27

Payge nodded. "I understand. I think you should come inside."

Rummaging in her bag, she drew the book out. "Here. Take it."

Payge laid it on his lap, brushing his thumb across the cover. "So much pain," he said. "If I meant you harm, I would have done it by now." He moved before Lottie had a chance to react, his hand seizing her wrist, not tight enough to hurt but tight enough to tell her escape was not an option. "Look at this street. Who is there to see someone dragged away to a hidden place?" He studied her, still holding fast. "I say again, I mean you no harm. Just the opposite. And you should have been more careful coming home from the library."

Lottie opened her mouth to speak, then clicked her jaw shut. Payge let his hand drop. She rubbed at her wrist. "You were there, weren't you? You followed me. Were you with him?"

Payge stood in a single fluid movement. "Come inside. We should talk. I'll make tea. Things are happening around you that you need to know about."

Lottie took a step and then made herself stop. "What does that mean?"

Payge ignored her as he pushed open the door.

"And I don't trust you." She flapped her hand towards the shop. "In there."

He paused for a moment. "I don't blame you. Why would you trust me? But you'll come in anyway, won't you? Because now you want to know. No, you need to know. Are you coming or not?"

Lottie drew in a deep breath. She looked at Payge as he held the door open for her. *I should go back. I've got tutorials. Essays. Reading to do.* She looked past him, into the shaded interior of the bookshop. "Yes, I'm coming. Don't you try anything."

Payge sucked in one of his cheeks. "If I did, you wouldn't see it. So you don't need to worry overly much about it. Not that I would. Through here."

She followed him along the narrow space between the bookshop window and the first set of shelves. She wanted to stop, to call out to him to wait, while she took down book after book, to sit on the floor, surrounded by them, to lose herself in them. But she followed. Through the arch at the end of the row of shelves and into the gloom of the second row. Here, the titles seemed to scratch at her mind with rat claws. Her fingertips itched with the need to touch the books. "Mr Payge?"

He turned, as smooth as a machine. "I'm just Payge. No mister needed. What can I help you with?"

Lottie gestured wordlessly at the wall of words in front of her.

Payge nodded. "I know. They call to you, don't they?" He looked away, a faint smile on his lips. "I don't hear it, but I'm told it's quite insistent."

"But they're just books. How can they?"

"They don't, of course. They're just paper. How can they have a life of their own?" He still held *Anatomy*. Opening it somewhere near the middle, gripping the top of it in both hands, he stared at it, and for one second, Lottie thought he would tear it in half. Instead, he closed it and slid it into a gap on a shelf. "It's all in your head. Come into the office. We can talk there."

He made for the narrow door set in the far corner. When he swung it open, bright light spilt out. Turning sideways on, he slipped through.

Lottie stood for a moment. "Walk away," a part of her said. Leave this place and never come back. Return to your studies and forget about all of it. Because nothing good will come of this.

And you'll never know.

This last thought came from nowhere, like a lost radio signal finding a receiver to latch on to. She scurried to the door without looking back.

The office was spacious and warm. A camp bed and a writing desk were tucked in one corner. In another, a small kitchen area made her notice the faint smell of home-cooked food. A big table occupied the middle of the room. On it sat an odd-looking mannequin. She drifted over, curious to see it closer up.

"Make yourself at home," Payge said, busying himself at the writing desk.

She studied the child-sized figure propped up on the table. "Wow, the guys in my gaming club would go nuts for this." She took in its green-tinged skin, its narrow face, its eyes like oval buttons of jet. "Brilliant level of detail." She glanced round for Payge. "I've always loved models and puppets and figures. Where did you get it from? And what's it for?" When no answer came back, she turned to the mannequin again. "Can I touch it?"

Payge looked up at her. "I wouldn't advise it."

30

The jet-black eyes blinked at her, and the mannequin said, "Hello, Lottie, how you doing?"

Lottie stepped back as the mannequin hoisted itself up and stood on the table. Her smile was huge as she turned to Payge again. "How are you doing this?"

"Doing what?"

"Making it talk. Making it move. Is it remote-controlled?"

"She's a bit on the rude side," the mannequin said. It stuck its hands in its pockets. "And she didn't scream or jump. Bit of a let-down really."

"I'm sure," Payge said. "Lottie, meet Jackdaw. Jackdaw, Lottie. You should know he bites. Hence the warning. And he cheats at cards. Don't play, if he offers."

Lottie narrowed her eyes. "Okay, I get it. Very clever. State-of-the-art animatronics." She reached out, then stopped. "It is okay if I touch him?"

"Do what you like," Payge said. "He's not my pet. Or the puppet you think he is. Puppets and pets don't stagger in at all hours, demand to be fed and pass out on your bed."

Lottie drew in a breath and stared at the unreadable black eyes. "Something tells me I'm being taken for a mug, my little animatronic friend. But I'll play along for now. Can I touch you?"

"Well, we've just met, and to be honest, you're moving faster than I would expect in a newly blossomed relationship, but on you go." Jackdaw gave her a wicked grin. "You may touch me."

"I meant *examine* you."

"Boring. Carry on."

She lifted its hand, as small as a child's but not delicate. The bones felt thick and heavy, the skin warm, warmer than her own. She drew her fingers up to its wrist. The pulse was unmistakable. Slow, much too slow, but with a steady, insistent beat. Lottie licked her lips.

"You're real. Living real."

"She's a bit slow on the uptake, if you ask me."

"Give her a chance," Payge said. "This is all new to her."

"What's wrong with you?" Lottie asked.

Jackdaw shrugged. "Besides a mild hangover, nothing really."

Lottie pressed on. "No, I mean, what condition do you have? What made you like this?"

"Definitely rude," Jackdaw said. He looked to Payge, who grunted back a reply. His black gaze turned back to Lottie, and he picked at a pointed fingernail that was as thick as a claw. "Nothing happened to me. This is what I am."

She took a wary step back so she could look at the pair of them. Her mind packed the reality of Jackdaw into a box and closed the lid. "I don't understand."

"Then I'll explain," Payge said.

Her calves bumped into something as she shuffled away from him. "I'm not so sure about this."

Jackdaw sat on the table edge, swinging his legs in the air. Payge rubbed at his bald pate. "A reasonable stance, given your circumstances, and I think I already said this. However, pay heed. I will not harm you. You can leave any time you like. I only ask that you listen to me, but if you don't want to…"

He gestured to the door, waited a moment, then drew a pair of wire-rimmed spectacles from one waistcoat pocket and arranged them on his nose. With studied care, he drew a small fold of paper from the other pocket. "This is a letter from Mr Steals." He cleared his throat and read. "My dearest Payge, you will take all measures to assure me Lottie is neither killed nor accrues significant loss of her faculties. You will suffer for it if she does. Your friend, Steals."

"Oh," Lottie said.

"Indeed," Payge replied.

"Would you like to sit down?" This was from Jackdaw.

"Yes. I think that might be a good idea."

Jackdaw craned round to speak to Payge. "Bring a chair over. And weren't you making some tea?"

Payge huffed at him. "I suppose."

Jackdaw jumped to the ground. "I'll make the tea. You tell her."

"Tell me what?" Lottie said.

Jackdaw dragged a chair over, its feet squealing on the stone floor. She watched the small figure in amazement, her smile growing wider as the lid of the box in her mind cracked open and a part of her began to believe. As he drew closer, he winked up at her. "There you go, you're looking better already. Now listen to what he has to say."

Payge lifted a leather-bound notebook from his desk and flipped it open. Clearing his throat again, he began to speak. "We've been keeping an eye on you. And your friends." He glanced at her before returning to his notes. "Lottie. Medical student. First year. Your tutor believes you will have no problem completing your studies, but you could do better if you didn't distract yourself so much. You have a small circle of friends. You do not drink to excess or indulge in narcotics. Your clothing is functional rather than decorative. Your internet activity is about normal." Here Payge paused as he flipped over a sheet. "Other than an unusual amount of time spent on sites devoted to" – he glanced at Jackdaw, who shrugged – "weird shit."

Lottie felt her anger rising. "You've been in my flat, haven't you? How else could you know that?"

Payge pressed on. "You're a member of something called the Knights of Chaos." He stopped his reading. "What might they be?"

"Uh, it's gaming. You know? Role-play. Swords and sorcery."

"You play with swords?"

"Um, yes. But not for real. Imaginary. We have adventures. Find treasures. Slay monsters. For fun."

Payge's mild regard never let up. "When you see what a sword can do to a living thing, you might not be so keen on playing with them."

"And I suppose you have?" She slung the words back at him. He never flinched, so she gathered herself for another go. "I asked you if you had been in my flat."

"I haven't," Payge said. "I sent him. He's far better at it than me."

She looked round to Jackdaw, who sat with his hands clasped in his lap and a look of friendly innocence on his face. "It's true. He's rubbish at breaking into places. By the way, Andrea has some nice underwear. You should ask her for some advice on that."

"So it's you that broke in and went creeping around our bedrooms when we were asleep?"

"No, I waited until you were all out. Then I broke in."

Lottie felt the flush spreading in her neck and face. She knew she should leave now. Go to the police. They'd admitted it. But her anger would not be swayed. And now she so badly wanted to know. "Wait a minute. The night I was attacked." She looked over at Payge. "Someone was at our door, trying to get in. I heard it. I saw it. So, you were trying to get in when we were asleep. You're lying."

Jackdaw and Payge exchanged a glance. "Not me, Lottie." Jackdaw's face changed. The easy-going look was replaced with something far colder. "And if you keep calling me a liar, we are going to stop being friends."

There was a moment of silence. Payge broke it. "I didn't realise they got past me. I was watching over your place the whole night."

"What did you do to that man? The one who followed me?"

Payge tapped at his notebook. "You know what I did."

Lottie licked at her lips as all the revelations of the last few minutes crowded into her head. She looked at Jackdaw. "I think you're just someone with a very strange medical condition. Some kind of growth disorder." She looked at Payge. "I think you're hiding something." After walking to the door, she turned on them. "I'm going to the police to tell them." Neither Payge nor Jackdaw moved.

"You're being hunted, Lottie." Payge spoke as if he was remarking on the particularly fine weather. "Someone means you harm. What happened the other night was part of it. A chance to make it look like a random crime. The police cannot watch over you all the time. I can and I will, because it's all I have to do. Are you leaving?"

She stood on the threshold, the door to the outside world. The memory of the previous night, the fear she had felt, was still a fresh wound. Her anger at being so helpless. Her need to know why. "If I don't leave," she said, "what happens?"

Payge gave a shrug. "I'll tell you everything you need to know. Come over here. Look at this."

She hesitated, but only for a second, before turning around and walking back.

Payge fetched a scuffed laptop and opened it up. Swiping a finger over the screen brought up a complex diagram of lines, symbols and numbers. "I don't expect you to understand any of this. And this will be hard to take in, but…"

Lottie crowded in beside him, frowning down at the screen. "It's like a flow chart. These numbers are probabilities?" She leant in to read the tiny writing. "That's my name. That's me in there." Her finger traced the lines on the screen. Her name appeared again and again, along with Liz and Andrea. All linked together with other names she didn't recognise.

"You can follow this?" There was a wary note in Payge's voice.

"No. Well, a bit. It's connecting up things and showing how likely they are. What's it for? Why am I in it? Why are my friends?" She poked the screen, jerking her hand back when it went blank. "That wasn't me."

The pattern reappeared, growing like a crystal. The lines it was made of were fewer and thicker. Her name was there again, the probabilities beside it grown larger, more certain. Lottie peered at it. "What just happened?"

Payge ignored her, his attention on the laptop.

"We should tell Steals about this," Jackdaw said. "Now. Right away and immediately. Or sooner."

"The owner of the shop?" Lottie said. "What's it got to do with him?"

Payge seemed to be lost in his thoughts. His attention never wavered from the screen.

"Payge," Jackdaw said. "We have to tell him."

"What? Tell him what? Would somebody tell me something?" Lottie said.

Payge's voice was low and even. "Steals's instructions were very clear. Protect Lottie from harm. Nothing more."

"No," Jackdaw said. "You don't get to do this. No way."

"Why not?" Payge said.

"Because he'll skin us if he finds out."

"He won't know. Because we won't tell him."

"Will one of you tell me?" Lottie said.

Jackdaw's shoulders slumped. "Okay, you win. We don't tell him. I still think it's a bad idea."

Payge traced lines on the screen with his fingertip. "If it helps, you could think of it as stealing something from him."

"Really?" Jackdaw twisted his bottom lip between his teeth. "I never thought about it that way."

Lottie hadn't noticed, until now, how pointed his teeth were. "What is this?" She went to tap the screen but stopped herself before she touched it.

Payge drew a deep breath. "It's a map of the future. Or futures. And the present. A pattern of actions, consequences and outcomes."

"I'm struggling with this. Why am I in it? My friends." She waved a hand at the screen. "These other people."

"So Steals can get what he wants. He made the pattern. He drew it around you and the people close to you. There is another person who doesn't want it to happen, who opposes Steals. If you're not around to follow the pattern, to work it through, then Steals loses and the other person wins."

Lottie stared at him, an uncertain smile on her face. "I have to do what's in this pattern. This is what you're telling me?"

"You don't have to do anything. But it might be better for you if you did."

"Suppose I walked away? Did nothing."

"You would still be in danger. Maybe your friends as well. Steals's enemy will still want to break the pattern by coming after you. You could go to the police, but what can you tell them? You can run away, but where would you run to when your life is here? Do you want your future to be like your journey home from the library?"

Lottie looked from Payge to Jackdaw. They stared back, Jackdaw with some sympathy, Payge with grim certainty. "Can we get out of here? This place… you two… I can't think."

"Maybe you need a drink," Jackdaw said. "I always reckon going to a bar is a good idea."

Payge scowled at him. "For once, you might be right." He sighed then, the look on his face softening. "This is difficult for you. A lot to take in. I appreciate that. Understand?"

Lottie nodded.

"Come on then." He touched a hand to her arm. "A walk, the fresh air and a quiet drink will give you some perspective."

On the sunlit street, Lottie felt a touch of dizziness. She watched Payge and Jackdaw walk away from her, Jackdaw drawing on a hoodie that was more than a couple of sizes too big for him. Just a man and a boy out for a stroll. Normal. Ordinary. What she had seen and heard in the bookshop crowded in on her. Payge called over his shoulder to her. "Will you get a move on?"

She trotted to catch up. "Is he coming with us? He'll never get served."

"I've other places to be," Jackdaw said. "See you later." He skipped a couple of steps before taking off down a side street.

"He's fast," Lottie said.

"You have a rare talent for stating the obvious." Payge strode in the opposite direction. Lottie struggled to keep up, breaking into little bursts of jogging between walking so fast her hips ached.

"Can you slow down?"

"No."

"You didn't lock your door."

"I never do."

"Aren't you worried?" She gasped for breath. "About thieves?"

"Not after I broke the last one's fingers."

"You're kidding, right?"

"In here." He nodded at a grubby doorway, painted in dull lilac.

Lottie looked at the sign above the door. "The Purple Pussycat? You want to go in here for a drink? With me? You know what this is?"

Payge gave her an unreadable look.

"It's a titty bar. You know, lap dancing? And I'm a woman?"

Payge seemed to consider this. "I've found if you want to go someplace where no one's going to look at you, this is the place."

"You've been here before?"

"A few times. And I'm telling you, they won't be looking at you."

Lottie glared back at him. "Like looking at naked women, do you? Gets you all turned on, does it?"

Payge grunted back at her. "Not your kind, no."

"I'm not going into a titty bar." She folded her arms and rocked back. They stared at each other.

"Fine. Come on then." He stalked away.

A minute later, he stopped again. "Will this do?"

"It looks a bit rough."

"Are you ever happy?" Payge snapped. "With anything?" She snapped back at him. "Sometimes."

He pushed through the door, and she trailed after him.

The inside of the pub was as mean as the outside, but it was busy. Lottie scanned the room, taking in the attention they were getting. The looks ranged from curious to sullen to hostile. She searched for a kindred female face and found none. She wondered how they must seem. An older man in a tweed suit and a young woman. She thought about turning around. But Payge was already at the bar, so she moved to catch up.

"What would you like?"

"An orange juice, please."

Their drinks secured, Payge ushered Lottie to a sticky-ringed table in a quiet corner. He downed half his beer in three big gulps. "Not bad."

Lottie slid her glass backwards and forward on the table. She hesitated to speak. Out here, what was said in the bookshop now felt ridiculous. "People keep looking at us."

"So?"

"I was just saying."

"Making you nervous, is it?"

"I'm feeling a bit jumpy, yes."

"Then we should have gone to the first bar I took you to."

"You're a real comfort."

"Sorry," Payge said. "You've every right to feel that way. But you needed to be told."

"I don't believe it. I can't." She moved her glass in tight circles. "I mean, I can get Jackdaw. He's just a man. With some weird disease. But I'm being hunted? Someone wants to harm me? To kill me?" She flicked a glance at Payge. "And this laptop that tells the future? That's just crazy."

"There's nothing special about the laptop, it's only an instrument for looking with. The pattern is the important part. I said it was a map of the future, but it's not. It's more like the landscape itself, and the laptop is the tool that lets you see it."

"The landscape of what?"

"Everything. What's the universe made of?"

Lottie pulled a face, nonplussed. "Atoms and stuff? Energy?"

Payge nodded. "What if everything is made of information? Information in patterns. Patterns that can be changed. Or created." He sat back. "There you have it."

"I'm not sure I do."

Payge finished his beer in a single swallow. Wiping his mouth with the back of his hand, he indicated if she wanted another.

Lottie shook her head. "You can do this, can you? Create these patterns?"

"No. I'm not a maker." He looked into his empty glass. "I'm having another."

"I don't get it," Lottie said.

"I get that. I just told you everything is made of information."

"Whoa, hang on a minute." Lottie peered across the table at him. "You're saying what I saw on the laptop was like… Like looking through a microscope? At reality? You'll be telling me next it's magic."

"Maybe it is. Sure you don't want another?"

He strolled off, leaving Lottie to stare at her glass. After a minute, she looked up and he was nowhere in sight. She craned round, searching the crowd at the bar. When she got some interested looks back, she stopped and went back to fretting over her glass.

"Buy you a drink, seeing as how you're all on your own?"

She looked up at the man who had asked the question. He was big, taller than Payge, and broad at the shoulders. She saw dirty fingernails and clothes that looked slept in.

"I'm with someone."

"Don't look like it to me." He slid into the seat across from her. "So why don't I buy you a drink. We can get friendly."

"I don't want your drink or your company."

Her glare brought a laugh in return. "You're just playing hard to get."

"Leave her be." She hadn't heard Payge approach.

The man barely glanced in Payge's direction. "Piss off, I'm with her now."

"You're not." Payge set his drink down and spoke slowly, his gaze fixed on the man. "You can leave, or I can hurt you. I like the idea of hurting you."

The big man stared back but Lottie could see it in his eyes. He was done, aside from trying to save face. He stood, knocking his seat over. "Ugly bitch." The words were spat back at her as he walked away.

"Sorry I took so long," Payge said. He righted the tipped chair before sitting down. "You handled the situation well. You were assertive. That's good. Next time, don't back away so much."

Lottie swept her gaze around the bar. "Can we leave now? He might have mates with him."

"You think? Let me know if you see them."

"What if they come at us? At you, I mean."

Payge took a swallow of his beer. "Then they'll regret it."

"You don't look the violent type."

"I'm not."

"So can we leave?"

"Once I finish this." Payge lifted his glass a fraction. "Is there anything else you want to ask?"

She thought for a moment. "This pattern. Why me? I'm just a student. What could be so important about me?"

"It's not about who you are. It's about what you do. Or rather, what you're going to do."

"What happened when I touched the screen and the pattern changed?" She challenged him with a glance. "Something happened there. Something you didn't expect. What was it?"

Payge sucked in a breath. "I don't know. I've never seen anyone do that before." He shifted to the sound of the bar's door opening. "Lottie, we need to leave. Right now."

"Why? You haven't finished your pint."

"Look to the door. I mean really look."

And she did. The person who'd come in was tall, not freakishly tall, but easily six foot six. He walked towards the bar, checking the crowd, but not looking behind, not seeing them tucked into their corner. She saw a face that could have been moulded from pale clay, done quickly, its features sketched in. Then Payge was hurrying her out of her seat and bundling her towards the door.

Outside the bar, he started running, pulling her along with him. Sprinting now. Her breath came in gasps.

"Payge. Stop." The two words took more air than she could afford. Her feet started dragging. "Please."

He veered into a lane between two buildings and let her go. Lottie bent over, clutching her belly, shuddering in swallows of air. "What was he?"

"They're called stalkers. They kill people."

"Was it…?"

"Looking for you? Without a doubt. They're not a subtle weapon but they are very effective. I doubt it would have attacked in there, but if it's moving openly, then it will attack soon. Probably at your flat, where it won't be seen. It will kill everyone it finds. I'm sorry. Something has changed. For the worst."

"How did it find us?"

"Someone set it after you. Steals's rival, most likely. There might be more than one. Wherever you go, it will follow your steps. It won't sleep. It won't stop." He glanced round the corner of the building before going on. "It would do to get you away for a couple of days. Somewhere safer than here. Somewhere I can more easily protect you. Until I can figure out what is going on. Will you come with me?" He studied her face. "You still doubt me. You still don't believe."

Lottie looked at the ground. "This is hard to take in."

"I think I can persuade you. If you come with me. I'll take you back to your flat. Pack a bag. Just essentials and a change of clothes. I'll wait for you outside."

"What do I tell my flatmates?"

"You're a clever girl. Make something up."

❧

In the park in front of Lottie's building, Payge watched as she disappeared through the main door. A small figure joined him.

"Get a message to Steals," Payge said. "Tell him it's working. She's in there right now, lying to her friends."

"What about her being able to change the pattern?" Jackdaw said. "How do you think she did it?"

"I've no idea. A stalker is following her."

"Shame. I liked her. What now?"

"I need to try to keep her alive a little while longer. I'll meet you at the gate. We're taking her to Ore tonight."

4

ORE

Lottie left her flat with her backpack stuffed with clothes and her cheeks burning. Andrea had believed every lie she had told, mothering her over this sudden need to hurry back to old foster parents she had never spoken of before. Liz had given her a look which said she understood, that sometimes there was trouble of the kind that you didn't want to talk about, and I know you're lying, but it's okay.

"You take care," Liz had said, as Lottie was halfway out the door, trying to drag herself out of Andrea's hug. Liz had made no effort to get up from her seat in the living room. "You just take care of yourself."

Now she was outside her building, her backpack sitting at her feet like an obedient dog. Payge was nowhere in sight. Lottie let out a squeak of frustration. Five minutes became ten, then twenty, and she still stood alone. With some reluctance, she stooped to pick her backpack up, cringing at the thought of what she would say to Liz and Andrea when she stepped back into the flat.

"Lottie."

She jumped at the sound of his voice behind her. Turning round, she glowered at him, thought about giving him a punch on the arm, then thought better of it. "Don't sneak up on me like that."

Payge sniffed. "I didn't sneak up on you. You just don't listen."

"Where were you? I thought—"

"I had abandoned you? After all I've said?" He gave another sniff. "Let's get a going. We can talk as we walk. I know you're going to ask."

"Tell me more about this pattern thing I'm in."

They walked for some time before Payge began to speak. "The patterns are made to try to achieve certain outcomes. They can't be made with absolute certainty, only a range of probabilities their makers then try to cut down to the one they want."

"What for?"

"You're asking me why powerful people do the things they do. Even if it means disrupting people's lives. Maybe even hurting them?" He looked away from her, sucking on his teeth. "You're still young, I suppose."

"Who are these makers anyway? Where do they come from?"

"Good question. There have always been makers, but it's a rare talent. It takes a lot of nurturing. Steals is only one of them. There are other makers with other aims, making other patterns. One wants this, another wants that. There's a power struggle. You get interference. You get conflict."

They walked in silence again. "This makes a lot of sense," Lottie said.

"I hope not. People should be left alone to get on with their lives in peace."

"No, I mean it explains why a lot of unlikely things happen. How total idiots get elected. Stuff like that. How we make the worst choices instead of the best."

"That's mostly your own stupidity."

Lottie looked up at him. "These patterns are just plots and conspiracies, getting people to do what you want. People have been doing those kinds of things since, well, since forever. What's so special about the makers?"

"They seek to manipulate and control."

"Control what?"

"Everything they can. People. Matter. Energy. Everything."

"Isn't that a bit fanciful? I mean, how would you even begin to do that?"

Payge drew in a sigh. "You really don't listen, do you? I already explained this."

"You did?"

"Everything is made of information, and information is arranged in patterns. Matter and energy behave the way they do because of the information coded in them. So do people. Patterns can be changed. Or made. That's what the makers do. They subvert the random nature of reality into something they want."

"Ooh, so it's like spooky mind control." Lottie wiggled outstretched fingers at him.

"No. It isn't. We're here."

He stopped beside a gate in a sagging wire fence. The gate screeched as he shouldered it open. Beyond the gate was a weed-spotted yard that spoke of long years of neglect. "Over this way."

Payge pointed to the derelict industrial building at the far end of the yard. Graffiti tattooed the building's walls in a continuous strip, all along its length. Among the usual obscenities and declarations, Lottie picked out symbols which seemed to cry out for her to read them but when she tried, the meaning slipped away, as smooth and slick as eel skin. Hard up against the nearest wall, a handrail sloped down into the ground, marking a sunken stairwell.

"Are you feeling alright?" Payge said. "You're pale."

"I'm fine," she lied. Damp sweat bloomed on her face as her insides cramped. She swallowed, feeling nausea swimming closer.

They tramped past the blackened circles of old fires, a litter of beer cans, burnt wood and broken glass marking their progress. Her foot caught an empty wine bottle, sending it spinning. The writing on the weathered label was not in English. It was in no language she recognised, the letters made up of groups of slashes and interlocked ovals, crammed together in tight rows.

They approached the sunken staircase. Even in the light of day, it formed a dark well into the earth. A hidden place, well acquainted with shadows.

"Hi, Lottie!" Jackdaw emerged from the bottom, giving her a wave.

"Why am I not surprised you're here," she said. Now

she could see where the crumbling steps descended to an iron door. The stairwell was covered in more graffiti, over-painted again and again, vibrant colours on top of older markings, rendering the whole into a chaotic frieze. Looking at it made her feel ill. She gripped the handrail, the reality of the cold metal lending her strength.

Jackdaw cocked his head to one side as he looked up at her. "You don't look too chipper, if you don't mind me saying."

"I'll be okay." Her insides were telling her a different story. "If this is some dodgy club or strip joint you're taking me to, I am going to kick your arse."

"I'm hurt you would say so. All the strip joints I go to are perfectly respectable."

Lottie smiled at him and felt better for it. As he led her down the stairs, she sensed the bulk of Payge at her shoulder, one step above. Jackdaw worked a door handle the size of a crowbar. The door opened on noiseless hinges.

"Shall we?" Jackdaw said.

Her stomach heaved, and Lottie swallowed hard. Acid burnt at her throat. She swallowed again, then twisted round to look up at Payge. "On the face of it, going in here with two strangers doesn't seem like a smart idea."

"You think I would waste my time bringing you here, if I meant you harm?"

"I know, you said before." Payge stepped forward, forcing her down the last step. "I'm going," she snapped. "Don't shove me."

The door led into a brick-lined tunnel with a dirt floor. To Lottie's surprise, it smelt dry and clean. She followed

Jackdaw a little way in, while Payge swung the door closed, killing what little light remained. The darkness felt palpable, like a blanket drawn over her. She waved a hand in front of her, striking something.

"Ow. That was my head. Mind what you're doing." Jackdaw's voice echoed slightly in the closed space.

"I can't see."

"Here." She felt Jackdaw's fingers close round her hand.

Payge rested a hand on her shoulder. "We'll lead you," he said. "There are no steps or turns. It's just straight ahead, level all the way."

"You can see in this?"

"Not well enough to do the crossword, but yes, just about."

She turned back to look at Payge before realising how pointless it was.

"Walk," he said.

Jackdaw led her, Payge's hand on her shoulder pushing her on. Lottie counted her steps. After five, she imagined she was having to work harder to keep moving. At ten, she was forcing herself forward. After another two, she stumbled, her balance lost, along with all sensation of the ground beneath her feet. "I think I'm going to be sick," she moaned. Ghostly lines of light appeared, intersecting each other in a complex geometry of angles. They hung in her vision, growing brighter. Lottie looked round, expecting to be able to see Jackdaw and Payge and her surroundings. She could see nothing but perfect darkness.

She felt Jackdaw give her hand a quick squeeze. Payge held her steady, steering her forward, gentle but insistent.

"Not far now, you're doing fine." They walked into and through the lines of light.

Another few steps and the lines faded to nothing. In their place, speckles of illumination lit up the tunnel. True light, she realised, for she could see the barest outline of a small figure in front of her. The speckles grew in number and brightness until the tunnel walls glowed with phosphorescence. Her unruly stomach declared a truce and Jackdaw's hand fell away.

"Nearly there," he said.

"Where?"

"You'll see in a second or two."

They had come to another door, similar to the first. Jackdaw pulled it open, letting in a warm draught scented with earth and minerals. Lottie stepped onto a metalwork balcony, clutching the handrail that surrounded it, as she took in the dizzying vista before her.

A vast cavern arched away in all directions, its walls covered with the same phosphor sheen that lit the tunnel. Sheets of light in white and blues and greens covered every wall, casting the huge space in a soft light, like a summer's eve. Beneath their feet, a rock wall swept down in a sheer drop of a hundred yards or more, to the flat plain of the cavern floor, where strings of lights picked out the streets of a small town. Beyond the town, light rippled off the surface of a dark lake. Above it all, far above, spikes and spires of stone, coated in the same glowing sheen, hung from the cavern's roof.

"Welcome to Ore," Payge said. "Do you think you can manage the stairs?"

"Can I have a minute?" Lottie asked.

"Take your time, love," Jackdaw said. Producing a small flask from a pocket, he took a pull from it and offered it to Lottie. "How did you get on coming through?"

She stared at the town below her, etched out in light. "It felt like something was pushing back on me, then it got a bit weird. I saw this kind of pattern of light. Lines and stuff." Still staring, she tipped the flask to her mouth. "Bloody hell!" She choked and coughed, waving the flask around. Jackdaw rescued it from her hand and held it out for Payge, who shook it away. "What is it?"

"Chilli brandy. Make it myself. Good, isn't it?"

"Good for cleaning floors maybe." She gazed upwards, then across, then down, then back to Payge. "We can't have gone more than ten feet down the stairs to the tunnel. How is this even possible? Where on Earth are we?"

"The free town of Ore has been around for a good long time," Payge said. "And we're not on Earth anymore."

"This is the bit most folk find difficult to take," Jackdaw said. "But you seem to be doing quite well."

"Not on Earth." Lottie's brows knitted. "On another world then?"

"Another world, yes. Another universe."

"Wow." Lottie looked around again, a big grin spreading on her face. "This is so cool."

"Yes, taking it very well," Jackdaw said. He took another pull from his flask.

"So what world is this on?" Lottie said.

Payge shrugged. "This is the world, as far as we know it. There might be light years of rock beyond this. Nobody has ever had the inclination to go digging very far." Lottie gave him an enquiring look, and he shrugged again. "Tough stone."

"And we got here through that tunnel?"

Payge shook his head. "They're called gates, for want of a better word. The tunnel is only there to keep the gate secure."

"Gates?" Lottie asked. "You mean there's more than one?"

He smiled at Lottie's expression. "Many more. Though not all like this. Look around. You see the other stairways fixed to the walls? And down there. You can see some openings in the ground? Some are fenced in or have doors set in them."

Lottie looked and the more she looked, the more she saw.

"Each one is the entrance to a gate. Ore is a crossroads of sorts. And home to some who want a place where you can get on without anybody telling you what to do."

"This is so cool. I just said that, didn't I? Wow. Cool." She tore her gaze away from the view and looked round at Payge. "You've travelled between these worlds?"

Payge nodded. "Yes. Many times."

"So where do you pair come from?" Lottie nodded at the door they had just come through. "Not up there, that's for sure. Are you from here?"

"No, not from here. Nobody is. Ore is, or was, an empty realm. Everyone who is here travelled from somewhere else. Enough talk. Let's get off this stair."

They made their way downwards, flight after zigzagging flight. Around halfway down, Payge stuck out a warning hand to stop their progress. He held a finger to his lips. From below came the stamp of footsteps as someone climbed up. The footfalls grew closer. A figure appeared, coming into view one stair at a time. Lottie saw tousled hair, a striking face, a young man in a faded Ramones tour T-shirt, carrying a large backpack.

"Payge, Jackdaw," he said. He favoured Lottie with a wink.

"Rafe," Payge said.

"How is it above?" Rafe asked.

"Quiet. Below?"

"Unsettled. Lots of new faces around. Watch yourselves." With a farewell nod, he carried on upwards.

"Ore thrives on trade. Information as much as anything else," Payge said. "Let's get on. Time's passing and I'm getting hungry."

"Wait," Lottie said, taking advantage of their enforced stop. "How does anyone live here? What do you eat? Who runs the place?"

"Jackdaw, will you please answer her questions and get her to shut up?"

Jackdaw fell in beside her and they marched down the stairs in step. "You have to like mushrooms if you're going to make Ore your home. Folk seem to muddle along fine deciding amongst themselves and there's general agreement among the neighbouring worlds to leave Ore well enough alone. The rest of it kind of sorts itself out."

"That's not much of an answer," Lottie said.

"I always find too much detail tends to confuse things."

"Who knows about this? Back on Earth? I mean, this changes everything, doesn't it?"

"Not many know. The makers on your world have worked hard to keep it hidden."

"I would have thought that would be quite difficult."

"Not really. Well, it wasn't until the internet came along. Personally, I think it's a losing battle now."

"How long has the gate been there?"

Jackdaw was slow to answer. "Your Earth is an odd place. All the gates on it stopped working about a thousand years, or so the story goes. Then opened up again around the time of your last big war."

"That's still quite a long time for nobody to notice."

He grinned at her. "You people have gotten pretty good at ignoring the obvious when it suits you. But the clues have been there all along."

"You can't leave it there," Lottie said. "What do you mean by that?"

Jackdaw picked up his pace. "Alfheim, Annwyn, fairyland. How many stories are there of strange other worlds and the people who live in them?"

"Yeah, but that's all they are. Stories. Parables. Ways of getting a message across. Manifestations of psychological – I don't know – stuff." Lottie waved a hand in the air to finish her point.

"Are they?" Jackdaw winked at her. "Really?"

The stairs ended, and Lottie found herself standing on the black dirt of the cavern floor. Her questions dried up when they approached the town. She was too busy trying to see everything at once.

First, they passed shacks scattered amongst the rocks and boulders littering the cavern floor. Closer to the town, the buildings became more substantial. Lanterns were strung on poles and fires burnt. There were stalls, small shops, people moving here and there, the buzz of voices. They entered a broad street, and she began to notice how many of the people didn't look human.

"It's rude to stare," Jackdaw said. "Well, not everywhere. In some places it's considered quite the compliment. Still, best not to."

"Sorry," Lottie said. She went right on staring.

Jackdaw took her hand and pulled her along, twisting between knots of people to catch up with Payge. They fell in behind him, walking in his wake as he ploughed through the crowd. People faded out of his way. When they didn't, he shouldered past them. Lottie could hear the growls and threats.

"What's his problem?"

"When he gets hungry, he's not himself. He gets irritable."

"No shit. What's he like if he's starving?"

Jackdaw shook his head and followed Payge up the wooden steps of a two-storey building. The smell of cooking wafted out in greeting.

"What's this place?" Lottie said.

Jackdaw grinned back at her before answering. "The one place nearly all worlds have in common. It's a bar."

Inside, rough tables and benches were spaced around a large common room. The bar looked as if it had been assembled from driftwood. The man behind it raised his hand in greeting as they entered. "Payge!"

"Christopher," Payge said. "You have a room? And can you feed us?"

"Depends."

"Ale?"

"That I can do."

"Steak?"

"Are you fussy about what it came from?"

"Have I ever been?"

Christopher laughed. "How you want it?"

"Bloody."

"For Jackdaw and the lady?"

Payge looked round. "Lottie? Are you hungry?"

She nodded.

"Roast chicken?"

"Sounds good."

"Good for me too," said Jackdaw.

The order made, they settled themselves at a table. Christopher bustled over with a laden tray, setting two large tankards in front of Payge, one before Jackdaw and a wooden mug in front of Lottie. She inspected it, sniffed at the contents, and then sipped. It was dark beer, rich and sweet. She took two big gulps.

"Nice," she said.

Payge emptied one tankard, dribbles running from the corners of his mouth. He wiped them away and set the empty vessel down. "Best in Ore."

"What now?"

"Now we eat."

"No, I mean now that I'm here. Can I go and look round?"

"No, you need to stay out of sight. The stalker must have passed through here to get to us. People will have seen it. We'll ask around, maybe get a lead on who sent it after you."

"You can't bring me to a place like this and keep me locked up."

Payge blew out a long breath and moved his empty mug an inch to one side. "I understand. But the thing is." He stopped and looked at Lottie straight on. "The thing is, we brought you here to keep you alive and well. Which is two separate things, the second being the more difficult. If we fail, it will end badly for me and Jackdaw. But I think I already told you so."

"I thought you might be joking. Or exaggerating."

"Two things Steals never does."

"There must be something I can do to help you. One for all and all for one, if you see what I mean." Lottie trailed off under their combined stares.

"I think you've been reading too many of the wrong kind of book," Payge said. "Anyway, here's the food."

A platter with two thick slices of seared meat was set in front of Payge. Smaller plates with bread and chicken legs came for Lottie and Jackdaw. She drew back at the feet still attached to the legs. Taking a cautious bite of the bread, she found it nutty and good. Payge picked up a piece of meat in two hands and bit into it, tearing sideways with his teeth. Blood ran down his chin and dripped on the table. Without pausing, he bit and bit again until the flesh was devoured. He eyed Lottie's plate. "You eating that?" He nodded at the chicken.

"I've kind of lost my appetite."

With a shrug, Payge picked up the chicken leg and popped it into his mouth. Bones crunched and cracked as he chewed. "You'll stay here to get some rest. Where you'll be safe." He started on the second hunk of meat and within a couple of minutes, lifted the plate to lick off the blood and meat juices. With a final swipe at his lips with the back of his hand, he stood up. "Right, I need to go. Jackdaw will stay with you until you're in your room. Do not leave it. Understand?"

Lottie threw him a sloppy salute. "Yes, sir."

He gave her a disgusted look and left.

"Come on," Jackdaw said. "I'll take you to your room."

"I can't believe this. I'm in a fantasy world, in a giant cave, with two people who aren't human. And I have to go to my room. Are you two for real?"

Jackdaw shook his head in sympathetic understanding. "I know. But what can you do?" He led her to the bar to collect a key, then to a set of narrow stairs.

"At least tell me a bit more," Lottie said.

"About what?"

"Anything. Everything!"

The stairs took them to a homely room of bare floors, wooden furniture and a brightly coloured quilt thrown on the single bed. "I need to go too," Jackdaw said. "You'll be fine here." He held the door open for her. "One question, no more."

"What are you? Oh. Sorry. That was really rude, wasn't it?"

"I'm not noted for my good manners. And I can answer it in one word." He uttered a melodic and incomprehensible series of sounds. "It simply means 'the people' in our tongue. Actually, it says a bit more, but it would take days to explain about clan and kin. Payge and me and all our kin are the people. You have lots of different names for us. Goblins, trolls, kobolds, bauchan, dokkaebi, pukwudgies. Orcs, even."

"You and Payge are related? You're so different."

"And you humans are all the same, are you?" His lips spread in a smile, showing his pointed teeth.

"I suppose not." Her cheeks flushed red. "Will you tell me about it? Even if it takes days?"

"Payge could do it better. He was more of the makar than I could ever be."

"Makar? I don't know that word."

Jackdaw's face screwed up in thought. "A makar is like a storyteller, a historian, a poet. As I said, Payge could do it better, but I'll tell you what I'm allowed to, and I'll feel fortunate I can do so." He stuck out his hand. "Deal?" Lottie reached for him, but he drew back. "Not so quick. In Ore, a deal's a deal. More than anywhere, they take it seriously. I will hold you to this."

"You couldn't hold me back."

He looked at her as if he was about to say something, then he smiled again, sad this time and shook his head. "Be careful. Don't leave this room for anyone but us. Lock the door behind me." Then he was down the stairs, leaving Lottie alone.

She pulled the bolt on the door and crossed to the room's only window. Looking out on the street, she could see no powered machines of any kind. There were some pack animals, including what looked like a miniature elephant pulling a wagon loaded with barrels. There were other beasts she had never seen, and she marvelled at each. But mostly, the traffic was people. Many of them weren't human people. A low-slung sled heaped with bales and drawn by six grey-skinned figures creaked past and Lottie finally looked away, her thoughts overwhelmed by strangeness.

She crossed from the window to the bed and lay down, listening to the sounds drifting up from the street. And whether the sounds lulled her or whether her own mind decided there was only so much it could take in one day, she passed from wakefulness to sleep without realising.

The sound of angry voices awoke her. Rolling off the bed, she crossed to the window to find the source of the noise. In the street, a knot of people had gathered around a stall where the trader and a customer were going head-to-head in an argument. Lottie checked her watch but its digital display was blank. Her phone, when she looked at it, was as dead as her watch. She felt spaced out, set apart from this odd place she was in. She looked at the bolt on the door. She looked out the window, then back at the door and made up her mind. Crossing to the door, she unlatched the bolt and stepped out of her room.

As she stood on the boardwalk in front of the inn, the place reminded her of a frontier town from the Old West. As she wandered away from the inn, she decided it smelt and sounded like one as well. The constant bustle and noise, which seemed to be a feature of the town, never let up for an instant. She cast her gaze up to what should have been the sky. To the stone roof of the cavern above the town. *Maybe you have to keep busy to keep your mind off that.*

She could feel it, she was sure. The immense mass of rock pressing down on the little bubble of air around her. Heedless of where she was going, she walked straight into something. The growl she heard made her realise it was someone rather than something. "Sorry," she stuttered out.

The words that came back were alien, but the intent was clear. The anger in them made her hurry across the road, threading in between the traffic, while she shot a glance or two behind her. The thing she had walked into tracked her with shark eyes sunk deep in pebbled skin.

Ducking around a corner to avoid that inhuman regard, Lottie found a side street lined with stalls offering street food. Cooking smells variously repelled her or drew her in with savoury enticement. Her stomach gurgled as she stopped beside a cart where a woman spooned what looked like rice into pockets of bread. The scent of garlic, tomatoes, and herbs circled around.

"You want?" the stallholder asked. She waved a stuffed bread in Lottie's direction.

Lottie nodded. "I… ah… I don't know how to pay. I've no money. I mean, I have money but not from here. I don't even know if you have money, to be honest."

The woman regarded her with a mix of pity and exasperation. "What do you have?"

Lottie dug through her pockets, gathering her few coins together. "I've only got this."

"Go on then." The woman took the coins and handed Lottie one of the bread pockets.

"Don't I get change?" Lottie said.

This got her a laugh. "You'll do fine here, I think." The woman offered up a few copper discs. "Ore money. Good in this town. And a word of advice. Don't let on you're new here."

Lottie took the coins, nodded her thanks and walked on. The side street led on to a busier road and she began to think the whole town might be one big market as she walked past stall after stall. Each one was devoted to selling a single product in a bewildering multitude of varieties, be it spices, swords, spirits or sausages.

The press of people around her thickened, pushing her this way and that. It became impossible to move forward but she was being shoved towards the middle of the roadway. Over the general clamour of the traders rose cries of surprise. Then of alarm. The crowd surged forward, taking her with it. Close by, a shriek of pain cut through the air. A glimpse of a struggling figure on the ground, trapped by a body on top of them.

The shouting grew. Her snack was knocked from her hand and trampled into the dirt. She was forced towards a narrowing in the street, a choke point where the shops and market stalls on either side created a gap no more than a few arm-lengths wide. People were clambering over the stalls to get clear of the crush in the middle. Still trying to push to one side, she was driven into this narrow gap, now filled with squirming, shoving bodies.

The surge forward lurched to a halt and like a wave hitting a breakwater, the crowd broke apart, shifting in the opposite direction. Space opened up around her. Further up the street, flames were licking through a window. Screams from that direction. A man and a woman barged past her, the woman saying it must be an attack. Lottie saw her chance, an opening which would take her to the side of the street, perhaps into the safety of a building. She raced for it. She almost made it.

The crowd closed up, thicker than before. The press of bodies lifted her off her feet, carrying her along until she was jammed against the boardwalk bordering the store fronts. Its wooden edge dug into her thighs. No way she could pry herself out of the crowd and get onto it. The crush heaved and swayed. Lottie lost her balance and fell.

Legs hemmed her in, a foot stamped on her outstretched fingers, making her cry out. Her cry went unheeded. She was being kicked, stumbled over, stood on. With a squeak of panic, she shuffled sideways, squeezing herself under the gap between the facings on the boardwalk and the dirt road.

She lay for a second, relieved to be out of the chaos on the street. Feet stamped the boards above her, dust and grit rained down on her. The wood groaned under the strain. In her head, she saw the planks collapsing, being driven into her body by the weight of people above her. Digging her feet in, she pushed and wriggled along on her back until she saw the crush of bodies thinning out. Then, sweating and filthy, she rolled from under the boardwalk and staggered to her feet.

As quickly as it had gathered, the crowd began to disperse. People fled from the street. Those that could. Some ran or walked. Some limped or crawled. Others lay still, alone or in small knots, their limbs twisted in unnatural ways.

Lottie stared, struggling to take in what had happened. Someone sprinted past her, shoving her aside. The impact spun her round and she saw a line of men, armed with spears and clubs, marching towards her. She raised her hand, to shout and wave at them, to let them know she meant no harm. Their pace was steady, relentless. Anyone who could run out of their way did so. Anyone who couldn't, fell before their weapons. After a moment's hesitation, she ran with them.

A narrow gap between two buildings offered itself and she bolted through, coming out in a quieter street, this one free from any armed attackers. Unsure where to go next, she caught the arm of a girl fleeing past, asking her the way to Christopher's inn. The girl's look of mute incomprehension and fear, her pathetic attempt to pull her arm free, made Lottie release her. She tried again, approaching an older man trying to shift a laden cart with two wheels stuck in a deep rut in the dirt. He went on pushing at his burden. "Help me," he said between grunts and gasps.

Seeing no immediate threat, she leant her weight against the cart, adding her strength to that of its owner. The cart lurched up and out of the rut, then rolled easy with the pair of them pushing. At the next corner, the man pointed. "Down there. To the right." He rattled off a couple of more directions for her to follow. Lottie nodded her thanks and ran.

She recognised where she was now. A final turn and she was only a stone's throw from the inn. A group of women and men stood in front of it, Payge and Jackdaw amongst them. They all held weapons of some kind, from swords to staves of wood.

"Lottie," Jackdaw called. He waved her over.

She caught Payge's look as she trotted up. "I'm sorry."

Payge shook her apology away. "There's no time." He called to Christopher, the innkeeper. "We have to go."

Christopher grimaced. "I could use you here."

Payge nodded, regret written on his face. "If there was another way…"

"I understand," Christopher said. "Stop by any time. If we're still here."

Payge bowed his head in thanks, then he was hustling Lottie away, sending Jackdaw forward to scout out their path. They ghosted through the streets, keeping close to the shelter of buildings. He kept hold of her hand, guiding her, pausing when they had to cross open ground, always wary. Jackdaw stayed ahead of them, barely visible, returning only to whisper advice.

They reached a quiet crossroads. In the time they took to wait for Jackdaw to return, Lottie asked what was going on.

Payge switched the short sword he carried from one hand to another and scratched at his head. "I thought it was maybe a raid by slavers but it's not."

"Slavers? As in people who take other people away to be slaves?"

"Exactly. It's a lucrative trade across the joined worlds. Yours included, I might add. So don't look so shocked."

"I wasn't. Okay, maybe I was. But you don't think that's what it is."

Payge looked around the street. The way he seemed to never stop looking around. He rubbed at his jaw before answering. "No, I don't think so. This is too organised. Too big an operation. This feels more like an invasion." His gaze stayed on their surroundings, hunting from place to place. "This is bad. There hasn't been an attack like this for years. Maybe since the peace began. I think it might be connected to you." He glanced at her before going back to his ceaseless scrutiny of their position. "And Steals. And whoever else is involved in this that wants you dead. The how and why of it, I don't know. Not yet anyway."

Before Lottie could ask anything further, Jackdaw returned, Payge hushed her to silence, and they stole away again.

They reached the edge of town and moved into the open space beyond it, using scattered boulders and outcrops of rock to provide cover, until they were within sight of the stairway they had used to reach the cavern floor. The foot of the stairs was now brightly lit and guarded by three men. Torches burnt along the pathway leading up to it.

"Damn," Payge breathed. "Damn, damn, damn."

"There," Jackdaw whispered. "Squad coming down the road towards us."

Payge spoke again. "It needs to be now. Three, we can handle. Three and that squad, we can't."

Lottie sensed the change in stance of her two companions. She watched them judging distances. The unspoken body language that passed between them.

"We rush them," Payge said. He looked towards her, catching her eye. "Use what surprise the dark will give us.

69

If we're quick, we'll be up the stairs and away before the others get here. Ready?"

Jackdaw sprang up and began to run, Payge a heartbeat behind him. She followed, running as fast as she could, the gap between them growing wider. Halfway there and the guards were alerted. She saw them readying weapons. Shouts echoed in the still air. Payge pulled ahead of Jackdaw, his legs and arms working like pistons. He was running straight towards a line of spear points. He ran all the harder. A snarl rose up from him, becoming a brutal roar of aggression. One of the guards cast a spear, a clumsy throw that Payge dodged around. The other two guards hesitated, shifting their own spears in their hands, gripping then re-gripping the wooden shafts of their weapons. Payge was nearly on them.

Lottie stumbled, a bad turn of her ankle throwing her out of her stride. Crying out as she limped to a halt, head down, clutching her knees, fighting to get her breath back. Sounds reached her. Metal striking wood in a quick one-two. The ring of steel on steel. A scream she never would have believed could issue from a human throat, a tearing screech of agony that was cut short.

Lifting her head, she hobbled onwards, trying to keep the weight off her twisted ankle, trying to move as fast as she could despite it. To where Payge and Jackdaw stood amongst three bodies.

"Quickly now. Up the stairs." Payge's voice was soft but urgent. His face was speckled with dark fluid. He offered her a hand, sticky with the same matter. The other still held the sword, its blade stained as dark as his hand.

As she let herself be pulled towards the stairs, she caught a butcher's shop smell of fresh-cut meat mixed with the thick scent of ordure. And she saw with sick horror what a sword could do to a living thing. Not much more than a minute had passed since they had run at the guards.

"No time, Lottie. No time. Up you go." Payge spoke to her in a lullaby voice, forcing her to the stairway.

They raced up the first few flights of stairs. Every few steps, Lottie gasped with pain.

"Are you hurt?" Payge asked.

"My back, my legs." The words wheezed out of her. "I got stamped on. Kicked a few times."

Jackdaw called out. "They're at the bottom of the stairs."

"Move it." Payge pushed Lottie ahead of him, heedless of her distress.

The stairway became an unrelenting treadmill of misery for her. Her heart thumped against her ribs. Her legs burnt in response to the demand that they climb and climb. When they neared the top and Payge called a halt, Lottie grabbed a handrail to stop herself falling over. Easing herself down, she perched on a step and groaned, stretching out her legs, the big muscles in her calves and thighs yowling in protest.

"Lost them. I don't think they're following," Jackdaw said. He peered through the latticed metalwork of the stairway. "I'll go down a bit and check, to be on the safe side."

Lottie only found her voice after he had clattered down a flight or two of stairs. "You killed those men. Because of me. They never did you any harm."

Payge nodded in reply. "I had no choice. They were in our way."

She swallowed. "It was horrible. Obscene."

"It usually is." He offered her his hand, and she took it, letting him pull her up. Jackdaw rejoined them, shaking his head at Payge's questioning look. They climbed the remaining stairs more slowly until they reached the door at the top.

"Won't they follow us?" Lottie asked.

"I doubt it," Payge said. "I don't think they were looking for us. They were only guarding the gate to stop anyone getting back here. It looks like somebody wants to split Steals's forces, cut him off from your world and the one he now calls home. We were lucky. Whoever that somebody is, they didn't pick people who knew what they were doing."

He looked past her, over the balcony, to the town below, where fires burnt hard and bright against the darkness. "Amateurs," he said.

Inside the brick-lined tunnel that led to the gate, Lottie counted her paces again. The phosphor glow of Ore faded out, replaced by blackness. The feeling of nausea she had experienced on her first passage through the gate was absent this time. The glowing lines appeared again. Brighter than the first time, clearer, in far greater numbers, growing into a nest of intersections. "Can you see them?" she asked.

It was Jackdaw who answered. "See what?"

"These lines. Blue light. Some are gold. It feels different from the first time we came though. Easier somehow.

Why can't you see them? They're right in front of us. We're walking through them now."

Jackdaw again. "I can't see anything. You didn't get a knock on the head, did you? That can make you see things."

Payge spoke from his place in the lead. "It's the gate. She can see the gate."

There was a note of cautious wonder in Jackdaw's voice. "Are you sure? I've never heard the like of that."

"Neither have I," Payge said. "Not for a long while."

Lottie reached out to touch one of the glowing lines. She jerked her hand back, startled at the static shock feeling she got from it. And the tugging sensation, like a weak magnet pulling at her skin. "Can you maybe tell me about it then? Because this is seriously freaking me out."

Payge again. "This isn't the best time to discuss it."

She felt her stomach lift, as it does in the instant of weightlessness when a roller-coaster passes the top of a climb and falls into a steep descent. The spectral lines vanished and there was only blackness. They stopped walking. She heard the scrape of metal. The door at the end of the tunnel swung open, letting in the electric shine of streetlights. Payge pushed her against the wall, shielding her body with his own, looking out to the sunken stairway and its coating of graffiti.

They waited. Seconds passed. They waited. Payge leant close to her, so close she could feel his breath on her neck. He whispered a single word to her. "Stay."

He crept up the litter-strewn stairs, the faint scuff of his feet the only sound. At the top, he motioned them on, the sword still gripped in his hand. Crouched there, he looked alien to her. Then her thoughts flipped. Payge was just Payge. It was the city beyond him that was a strange and unknown place.

Starting up after him, she missed her footing. Jackdaw caught her arm to steady her.

"I don't feel so great." Her stomach roiled and a wave of weakness washed through her limbs, making her feel shaky and unsteady on her feet.

"I'm not surprised. But you did well back there. Better than most would have done."

He stayed by her side until they emerged from the stairwell. Payge stood a short way off, waiting for them to catch up. "We go back to the bookshop," he said. Casting his sword away, it whickered through the air, landing with a muffled thump amongst the weeds.

"Will we be safe there?" Lottie asked. She got no reply. Payge took up a place on her right, Jackdaw by her left. A light drizzle met them as they left the yard and she shivered with cold and fatigue. "It's late."

"That it is," Jackdaw said. "That it is."

5

HOME AGAIN, HOME AGAIN, JIGGETY JOG

Payge bolted the door of the back room of Mr Steals bookshop. Sodden jackets were cast off. Lottie looked with dismay at the filth ground into the front of her fleece top then at her two companions. The bright glow of the lamplight in the room showed every spot and splash of blood on them. She looked around for something else to look at.

"Get me something to eat," Payge said to Jackdaw. "Anything." As Jackdaw went to rummage in an ancient fridge that sat in a corner, Payge turned to Lottie. "Strip," he said. "We need to tend to your injuries."

Jackdaw returned with a lump of roasted meat. Red juice oozed from it. He took a bite and passed it to Payge, who nodded his thanks and tore two chunks from it with his teeth before handing it back. Their hands left dirty marks on the roast. They continued passing it back and forth until it was gone. Payge licked at his fingers, looking at her. "You haven't taken off your clothes yet." He turned to Jackdaw. "Find something to drink, there's whisky over there."

"I don't know if I should. I think I'll be fine," Lottie said.

Payge dug through a cupboard, pulling out a first-aid box. He wiped at his face, smearing dirt and dried blood. "You're going to treat your own back?" When Lottie said nothing, he answered her troubled look. "I've done this a lot. More times than I can count."

"True, he's quite good at doctoring," Jackdaw said. "Some people he treats actually survive." He held up a bottle and three glasses like a prize. "Single malt. The good stuff. He normally doesn't let me near it."

"That's because you're an uncivilised heathen who thinks rum and cola is the height of sophistication."

Jackdaw set down the glasses. His fingers left smears inside them. He poured three shots and handed them round. "You know," he said, "I enjoyed that. It's been a while since we had a good fight."

"Aye." Payge tipped his drink towards them both. "To the dead. And the living."

Jackdaw raised his own glass in return and drank. The two of them looked at her, waiting, expectant. "It's our way, Lottie." Payge spoke gently. "I only ask you respect it." Lottie raised the whisky to her lips. She tasted blood, dirt, the wash of clean spirit burning her tongue.

"Now are you going to take your clothes off, so I can treat you?" Payge asked.

"We won't eat you or molest you," Jackdaw said. "You're too skinny and you're not our type."

She stood up. "Wash your hands first." Turning away from them, she peeled off her fleece and T-shirt, then after a moment's hesitation, wriggled out of her trousers. She heard Jackdaw suck in a breath. She could just see Payge over her shoulder. The sound of a lid being unscrewed. "What are you putting on me? It smells like wee."

"Funny thing," Jackdaw said. "The other night he asked me to piss in a jar just like that when he said he was making up ointment for bruised backs."

"Will you shut up?" Payge said. "It's just a salve we use. It will sting at first, not for long, then it'll ease the pain and help you heal."

"You make it yourself? I can't believe I'm letting you—" Anything else Lottie would have said was halted as she winced. Payge's fingertips made circles around the bruises and scrapes on her back, the stinging was fierce, but it faded in seconds, replaced by numb warmth. Forgetting she was in her underwear, she allowed Payge to lead her over to a camp bed, where he helped her into a set of baggy pyjamas. "Interesting," she said. Her voice came from far away and was padded with cotton wool. "Fast anaesthetic and narcotic properties. I'm guessing an opioid of some kind."

Payge smiled at her. "Nothing you would find on this world. Now stop asking questions and shut your eyes."

She lay with her eyes closed, enjoying the dark and the comfort and the secure warmth. As she slid towards sleep, she heard them talking but the sense of the words melted away as soon as they were spoken.

"What now?" Jackdaw said.

"Now she believes. Now we take her home and get her to do what Steals wants."

"I don't know, Payge."

"What don't you know, Jackdaw? That you don't want to keep the skin on your back? That you want to keep doing Steals's bidding forever?"

"She's different. She can see the gate. What does that mean?"

Payge shook his head. He swirled his glass, making the whisky dance. "Nobody makes anything like this, not in all the worlds I've been to. It's unique. I don't know what it means but I think we can use her."

"For what?"

"I need to speak to Raven first. Can you find her? Bring her here?"

"You know we're not on the best of terms. And what she thinks about you."

"All too well. But she's still your sister."

"I'll try."

ↄ

Lottie opened her eyes, with no idea of where she was. Only that she wasn't cold, in the dark or in pain. She smelt clean sheets, her back ached and she felt hungry. She sat up, rubbing at her eyes and running a hand through matted hair. Then she saw Payge. He was carving up a loaf of bread, his shirt sleeves rolled up, his tweed waistcoat back on, looking like nothing more than a heavily built shopkeeper.

"Hungry?" he said.

"Starved."

"Over here then."

She clambered out of bed and padded across to the table. There was tea, bread, cheese and jam laid out and she set to lathering a slice.

"How do you feel?" Payge asked.

"Odd. Spaced out. It's a lot to take in."

"I meant your back."

"Oh. It hurts but not nearly as bad."

"Good." Payge watched her as she ate. He poured tea for her. "Going to Ore was a mistake. I put you in harm's way and I'm sorry for doing it. I should have known better. What you did though, leaving the inn? That was plain stupid. You need to be smarter."

"Why?" She glared at him across the table.

"Because you're going to get yourself killed. You saw what happened in Ore. The makers don't hold to your society's rules. They don't answer to anyone, except other makers more powerful than themselves." Payge sat back and blew out a sigh. "Telling off over. I don't know why I'm bothering. I'm not your family. What did you think? Of Ore?"

Lottie chewed and spoke. "I actually quite liked it." She reconsidered. "Some of it, I mean. No, more than that. It's difficult to say what you feel when someone's shown you the impossible."

"Not impossible then, is it? And close your mouth when you eat."

She went to reply, thought better of it and swallowed first. "You know what I meant."

"We could have lost you." Payge poured himself more tea. He motioned to Lottie with the tea pot, and she nodded. When he put the pot down, he spoke again, his words coming out with care. "I need you to do something. You're not going to want to do it, but it will help."

"Help with what? And why should I do something I'm not going to want to do?"

"Help get you out of danger. Is that reason enough?"

Lottie bobbed her head up and down. "I'd say it's a fair point."

"You need to take this seriously."

"Is the charm offensive over for the day, then?"

Payge's face darkened. Then, to her surprise, he smiled. "I'll show you what I mean." Clearing a space on the table, he fetched the laptop he had shown her before.

"The pattern?" she said.

"Here." He pointed to a symbol on the screen. "This represents Ore. You see how the line to it ends then transfers to here." He swiped one finger across the screen, pulling more lines on to it. "See how the pattern is becoming simpler? It's reaching an end point. When it ends, you'll be safe. Your actions will push it along, get it to the end point faster."

"Can you teach me to read all of this?"

"No."

"Then why show me at all?"

"To help make you understand."

Lottie fell silent. She made a pretence of studying her breakfast leftovers. "Those three men you killed. Three innocent people dead because of me. How am I supposed to understand that?"

"I doubt they were innocents. They were soldiers. Mercenaries, in all likelihood. They wouldn't have stopped for a second to do the same to us."

"So that makes it all right?"

Payge shrugged. "It does for me."

"But they're dead!"

"When you make war on someone, these things happen."

"But—"

Payge pursed his lips. "I was a soldier for a long time. I suppose you get used to it. I can't really say anything else to try to make you feel better but if it helps to talk about it…"

"I don't know what I think. It's like there's just a mess inside my head." Lottie looked for insight in her mug of tea and found none. "I was really scared when I got caught in the crowd back in Ore. Then I felt happy because I escaped. Well, not happy. Maybe relieved is more like it. Then I felt bad because I hadn't done more to help the people who were hurt and couldn't get away. I felt a bit guilty about abandoning this old man and his cart. It was maybe all he had in the world. But I did help him a little. Before I ran away and left him. Then you murdered those men."

"I didn't murder them. I was protecting you." Payge rubbed at his eyes. "I was younger than you when I fought in my first battle. It lasted for days. I went through everything you've just described."

"Oh," Lottie said. She stared back at him. "I can't picture you being scared. You just don't seem the scare-easy type. More like you doing the scaring, to be honest."

"I've learnt to deal with fear, but it doesn't mean I don't feel it."

"I suppose that's what courage is."

"Courage comes easy when you're surrounded by an army and the flags are flying and your blood is hot. It's when you're alone and in pain and you have nothing, that's when you find the measure of your courage."

Helping herself to another slice of bread and some cheese, she dug a knife into the butter. "Have you been in many battles?"

Payge pulled at his chin. "I've been in a fair few. I fought in the Long War. And the Short War. I was at Bitter March, though I'll always wish I wasn't. The civil war in the Wildings. I helped Handsome John to his throne, and I helped lever his fat backside off it again. I put a spear in the Iron King's champion and watched as Fair Uriel put her sword through the Iron King's throat." He fell silent, rubbing at the back of his hand, as though nursing an old wound that had never been forgotten or quite healed. "She was the only one I ever fought for willingly."

"I don't recognise any of those names."

"You wouldn't. None of them happened here."

"Oh. I'm still having trouble getting my head round all this."

"It can take a while for the idea to bed in."

"And now you sell books."

"And now I keep books."

"And save students in distress."

His smile was small and thoughtful. "That too."

Lottie looked at the table. "What do I do now?"

"Give yourself a bit of time. Reflect on what happened but don't dwell on it."

"Thanks, but I meant what we do now about this." She pointed to the pattern. "What's this thing you want me to do."

"I'll explain." His fingers traced around two symbols on the screen. Names were typed in boxes below the symbols. Andrea. Liz. "Your friends. Wait, I need my notes."

Payge crossed the room to look through his desk, leaving Lottie to stare at the pattern. She tried to make sense of it, but it was like looking at sheet music and having no idea what the notes sounded like. "What's this got to do with my friends?"

Payge continued to rummage through his desk. Lottie poked at the laptop, pushing it askew on the table. "Why the swords and spears? Why not guns? In Ore, I mean."

"Why don't you people use nuclear weapons every time you have a conflict?" Payge said.

"Um, because there are treaties and conventions and the like?"

"There you go then."

"But guns are a fair degree away from atomic bombs."

"Not for some worlds. They would shift the balance of power too much. And you have to be careful with guns, in case somebody comes back at you with something much worse."

"Like what?"

Payge made a satisfied noise as he dug a notebook out of a drawer. "Over a century ago, there was a war between different factions of makers. Whole worlds were lost. Poisoned. Laid waste. Yours might be the only world with nuclear weapons but you're not the only ones with weapons of mass destruction. Very far from it. A certain amount of coming to senses went on, accords were made, tacit agreements reached. The peace began some seventy years back. It's held, more or less, ever since. But greed and desire are universal. Power lies in the Low Countries now, spread between different factions. It's a complex situation. And a volatile one. The trouble is some see it as an opportunity. Here we go, your friends."

He read from his notebook. "Elizabeth McReadie. Second-year student, politics and economics. In the early stages of alcohol dependency. Her tutors doubt she will make it through to her third year. Considerable personal debt. Accurate description, would you say?"

"I don't know. Liz doesn't talk about her family. I never realised before. Or about the drinking. Or money." She looked at Payge. "Things a friend might know."

Payge answered by flipping over a sheet and carrying on. "Andrea Ross. Second-year law student. Average grades but struggling. Moderate drinker, occasional cannabis user. No debt. Has just started an affair with one of her tutors."

"No!" Lottie stared. "Andrea's having a fling? Bloody hell. And blow? Her dad would have a fit."

"It's her father Mr Steals is interested in. Do you know him?"

"He's been around the flat, said hello, but I wouldn't say I know him. Seemed nice enough, though a bit overly protective, from what Andrea has said."

"Steals believes Andrea's father could, with the right help, reach a position of significant influence. Steals wants that influence in his pocket. You are a key part of achieving it. It's much less likely to happen without you."

Lottie looked at him, and Payge looked back. She hoped he would say this was all a put-up, that he was just pulling her leg. His mild look told her different. A small part of her thought maybe she was walking on the edge of a precipice, a sheer drop-off she didn't even know was there. "This is quite something." She turned her attention back to the pattern on the screen. "You said before, Liz and Andrea are in danger?"

Payge took his time answering. "Yes. The longer this goes on, the more they will be."

"Because of me? Because I'm around them?"

"Yes."

"What if I just leave? Will this end?"

"No, it won't end. It will fall to your friend Elizabeth."

"I was first choice?"

Payge nodded slowly.

"So that's my out, is it? I have to do Mr Steals's bidding?"

"It's a lot better position than some are in."

"You don't look as if you're doing too badly."

Payge tapped his finger on the table; it made a *dunk-dunk-dunk* rhythm of irritation. Then he sighed, and the fire seemed to go out of him. "I could tell you, but would you listen?" After a few moments, he rose and began to busy himself with tidying the table.

Lottie stayed seated, her anger draining away in the face of Payge's climb down. Feeling awkward, she struggled for something to say. A memory of a conversation came to her. "Payge, were you always a soldier? Only Jackdaw said you were a makar, which is a bit like a poet, I think—"

He pivoted round to face her. "Jackdaw told you this, did he?"

"I didn't mean to get him in any trouble. I don't want to cause offence or anything, I'm just trying…" She had to stop, her voice was trembling too much, and tears were too close. "I don't know why I'm crying." Sniffing, she wiped at her eyes with the back of her hand.

Payge came over to the table and sat beside her, passing her the dish towel. "It's stress. A reaction to what you've been through. I've seen men who thought themselves brave, who couldn't string two words together for days after their first fight. And yes, I was a makar. But it was a long time ago, before I was a soldier." He reached out to take her hand, and she let him. "Since then, I've had no choice but to do what I'm told. Like most of my people. I wouldn't wish it on anyone, so I'm doing what I can to stop it happening to you. Do this and get away. Get out of the pattern."

"What do I have to do?" Lottie asked. She dabbed at her eyes with the dish towel. She thought about wiping her nose on it but laid it back on the table instead.

"Andrea's father has a flat in the city. He uses it during the week when he's working. I need you to get his mobile phone number from Andrea."

"I can't just ask her for her dad's phone number. Why not phone his office if you want to speak to him?"

"I don't want to speak to him. I want to confirm he's where I think he will be this evening. You need to do this today. As soon as you can. Yes?"

Lottie nodded.

"Good girl. Right, let's get you back home. Don't leave until you get the phone number. I'll be watching for you."

6

LIE, STEAL, CHEAT
AND DECEIVE

The flat was empty when Lottie unlocked the door. She walked from room to room, listening to the quiet and smelling the scents of her living space. She made tea and waited for her flatmates to return, wondering what to tell them and what they would say if she simply told them the truth. After a brief debate with herself, she settled on her original lie, adding an administrative mix-up and a nightmare of missed travel connections on the journey home.

When Liz and Andrea arrived home, they fussed over her, sympathised with her, made her dinner and listened to her story. "They should be ashamed," Andrea said. "Making you go all the way there then saying they got the wrong person. It's not right."

Lottie agreed with her, saying less and less as Andrea said more and more, while Liz watched them both in silence. The discussion ran its course, Andrea announced she was going for a shower, leaving Lottie alone with Liz.

"Were you in a fight or did you fall off the bus?" Liz asked.

"What?" Lottie said.

"Your hands are all scraped, there's scratches on your face and you're moving around like an old woman."

"I, uh, yeah, I did take a bit of a tumble. Banged my knee. And my elbow."

"Is that a fact?" Liz said. "You need to be more careful."

Lottie nodded, trying with desperate hopelessness to stop her cheeks flushing red.

Liz spoke again, the edge gone from her voice. "Whatever it is, don't keep it to yourself. It'll tear you up inside. You hear me?" Lottie made no reply.

Slapping the arms of her chair, Liz made to get up. "Right, I'm going down the student union for a proper drink. You coming with me?"

"Liz, it's a Wednesday night, maybe you shouldn't…"

Her friend gave her a puzzled look. "Where have you been? It's Friday, you muppet."

"Sorry. It's been a hectic few days. I must have lost track."

"Sure you won't come with me?"

"No. Yes. I might."

"Well, make up your mind."

Lottie stood up. "I will but I need to phone someone first. I'll ask Andrea. My phone's totally dead."

"Here, use mine." Liz slipped a scuffed smart phone from her pocket and proffered it to Lottie.

"No, it's okay. I'll get Andrea's."

"Go on. I don't mind."

Lottie tried to make herself sound casual, but she was sure her voice was coming out in a reedy squeak. "I don't know how long it will take."

Liz smiled at her. "And I can't help a friend in need? Hang the expense, dear muppet, and phone away."

Prickly with discomfort, ashamed of herself, Lottie answered her. "Andrea can afford it, can't she? Her rich daddy? Me and you, we're different."

Liz stared back, the smile on her face fading to disappointment. "Go on then."

Lottie made her way to the bathroom door. "Andrea, can I use your phone? I broke mine."

Andrea's reply was muffled by the thin barrier between them. "Sure. I left it in the front room."

"What's the number to unlock it?"

"Hang on five minutes and I'll be done here."

Lottie bit her lip and squeezed her hands together. Her fingers squirmed over each other. "I need to make the call now. It's to an office and I'm scared I'll miss them. It's quite important. They might be closed in five minutes."

"Oh. Okay then. It's one, nine, eight, four."

"Thanks," Lottie mumbled.

She stepped away from the door, back into the living room, where she picked up Andrea's phone from the table. Liz watched her without speaking. Putting in the security code, an awful realisation struck her; she would have to phone someone to complete her fiction. She swiped her way to the address book, giving Liz a weak smile. "Need to find the number."

"Really?" Liz said.

There were three numbers listed as "Dad" in the phone. "Need a pen," she said. Liz made no effort to help her. Behind her, Andrea called through as she left the bathroom.

"How are you getting on?"

"Fine, fine. Writing down the number for next time." She scribbled on a piece of scrap paper, then put the phone down.

"Not making the call?" Liz asked. There was a razor in her question, hidden in a look of innocence.

"I better take this through to my room."

"No need. You get on and make your call. I'll get out of your way." Liz was out of her chair, snatching up her coat and bag, closing the door of the flat behind her with a bang. Feeling utterly miserable, Lottie went to her own bedroom and closed the door.

Andrea called to her. "Did you get through okay?"

"Sure," Lottie said. She stopped to quell the hitch in her voice. "I left your phone on the table." Cuffing away silent tears and pulling her sleeves down to cover her hands, she drew her knees up to her chest, cradling her arms around them. The noise of Andrea bustling around the flat was a sound from another place that existed behind a high wall she could not climb.

"What do I do?" She wasn't aware she had said it out loud. She bit at her bottom lip and stared out of her window, her body rocking in tiny arcs. "What am I doing?" A fantasy flitted through her head. *Grab a bag and disappear. Leave everything. Leave Liz and Andrea to deal with whatever comes next?*

Looking round her threadbare room, she thought about Payge and Jackdaw, how quickly they had fitted themselves into her life. *Are they my friends now?*

When no easy answer came, she stood up and went to the door, calling out to Andrea as she left the flat. Outside, it was more than halfway to night-time. The air was cold, filled with the damp smell of autumn. She shivered inside her coat but welcomed the fresh touch of the evening on her face.

"Did you get it?"

She spun round, her heart thumping. Payge stood by the path, his hands in his pockets.

"You scared the shit out of me. Stop it."

"Did you get the phone number?"

"Yes, I got your bloody phone number. Happy now?" She stomped down the path, passing him as she did.

"Can you give it to me, please?"

"I'll bloody give you something."

"Lottie." He called to her, and she stopped, a good half dozen paces beyond him. He sounded tired. He looked tired. There were dark stains on his jacket. Mud or something else. Under the harsh contrast of the streetlights, it was difficult to tell.

Payge rubbed one of his big hands over his face. "Things are... not good. It's not safe here." He hesitated, as if uncertain how much to say. "Walk with me. Please? Just to the road. Then we'll get a taxi or a bus."

"Where to?"

"Away from here will do for now." He looked around, as if catching a sound Lottie could not hear. "Just a dog walker."

"Will you tell me what's going on?"

"Once we're away."

"Okay."

They crossed the small park in front of Lottie's building, onto the busy street that bordered it. They passed the alley where Payge, she was now sure, had killed a total stranger on the night she was followed home from the library. Up to the bus stop where she had faced that stranger and had fled from him in panic.

Payge moved close to her. She let him, his solid bulk reassuring beside her. They waited at the kerbside, Payge looking round constantly. There was a taut energy in him. It was infectious. She began to feel jumpy herself. When a bus drew up, Payge hustled her on.

"Where's this one going?" she asked.

"No idea and it doesn't matter," he said.

Ten minutes later, they got off at a random stop. The tension leached out of Payge, and he went back to looking tired. "Let's find a bar or a cafe or something. I need to eat. I can't think straight when I'm this hungry. We need to rest too. It's going to be a long night."

"I've seen you eat. They'll throw us out."

He smiled down at her. "Don't worry. I can mind my manners when I have to."

After some searching around, they found a bar, ordered meals, and installed themselves in a booth near the door.

"So?" Lottie said.

Payge said nothing. He picked at his fingernails, not looking at her.

"You said you would tell me."

"I know. I'm just not sure how to say this."

"Say it as it comes. That usually works for me."

"It does? Remarkable."

"Get on with it. You're being evasive."

"Sorry." Payge went back to work on his fingernails.

"You do that a lot, I've noticed. Apologise."

"Guilty conscience."

"Somehow, I doubt it."

"We need to get things moved on. As quick as possible." Payge frowned down at his hands. "To the point where you don't matter." He gave her a brief smile. "I'm not saying you don't. What I am saying is, you will be safe. That's the important bit. Because Jackdaw isn't here, I need you to break into Andrea's father's flat and hide a package. That's what you have to do. To be safe."

"You want me to break into someone's house?"

Payge nodded.

A young man approached their table, bearing two plates. "Two mixed grills?" he asked. "On one plate?"

"Here," Payge said. He licked at his lips as a heap of meat was set in front of him.

"And the vegetarian chilli?"

"Here, please," Lottie said.

Their server bade them enjoy their meal and left them to it. Lottie eyed the glistening pile in front of Payge. "Don't you worry about your cholesterol?"

Payge picked up a chop and attacked it with obvious relish. "No. I doubt I'll die of a heart attack. Not in this line of work."

"And this line of work now involves burglary."

"Look, it's no big thing. Nobody will get hurt. I'll be outside, keeping watch. You go in, do the job, back out again. It'll only be minutes."

"Yes, but it's somebody's home. It's breaking the law. And besides, I don't know how to get through a locked door."

"Lucky we have a key then, isn't it?"

"How did you get it?"

"Your friend Andrea had a set of keys. From when she stayed there during her first year of study. Jackdaw borrowed them. I copied them."

"Why can't you go in?"

"Because I'll be outside, keeping watch, making sure there's no bother. And to warn you, if there is."

Lottie stirred her chilli. "I don't like this, it's wrong."

Payge nodded and munched. "Of course it's wrong. Let's face it, there's nothing very right about this. But still, what do you do? Die instead?" He looked at her. "Ready to do that? Or do this one simple, easy thing?"

"I'm not used to this. I'm not you or Jackdaw with your... adventures. I'm just a student. Just ordinary."

"You're coming dangerously close to whining."

"Jeez, you're a miserable, cold-hearted bastard."

Payge pointed his fork at her, a chunk of sausage speared on it. "Better. Much better. You've got a bit of fire in you now. This is when I see you at your best." He popped the sausage into his mouth. "You're right. I should try harder. So, what's it to be?"

Payge gnashed at the rind of fat from his steak before swallowing it in a huge gulp. Lottie chewed a spoonful of her chilli.

"I think you know the answer already."

"Good. Now can you finish up that stuff you claim passes for food, and can we get this done?"

Lottie gave a small nod in reply and after a half-hearted attempt to finish her meal, she pushed her bowl away.

⌁

They walked across the city for almost half an hour before stopping. "This is it," Payge said. He pointed to a cluster of low-rise apartment blocks across the street. The area spoke of quiet prosperity, tidy pavements, expensive cars, boutique shops. No graffiti in sight.

Payge took out his mobile phone and tapped at the screen. "This is why I needed his number. Hello, Mr Ross?" His voice was bright with enquiry. "Jim Prentice from the *Evening News* here, I was just wondering if I could— How did I get this number? I called your office earlier and they said— Oh. I see. Well, I'm sorry to have bothered you, sir. I'll call again—" He held the phone away from his ear and looked at it. "Rude. Still, he's at dinner, where he should be."

Digging in his pocket, he produced a set of keys and shook them at her. "This one gets you into the lobby. This for the front door. First floor, Flat 1B." Now he handed her a padded envelope. "There's a memory stick in here. If he's got a desktop computer, plug it in at the back. Failing that, find the Wi-Fi router and plug it in there. Or the TV, if it's a smart one. What's left in the envelope, you hide. Somewhere it won't be found by accident. At least not for a few days."

"What about CCTV?" Lottie asked.

Payge reached out to her, and she jerked back. More slowly, he reached round to pull up the hood on her jacket. "Keep your head down. Just a precaution. There's nothing suspicious about someone going into a building using a key, is there?"

"I feel a bit sick."

"Understandable, given the circumstances." He looked at her a moment longer, appraising her. "This will help you. Trust me, it will."

Lottie nodded and swallowed. They walked into the shadows under the canopy of a closed-up shop. Payge pointed across the street. "I've got sight of the front door from here. I'll stay in this spot the whole time. Now on you go."

Just do this. Just do this. Just do this. The repeated thought matched the cadence of her steps, keeping her going as she marched across the road. But as she approached the main entrance to the apartment block, she slowed down, aware of the cool slick of sweat on her back and that she badly needed to pee. She glanced back and saw Payge, his hands tucked in his pockets, staring at her. She lifted her hand to wave at him. He made no effort to wave back. Her own hand, half-raised, dropped back to her side. Pulling the key out, she opened the outside door and made her way into the lobby. *This is okay. I'm still not doing anything wrong here. I could explain this. Sort of.*

Ignoring the lift, she took the stairs to a wide landing with only two doors, marked 1A and 1B. *Payge said the place would be empty. What if it's not? What if there's someone at home? Andrea's mum, come to visit?* She waited for a moment, listening. *If there's a noise from inside, I'll go back.* The silence answered her. *Do I switch the lights on when I go in?* Lottie chewed at her lip, thought about going back to ask Payge, thought about phoning him and realised she had no way of doing so. *He should have given me a phone. So he can warn me. Did he forget?*

Casting an anxious look over her shoulder, she slotted the key into the lock on the door of Flat 1B. The key turned, the lock clicked, and the door swung open. She was inside. Inside someone else's home. *This might take a bit more explaining.*

There were three doors off the hallway in front of her. Two of them stood open, allowing dim light to filter through. The third was closed. *No lights on. That's good, nobody at home. Unless they're in bed. Why didn't I go to the loo when I had the chance?*

The thick carpet muffled her footsteps as she cat-walked to the end of the hall and peeped into a living room and kitchen area lit by the glow of the streetlights outside. The place was pristine, tidy to the point of obsession. She backtracked to the next open door. A bathroom that out did the living room for neatness. Looking round the small room reminded Lottie how desperately she needed to make use of it. One door unopened. One room left. The bedroom.

She faced the final door, gripped the handle and turned it. The door opened without a sound. The curtains were drawn, making the room a pit of darkness. In the meagre light coming from the hallway, she could just make out a double bed. Made up and not slept in.

Lottie whooshed out a huge breath before making her way back to the living room. Reaching for the light switch, she caught herself and drew her hand back. Moving over to the windows, she took out the packet Payge had given her and opened it. Inside was a memory stick in a ziplock bag and slim bundles of pristine bank notes, fifties and twenties. Pulling one bundle out, riffling the edge of it, she thought there must be thousands of pounds. More troubled than she wanted to admit, she slid the bundle back in with the others.

Her bladder was letting her know it couldn't wait any longer. Stuffing the envelope in her pocket, she scurried to the toilet. Sitting herself down, she swung the door shut out of habit, the tiny window high on the wall giving her just enough light to see by. Blessed relief mixed with growing anxiety. Voices and the sound of footsteps reached her from outside the flat. She shot up, heaving at her clothes, praying the sounds were being made by whoever lived next door.

A key rattled and clicked in the front door. Lottie stopped breathing. With utter horror, she listened. Two voices, a man and a woman. He was laughing, she was giggling. The front door was opened, making the voices sound much louder and much closer. A switch clicked, spilling a fan of light under the bathroom door. The front door banged shut. The man said something. Too low to hear. The sound of clothing rubbing on clothing. The sound of kissing. A low moan.

The man, urgent, insistent. "Here, right here."

The woman. "Easy, take your time."

The soft bump of a body pushed against the wall. The woman, a smile in her voice. "Mr Ross. You are a bad, wicked man."

The man. "Only because you make me."

The whisper of clothes dropping to the floor.

Lottie stood, petrified. But her thoughts raced around in giddy spirals. *It's Andrea's dad. Not with Andrea's mum. It doesn't sound like her mum. Her mum wouldn't do that. I don't think. Would she? What if one of them needs to go?*

The noises from outside became more insistent, a heel thumped against the wall, a deep male grunt, a female sigh of pleasure.

The woman again. "Not here. The bed. Take me there."

Lottie blushed to a hot glow. Movement in the hallway. A door opened, a laugh and a happy shriek. Lottie felt like she might vomit with anxiety.

Wait, some cool voice told her. *Wait. Until they're… more occupied.* So, she waited, while every other part of her screamed at her to bolt for the door. And there was still the envelope in her pocket. No place in the bathroom she could see to stash it. Gathering up what courage she had, courage that was draining away with each passing moment, she ghosted the door open and stepped into the hall. Light from the open bedroom door cast a bright band on the carpet.

Just cross it and you're in the living room. Slip the envelope under the sofa. Plug in the memory stick. A few seconds. Once you're running, there'll be no catching you. Get it done.

The sounds from the bedroom had become more urgent, more liquid. She took her chance. With soft steps, she made her way to the bar of light sectioning the hallway. She paused to take a breath. She stepped into the light. She couldn't help but look into the bedroom.

The woman, a young woman, not Mrs Ross, was on the bed, down on forearms and knees, long hair obscuring her face. Behind her was Mr Ross, his hands clasping the woman's hips. He was looking straight out the door. To where Lottie stood in the light.

She froze, her gaze hooked on Mr Ross. She watched him struggle to make sense of what he was seeing. His bafflement morphed into shock. Lottie's nerve snapped. She spun round, her legs tangling in each other, and she fell hard. Frantic voices reached her from the bedroom. She scrambled up and launched herself towards the front door. She reached it as the shout came from behind her.

"You. Stop."

She turned without thinking, in blind obedience to the voice of authority.

Mr Ross stood in the hallway, naked, one hand clutching the bedroom door. "Wait. I know you. You're one of Andrea's friends. How did you get in? Did you break into my house?" He started towards her. "Don't you move. I'm calling the police."

Lottie's gaze dropped to where the remains of his erection waggled at her as he approached. Realisation dawned and he stopped, his hands reaching to cover his groin. Taking her chance, she threw open the door and pelted down the stairs. Through the entrance lobby and outside, sprinting across the road to the shadowed shop front where Payge had said he would meet her. It was deserted. She looked back in desperation, half-expecting to see the naked Mr Ross chasing her, his hands still cupped over his crotch.

"Payge?" she called. "Payge?" It was a shout this time, bringing worried looks from a passing couple. "Payge," she said to the empty street. "Where are you?"

She waited and there was no sign of him. She waited long past the point where she knew it was hopeless. Then she turned her back on the apartment block and slunk away into the city.

⁓

She felt so weary when she walked into her own flat. The sight of Mr Ross sitting beside his daughter on their battered sofa set her heart beating faster, but her body told her it'd had enough adrenaline for one night. She eyed him up, waiting for the storm to break.

"I think you've got some explaining to do, young lady." His mouth set itself in a prim line after he spoke.

Lottie did not reply. Her jaw clenched. The lines on her own face might have been cut in stone.

"Aren't you going to say anything?"

Still, she did not answer.

"Andrea, are you going to get your friend to say anything?" Mr Ross shifted in his seat, the better to see his daughter.

Lottie looked to Liz, sitting off to one side, her expression studiously neutral. Andrea clutching her father's hand, looking worried and confused. Dad just plain angry.

"Don't speak to me like I'm a child," Lottie said. "Save it for your daughter." She knew she had said the wrong thing. There would be no recovering this now.

Dad was out of his seat. "You were in my flat. You broke in. I saw you."

The accusation made. Andrea had begun to sob in quiet breaths. Lottie chewed at her bottom lip. She looked to Liz for support but there was neither sympathy nor condemnation there. So, she started to work out how to say what she had seen. How to phrase the destruction of her friend's family.

Dad spoke first. "It was you. I've got a witness. My assistant was with me. Helping me with some files. She saw everything." Dad was shrill in his announcement. He produced his phone and began jabbing in a number. "I'm calling the police right now."

His lie struck at her. How easy he made it. Distorting the world to his will. Lottie thought about how her truth would weigh up against the falsehoods of this man and his girlfriend. Better to say nothing, spare Andrea the pain. *Anyway, what can I say about why I was there? That doesn't sound like I've lost it completely.*

She felt the weight of the package still in her pocket, forgotten since she had left the flat. A weight that would pull her down. *I need to get rid of this damn thing.* She started for the door as Mr Ross finished his call.

"They're on their way over," he announced to the room. "Hang on. Where are you going?"

"Out," Lottie said.

"I don't think so." He moved to stand between her and

the door. Lottie carried on past him and as she did, he grabbed her arm. "You're going nowhere."

Lottie looked from her arm to the man's face. "Let go of me."

The grip on her arm tightened. He began to pull her back into the room, back towards the sofa, using his physical strength where his authority had failed. Lottie kicked him in the shin. Mr Ross yelped and let go of her. It crossed Lottie's mind to kick him again.

"You hit me," he said.

It sounded like a querulous whine to Lottie, so she did kick him again, catching him on the knee. He staggered and went down, crying out in distress. Andrea was out of her seat, rushing to her dad, the teary look she gave Lottie somewhere between fear and disbelief.

Lottie glanced over to Liz. "Liz, you've got to believe me. It wasn't like what he's saying. I did go there, but not to…" She didn't know how to go on. Her friend's face was a closed door. No words would open it. Something was breaking inside her, shearing with awful finality and she felt the hurt of it, distant but growing. Big enough to fill her, big enough to drown her.

"I'm sorry," she said. "That's not how it happened. Not all of it. I just want someone to hear me out." But no one was listening.

She walked to the front door and laid her hand on it. Behind her, Mr Ross was once more declaring his intention. How he would have her arrested for assault, along with breaking and entering. Angry, tired and heartsick, Lottie closed the door on his yammering, leaving behind her friends and her home, exchanging them for the night and the only place she had left to go to. Mr Steals Books.

7

WHO COULD THAT BE,
ON THIS VERY DARK NIGHT?

The streets were busy despite the late hour, clumps of people spilling out of bars as closing time was called. She walked among them, unnoticed and unremarked on, making her way to Gallowgate Lane. *Less than half an hour and I'll be there. Or leave it until the morning? Maybe better to get a night's sleep. Where am I going to sleep?* It dawned on her there were thousands of pounds in her pocket. *A hotel or something?*

She started to look round, checking the opposite side of the road, led by her last thought. Her gaze stopped on a tall figure moving into the shelter of a doorway. She looked away, a worm of dread working at her insides, then made another quick look to be sure. Still there, cupping its hands to its face. A match flared, illuminating its features. The glow of a cigarette at its lips. The creature Payge had called a stalker. She remembered how quickly they had fled from it in the daylight.

A taxi swept past, and she cursed her own stupidity for not flagging it down. Further down the street, a couple were climbing into another. Lottie sprinted towards them. "Excuse me," she called. One half of the couple, the woman, lifted her head. Lottie called again, waving her arm as she ran towards them. "Excuse me." Now the man followed his partner's stare with his own wary look. Lottie stopped in front of them, the words tumbling out of her in breathless haste. "Do you mind if I have this one? I'll pay you." The uncertainty on the faces of the couple hardened into suspicion. Lottie fumbled in her pocket, trying to snare the envelope. "I can give you a hundred. If I can have your taxi."

"Bloody druggies." The man spat the words out, bundling his partner into the taxi. "Out of her head."

The door slammed shut and the taxi pulled away, leaving behind the stink of diesel fumes. The street was quieter now, near deserted. Tinny music and the smell of burger meat wafted from a takeaway some short distance further along the street. She hurried to it and stopped outside, lingering in the oasis of light cast by the takeaway's sign. Checking back down the road and sure enough, the creature was still there. It had moved from its doorway, keeping the same distance between them. Stalking her.

I'll give myself a minute here. Just to rest.

It was easier than admitting how scared she felt, hanging around outside the takeaway as people came and went less frequently and the minutes until it closed grew fewer and fewer. She watched the figure across the road watching her, time marked out by cigarette after cigarette.

"Are you okay, miss?"

The question caught her by surprise. She turned to see two policemen walking towards her. When she didn't answer, they looked at each other, silent communication passing between them.

"Have you been drinking?" one asked. "Or taking anything?"

Her heart thumped against her ribs. Her sweetest smile came out, "I don't drink." She gave them a long-suffering look. The lie came easy. "But I'm waiting for some friends who do."

"Are you sure?" The pair of them crowded in front of her. Two big men made bigger by the bulk of the protective gear they wore. Looming over her. Lottie pressed herself back into the wall.

"Are you sure you're waiting for your friends? Are you sure you aren't waiting for something else? Waiting for someone to pick you up?"

Lottie opened her mouth to answer, then decided not to.

The first police officer spoke again. "Perhaps you should go home. Now."

"I, uh…" The crazy thought skittered around her head that she had to do something. Tell them what she had done. That she had broken into someone's home. That she was a thief. Give them a reason to arrest her. Show them the package. Let there be an end to it. Just give in.

But I didn't steal anything. I didn't break in. I had a key. Okay, maybe I did break in…

"Fine. I'm going." She made to leave but the policemen stayed put, blocking her way. Lottie bit down on the anger she felt at what these two men had assumed about her. "Sorry. Can I go now?"

One of them stepped aside without a word, and she started away, moving quickly, plotting a path to the bookshop in her head, going over and over in her mind what she must do. *Stick to the main streets. Stay in the light. Make sure there's people around.* It occurred to her the bookshop was on a quiet side street. Where she had never seen a single soul. And it would be closed. She carried on anyway, driven by need, her thoughts narrowed down and pared away by swelling fear. Until she heard her name being called.

She stopped, squinting down a dark walkway between two office blocks. A small figure stood in the gloom, beckoning to her. Lottie hesitated, unsure. The figure stepped towards her, into better light. At first, she thought it was Jackdaw. Same height, same build. Only Jackdaw didn't have long braids of black hair. Jackdaw didn't have swirls of tattoos on his face, nor gold piercings that glittered when he moved. The same almond-shaped eyes though, but more slanted, the skin more olive, the teeth more pointed. And female, clearly female.

"Lottie, I'm a friend. Jackdaw, Payge, the three of us. We're all looking for you. We need to get you away. Don't speak. Come with me."

Looking back, the stalker was perhaps fifty yards distant, the light of the takeaway's sign at its back. Not moving. Standing still. Watching her. Lottie spoke quietly. In a whisper. "How do I know I can trust you?"

"You don't. Only, know that Jackdaw is my blood-kin and although he is a thieving, obnoxious, sarcastic annoyance, I love him dearly."

Lottie bit at her lip, then ducked into the passageway. A hand grasped her own. "This way."

She was led to the rear of the office blocks, threading between refuse bins and parked vehicles in a back yard. Onto another street, across it, through a garden, making random turns until they stopped in the overhang of some scaffolding rigged along a row of shop fronts. The small woman pushed Lottie deeper into the shadow of a doorway and scanned the street they had just crossed. With a nod of satisfaction, she turned back to Lottie. "I'm Raven. Jackdaw's blood-sister. I'll take you back to the bookshop. From there, we'll get you somewhere safe."

"The shop isn't safe?"

Raven shook her head, looking at the street once more. "Maybe. Maybe not. I don't know if whoever is doing this is ready to move directly against Steals yet." She pressed her fingers to Lottie's lips. "Quiet. Let's go."

Raven took the lead, steering Lottie from one concealed place to the next. Always looking back, always checking before moving, then running at a pace Lottie could match. They reached Gallowgate Lane. Payge was standing outside the bookshop to meet them.

"Where's my brother?" Raven asked.

"He's not far away. Having a look round."

"I'll go find him. Get her inside. We need to leave."

Payge nodded his agreement and ushered Lottie through the door. "Haven't you got some explaining to do?" she asked. "You left me in Andrea's dad's flat and he came back and found me. Weren't you supposed to be watching my back? Warn me of any trouble? What happened there? I can't go home now. The police are after me. My friends think I'm a criminal. In one night, you've ruined my entire life."

Payge rubbed at his chin. "I can see you're upset."

"Upset? Upset doesn't come close to what I'm feeling right now."

"Lottie, this isn't the best time to be doing this."

"I don't care—"

A flicker of movement outside caught her eye. A small body thumped against the shop window, sending a jagged crack down its entire length. Payge shoved Lottie to one side. The door exploded inwards in a hail of broken glass as the stalker burst through it, crashing into Payge, the two of them careering into the bookshelves, going down in a tangle of flailing limbs.

Payge was on his feet first, positioning himself between Lottie and the intruder. She looked over his shoulder as the stalker arose up, a full head taller than Payge. Thick blood oozed from cuts on its face and hands. It flicked her a glance from yellowed eyes.

"Lottie," Payge said, "go through to the back room. Find the way out."

The stalker reached into its coat and drew out a long, serrated blade. A tool for killing. No fingernails on the hand holding it, Lottie saw. A crazy, pointless observation her mind cranked out for her. "What about you?" She heard the waver of fear in her voice.

"Go," Payge breathed.

The stalker moved with blinding speed. Payge side-stepped faster still, catching its wrist in a two-handed lock, using its own arm as a lever. A dull crack and the blade fell to the floor. Lottie watched the stalker's face as its bones gave way. Not a trace, not a flicker of pain. It swung the arm Payge still gripped, pivoting itself round, using its momentum to lift Payge and throw him into the bookshelves. Volumes cascaded down again, pages swooped and fluttered. The stalker was on Payge before he could pick himself up, using its hand like a hammer, sweeping it into Payge's temple. His head snapped round, and he slumped, motionless.

It turned to Lottie, took a step towards her. She took one back. She shook her head at it, as if her negation of it could drive it away. "No," she said. "No, no, no. No!" She screamed at it, grabbed a book and threw it with all her strength. Her missile struck it in the eye. The stalker stopped, tipped its head to one side. Lottie threw another book. The stalker flinched no more than it had with the first, which was not at all. Then it was on her.

It grabbed her jacket and hauled her off her feet. For the barest instant, she felt herself sail through the air. She was on the floor, too stunned to move. The stalker stepped over her, pinning her shoulder with one foot, its good hand gripped her wrist and pulled her arm upwards. She screamed in mortal pain. Her shoulder creaked in its joint. Some distant part of her realised she was going to be torn apart.

The sickening pull on her arm ceased, the grip on her wrist loosened. Her shoulder joint still roared with hurt. She drew in a breath, looking up at the stalker, dumbfounded, watching as the point of a blade slid out of the stalker's throat, just below its chin. The stalker slumped forward, a keening noise escaping from it. Raven crouched on its back, forcing the handle of a dagger into its neck with her palm.

Lottie pushed herself away with her feet, clutching her injured arm. "Is it dead?"

Raven slid off the creature. "Not yet. But the poison on the blade should keep it still long enough." She drew her dagger out of the stalker's flesh, twisted its head around and stuck the knife into its eye socket. The stalker jerked and twitched. Lottie's gorge rose as Raven jammed the blade in and out, as if she was perforating the top of a coffee jar. Each time she struck, and the stalker moved, she stabbed again, until the creature was still. She stuck it in a couple more times. "Need to be sure. They'll get back after losing limbs." She gave Lottie an appraising look. "How's your arm?"

"Hurts. A lot."

A nod of sympathy. "We'll get to it as quick as we can." She turned to Jackdaw, who was tending to Payge. "How is he?"

Jackdaw looked up. "Alive. He'll be fine when he comes round. Hi, Lottie. You've met my sister. She's really quite nice. When you get to know her."

"You're an idiot." Raven kicked the body of the stalker. "Tell me when he's awake. I need to speak to the pair of you." The look on her face said this would be no pleasure. She turned to Lottie, her expression softening. "Come with me. We'll get a look at your arm now."

Lottie let herself be led into the back office. "Thank you," she said. "For out there. I thought I was… you know?"

Raven's black eyes were unreadable. "How are you feeling?"

Lottie thought about it. "Shaky. Scared. Angry, maybe?"

"Good. That's good. Most people don't walk away from an attack by those things. Sit down. Turn around."

She did as she was told. She felt Raven's hand on her shoulder, then a pressing of her fingers. Lottie hissed and jerked away.

"Can you take these off please?" Raven tugged at her jacket.

Lottie tried to slip out of it, gasping in pain when she had to lift her arm.

"Here, let me help."

Slowly and with care, sliding and easing, they worked together to get Lottie out of her jacket and fleece sweater without her crying out too much. Raven lifted Lottie's T-shirt, enough to see her back and shoulder. There was a moment of silence. "Who did this to you? Was it him? Payge?"

"No." Lottie tried to twist round and yelped at the hurt it brought on. "Payge is… I'm not sure what he is, to be honest. He treated me, put some salve on it that helped."

"He has some skill with medicine. I'll give him that." Lottie felt Raven's fingers on her skin, probing at her shoulder, lifting her arm, moving the joint.

"Ahhh. Sore. Ouch, ouch, ouch."

"Sorry. Here, this'll help." The hand clasping her shoulder grew warm against her skin. The pain faded to a dull ache. The fingers traced the bruises on her back, and they too gave up their chorus of hurt.

"It'll give you a bit of respite for a day or so, give you time to heal some," Raven said. "You're lucky. I don't think there's any serious damage."

Raven's hand smoothed over her shoulder again. Warmth soaked through her skin, loosening the muscles below. "That feels a bit weird. But nice. What did you put on me?"

Raven smiled at her. "Nothing. It's just something our people can do. I could tell you I'm secreting a very mild neurotoxin through my skin but that might freak you out. Let's leave it as an old healing ritual of my clan. My brother could have done it but he's too lazy to care."

"I heard the way you spoke to him. You don't get on with him, do you?"

"You like him?" Raven said.

Lottie nodded. "I think maybe we're friends."

Raven made a face. "We get on well enough, I suppose. He's my brother and I love him dearly but he's like all men. I prefer other ways."

"What ways?" Lottie asked, pulling her top down over her bare skin.

Reaching out to her, Raven brushed an errant lock of hair back into place. "The way women do things." She smiled, showing a mouthful of pointed teeth.

Lottie smiled back at her, straightened her shoulders and stretched, feeling good. Part of her whispered that she shouldn't feel this good. Not after what had just happened. But it was easy to ignore. She felt good. She wanted to talk. "Are there many of you? In your family?"

"Sure," Raven said. "There are my blood-brothers. Jackdaw and his twin, Rook. Couple of kids, really. Crow, who's the oldest. There's the Magpie. I don't want to know where he is or what he's doing. And there's Jay. Who hasn't decided yet. And me."

"No sisters?"

Raven gave her head a wistful shake. "No. None of them chose female. Jay might but I don't know."

"I wish I had family. It must be something to know there's someone who will always look out for you."

"Magpie would probably sell me before he looked out for me, but I get what you're saying."

"Hang on." Lottie stared at Raven. "You said you chose your gender? Did I hear you right?"

"You did. We're born neutral, grow up that way. When we reach puberty, we can decide what we want to be. Some folk just let nature take its course, see what they end up as. Others make a choice." She stopped to regard Lottie. "Jackdaw was right about you."

"What?"

"Look at you. You would sit there all day and ask questions. You're happy."

"And that's a bad thing?"

"Being happy? Absolutely not." She took Lottie's hand in her own. "You need to be careful. There's more going on here than Payge is telling you. There's more going on than he knows about."

"I shouldn't trust him?"

"Do you?"

Lottie pulled her hand back. "I think I do. He's saved my life. He's difficult to like and he doesn't want to get close to anyone. But yes, I trust him. Do you think I shouldn't?"

"I can't tell you, it's for you to decide."

"What do you think is going on here? Jackdaw must have told you."

Raven pulled at her lip, her fingernail clicking over a golden stud pierced through it. "Two makers. Seemingly at war. Or close to it. And there's you."

"Me?" said Lottie.

Raven smiled at her, showing those sharp teeth again. Lottie wondered how she had warmed to this fierce woman so quickly.

"My little brother told me about how you could see the gate." Raven leant in, reaching for Lottie's face with her hand. Lottie thought to shrink back then held herself steady. Raven touched her skin, fingertips just resting on her cheek bones. She turned Lottie's head to one side, then the other, studying her face. "How did they get to you? A book, was it?" Lottie nodded, and Raven dropped her hand away. "Steals still pulling that old one. The gates. Being able to make one. It's a rare talent. And even then, it's buried deep and needs to be coaxed out by training and practice. Few races even have the ability. Humans do, though. More than most. But being able to see one?"

Lottie wanted to ask at least six questions but before she could get out one, the door opened, and Payge came through.

"You're alive then," Raven said. "Ready to serve your master another day."

"Don't start." Payge walked as though every step brought pain.

"I'll stop when you come back to our people."

"You know I can't do that."

"Then you should die and stop being a disgrace to us."

Lottie watched Payge pull himself up, dark anger rising in his eyes. Just as quickly, it drained out of him. He slumped in a chair. "Still living the tired, old dream then? Waiting in the shadows for the day that will never come."

"At least I can say I live with some hope. What have you got, each morning you open your eyes? Another day being Steals's yard dog? And as for you." Raven shot over to Jackdaw and landed a clout on his head.

"Ow! What was that for?"

"For being stupid enough to follow him."

"You know what I owe him."

"So you follow him into slavery for a stupid oath?" She calmed herself with a visible effort. "We can't stay here. They'll send another stalker. Or something worse. We need to get Lottie away."

"She needs to stay," Payge said. "No one knows what she can do, except us. She needs to complete the pattern. Then she's free and her ability stays hidden."

"Yeah, about being free," Lottie said. "Why did you leave me to get caught?"

Raven spoke before Payge could answer. "They're not going to let her live once they find out what she can do. Because they will all want her." She paused for a moment, looking at Payge. "You've got an angle on this, haven't you? What are you planning on doing with her?"

Payge opened his mouth to speak, then froze. They all heard it. The snap of a piece of glass breaking underfoot. He rose silently, pointing to a door at the rear of the office. They hurried over to it, as he moved to bolt the door into the office, scoop up the laptop and follow them out. The rear door to the office took them out of the bookshop and onto the night-time streets. They kept up a fast pace to begin with, Payge beside Lottie, Raven and Jackdaw moving ahead and behind. After an eternity of running and walking, Lottie, dizzy and sick with fatigue, pulled Payge to a halt. She wanted to sit down. Better still, she wanted to lie down. "Is it much further? I don't feel so terrific."

"We're going to a lock-up I've got. No one knows about it, not even Steals. A couple more miles to go."

"Oh," Lottie said. She hung her head. She felt a small hand lift her chin.

"Hey," Raven said. "You're doing fine. We're nearly there."

Lottie nodded and believed the lie because it was the easiest thing to do. She walked on, concentrating on putting one foot in front of the next. Dimly aware they had passed into a meaner part of the city. Houses with boarded-up windows and abandoned kitchen appliances in their front gardens. Pavements scattered with diamonds of broken glass. At some point, her sleep-fuddled brain realised she was moving but her legs were not. As she tried to work it out, cradled in Payge's arms, she fell asleep.

8

SATURDAY NIGHT AT THE UNION

Lottie woke into pain, stiff limbs and a tartan blanket that gave off a miasma of smells laid over her. Levering herself more upright in the decrepit armchair she found herself in, moving a fraction at a time, she tried an exploratory stretch. Her muscles yowled in reply. Looking round, she saw a sparsely furnished garage, steel cabinets, a kitchen table where Payge and Jackdaw sat, a punch bag dangling on a chain. The place reeked of oil and damp concrete.

"Good. You're up." Payge said. He pointed to a collection of paper cups and wrappers on the table. "We got you something to eat."

Lottie shuffled over, the blanket and its smells wrapped around her. "I don't know which bit hurts the most." She licked at her filmy teeth. Her slept-in clothes felt scratchy against her skin. "I don't suppose you've got a shower and a toothbrush?"

Payge gestured round. "It's a garage. What do you think?"

"Good morning to you too." She sat at the table, pulling the blanket tighter around her shoulders. "It's a bit cold in here."

"Anything else?"

"What's for breakfast?"

Payge held up a squashed-together lump of meat for her to inspect.

"Raw burgers? For your breakfast?"

"We got you a pork pie and some crisps," Jackdaw said. He slid out of his chair. "There's hot tea."

"How's your arm?" Payge asked.

"Stiff. It hurts."

"Bad?"

"Well, somebody did try to pull it off."

Payge rose from his seat and crossed to one of the cabinets. When he opened the dented and oil-stained door, it revealed a spotlessly clean, white-painted interior. He selected a stone jar from a shelf and returned to the table.

She watched him open it. "Is it the stuff that smells like pee?"

"No. Let me see your shoulder."

Through clenched teeth, Lottie let Payge examine her aching joint, then rub paste from the jar into her skin. "Any better?" he asked.

She moved her shoulder with care, testing it out. "It feels better. Thanks."

"Good. I've never tried it on a human before. Now eat your breakfast."

"Yes, Mum." She unwrapped her pie and took a big bite. It managed to be both crumbly and stodgy at the same time. Pastry stuck to the roof of her mouth. "What do we do now?"

Payge drew a breath and rested his hands on the table. "There's been a change in the pattern."

"What is it? And where's Raven?"

"She's on the roof, her turn as lookout."

"Won't that draw a bit of attention?"

"A kid on a garage roof isn't going to draw attention in this part of town."

Lottie sipped her tea and forced herself to take another bite of the pie that she was beginning to think had little to do with pork. "Is this your secret hideout then?" Fragments of pastry blew onto the table as she spoke.

Payge scowled and swept the crumbs on to the floor. "That's exactly what it is. The only place I've got that's mine. And I like to keep it tidy."

"Sorry," Lottie said, huffing out more crumbs. Payge glared at her. She slowly wiped the crumbs away with her sleeve. "About the pattern?" she added.

Payge shifted some of the breakfast debris on the table, set down the laptop and flipped it open. "See here and here. This branch is where it went wrong in Mr Ross's flat."

Lottie peered at the screen. "You still owe me an explanation about that."

Payge pointed to the screen. "This is your friend, Elizabeth."

"Liz is in danger?"

"She's not in any danger yet. We've got time."

"How much time?"

"Enough."

"Problem?" Raven appeared beside her. She shrugged out of a huge anorak and threw it at Jackdaw. "Your turn."

"I haven't finished my breakfast!"

Raven only looked at him and Jackdaw withdrew, muttering under his breath.

"Feel any better?" Raven asked.

"Some," Lottie said. She trailed off, thinking to herself. "Why Liz? Why now?"

"Because she's now closer to your friend Andrea than you are," Payge said.

"Oh." It was a small, quiet sound, spoken to the tabletop.

"If you had done what I asked you to do, it would be different."

Lottie looked up at him. "How is it my fault? I did what you asked. You disappeared on me."

"You didn't do what I asked. The package was still in your pocket."

"You went through my pockets?"

"Of course. I needed to know if you got the job done."

Lottie rocked back in her chair, folding her arms. "You don't go through my pockets. Not ever again. Not without asking."

"I'll do what I have to."

Lottie slapped at his forearm, where it rested on the table. "No, you won't."

"Stop it, the pair of you," Raven said. She turned her attention to Lottie. "Someone still wants you dead. Remember that. We need to get you away. I can take you to a safe place amongst my people. It's a few days' travel but you can stay there as long as you need to."

Payge glanced at Raven before turning his attention back to Lottie. "You don't need to run away anywhere. You can stay right here."

"Who is this person that wants me dead?" Lottie asked.

"You need to follow the pattern. It's the best way out of this."

"I need to help my friend."

"Lottie, please sit down."

"Will the pair of you stop telling me what to do all the time! I'm not your bloody pet." She clutched her arms tight about herself and glared at them.

Payge held up a hand. "You're right. We shouldn't. Me especially. Look, your friend isn't in any immediate danger." He pulled the laptop towards himself. "See here." His fingers touched some lines and numbers. "It's only one probability among others, stretched over a period of a few days."

Lottie pressed her lips into a thin line. "I want to go outside. Get some fresh air. Am I allowed to do that?"

"Of course," Payge said. "Jackdaw will keep an eye on you."

"Fine. How do I get out of here?"

Payge indicated a side door. Stamping her way over to it, she left without looking back.

ᥫ᭡

Raven waited until Lottie closed the door behind her before turning to Payge. "She would have been safe with me. You didn't have to tell her any of that. You could have said anything you wanted but you made sure she wants to stay here."

"You'd rather I lied to her?"

"If it keeps her from harm? Yes, I would. She's too precious to put at risk. If she is what I think she might be."

"You want her, don't you? For what she can do."

"Only when she's ready. And when she agrees."

"Then you know we need to keep her ability hidden. Look, I know it's a risk, but if she stays with me, I can make her safe. Truly safe." Payge regarded his hands for a moment. "Will you trust me on this? Two days are all I need. If it doesn't work out, you can have her."

"Two days?"

"At the most."

Raven considered. "If you let me try something with her first. A test of sorts. To see if I'm right about her."

"Dangerous?"

Raven shrugged. "Not to my knowledge."

"Do your test. I'll take my two days. If this goes the way it should, it'll be done."

"What way is that?"

Payge tapped the edge of the laptop. "The pattern has changed. Lottie's friend, Elizabeth. Lottie has to see it. To be there when it happens. To take it back to her other friend, Andrea. Who'll then take it to her father. Who'll do anything to keep his daughter safe."

"Steals wants this Elizabeth killed?"

Payge shook his head. "I'm not sure. Murder usually

isn't his style. But that still leaves a lot of scope for unpleasantness."

"He shared this with you? You're going to be part of it?"

Payge shook his head again. "No. I got a message yesterday evening. He's keeping me out of this one. All I have to do is set it up. Get Lottie to where she needs to be."

"Why's he keeping you out of it? I thought you were his top dog?"

"You never miss a chance, do you?" Payge glanced away. "I failed. Steals wants this Mr Ross in his pocket. The idea was to get into his home, hack his computer, hide some cash. It didn't work out."

"Why not?"

"The father wasn't where he was supposed to be. He should have been at dinner with his assistant. As he does every week. Instead, he came back when Lottie was still in his flat."

"And then what?"

"I left her to get caught. I thought there was a fair chance it might end the pattern. Or at least, her involvement in it. I didn't think she would manage to escape. Turns out I underestimated her." He stopped to rub at his face. "Turns out I was wrong about ending the pattern as well."

Raven gave a grim smile. "Makers and their servants. So now Steals wants to do something more brutal. What's his play? Use this Elizabeth to send a threat to the dad? That the same will happen to his daughter if he doesn't dance to Steals's tune?"

"Maybe. Maybe not. It might be more subtle. Just plant the message that his daughter isn't safe. That he needs to be more powerful to be able to protect her." Payge hesitated for a moment. "Steals has something in mind for Lottie. More than just this set up of Andrea's father, I'm sure of it. She's trusting, easily manipulated. Easy to recruit. And now she knows about all of this." He looked at Raven. "She changed the pattern. With a touch of her finger. I watched her do it. She's changed it just by being around it. Who can do that?"

Raven shook her head in reply. "This Elizabeth person. Rape? Assault? Maybe dead?"

Payge nodded. "Likely."

Raven let out a breath. "I can live with that. As long as you keep Lottie safe. If any harm comes to her, I'll put a blade in you."

"I'll bear that in mind."

⁓

Lottie stared at the rectangle of scabby asphalt boxed in by ranks of lock-up garages. Somewhere beyond the garages, a car alarm bleated unheeded. She shivered but didn't feel like going back inside. Jackdaw appeared beside her, flapping his jacket sleeves where they hung down past his hands. "Think I'll grow into this?"

"Don't try to cheer me up."

"Bad mood, eh? Want to tell me what's up?"

Lottie dipped her head towards the garage door. "Those two."

"Aye, they do that to you."

They stood in silence for a moment. "Want to go to the shop?" Jackdaw said. "I'll go with you."

"The way you look? Is that a good idea?"

"I'll pull my hood up. Come on, I'll buy you an ice cream."

"Why?"

"Because it'll cheer you up."

"Won't they miss us?"

"No chance, they'll be too busy arguing." He began to walk away, and Lottie fell in beside him. "With any luck, they'll kill each other by the time we get back. I'm kidding. They'll probably stop are major injuries. I hope."

"What is it with the pair of them anyway?"

Jackdaw grimaced, his lips pressing into a thin line. "They both want the same thing."

"Eh?"

"Yeah."

"I'm guessing it's the 'how' that separates them."

"Give the girl a cigar."

"Ugh, no thanks. A shower would be nice though. What is it they can't agree on?"

Jackdaw went quiet.

"Is it a secret?" Lottie asked. "Sorry, I didn't mean to pry. You don't need to tell me."

"No, it's okay. It won't do any harm. You're part of the gang, after all." He smiled at her. "I've learnt to shut my mouth about it round the pair of them, as it usually ends with stuff flying through the air. Sometimes sharp stuff. Heavy stuff too." Jackdaw scratched at his head. "See this dent here? Raven did it. Threw a hatchet at me one time. Her aim is lousy; she couldn't hit the ground if she threw a stick at it. Got me with the blunt end. Hatchet's difficult thing to throw, mind. Balance and all. You're better with a knife, if you need to throw. Or a spear. Good for close combat too, the spear. Most folk don't realise that."

"And the reason they fight so much?"

"Oh. Right. Our home. Our new one, I mean."

"Sorry?"

"Here's the shop," Jackdaw said.

"Why do you need a new home? What happened to the old one? What was it like, anyway, your home?"

Jackdaw shrugged. "I don't know. They tell me it was nice. Like Scotland but without the long, hot summers. We left before I was born."

"Your family?"

"No, all of us. Our entire people. At least the ones who weren't sick. We had to leave so many behind."

"It sounds awful. Was there an earthquake or something? A disaster?"

Jackdaw nodded. "A disaster. That about sums it up. There was a war. The makers. Again. One of them let loose a plague on our world. Terrible it was. Maybe a quarter of everyone who caught it died. Many more were… changed by it." Jackdaw sniffed and wiped at his face. "We fled, all of us, to get away from it, before it took us all. To whoever would take us in. And many did take us in, but at a price. What better gift could you ask for in the middle of a war than a slave army? That's pretty much been our lot ever since."

"How long ago was this?"

"I don't know how you would reckon it in your years. A while now. Depressing, isn't it? Makes you want an ice cream. I think this needs raspberry sauce as well."

"I think you're right."

As Lottie entered the shop, her thoughts turned back to Liz. As she asked for two ice creams, she thought about the people around her now. As she paid, she made up her mind about what to do next.

They walked back, comparing notes on the relative merits of Mr Whippy versus plain, old, scoop-it-out ice cream. Lottie kept up her end of the conversation as she thought about what she was going to ask. Feeling a touch guilty, she pitched her first question. "You and your sister are close?"

"Oh yeah, we've always got on. Me, Rook, Jay and Raven." He laughed. "I remember the day Raven said she was taking another woman as a mate. The elders, they had a fit." Jackdaw's smile faded. "She faced some hard times afterwards. I stood with her. We all did. Then they exiled us. Didn't see that one coming." He licked at his ice cream. "I met Payge not long after. He pulled me out of the mud at Bitter March. It cost him a sword wound to do it. He could have left me to die but he didn't. That's Payge."

"How long have the pair of you known each other? How long have you been here? And how old are you anyway?"

"Slow down there." Jackdaw laughed at her barrage of questions. "It's hard to say. Time runs different in each world. We've travelled to so many places, I kind of lost track along the way. The years don't mean much, it's only what you do that has any meaning. We started working for Steals, maybe ten years ago?"

While he popped the last of his ice cream into his mouth and crunched away at it, Lottie drew a breath and asked her last question. "Why do you work for Steals at all?"

She wanted to say something more, but she held herself back. Waiting. Jackdaw walked along, lost in his own thoughts. When he spoke again, there was a distance to his voice. "Payge works for him because Steals owns him and his clan. Our people were slaves before Steals. We were slaves because our fathers and mothers were." He looked at Lottie, and his dark eyes held nothing for her, but his face was written with bitterness and lost hope. "Sorry. I think the ice cream just wore off."

She held back from giving him a hug, afraid it might stop him talking. "Why don't you just run away?"

"There's more to being captive than just walls and cages. Raven did run away. She went off and started up her own clan. Set themselves up as a free people. But they came after her. Her owners."

"But she did escape."

Jackdaw gave her a sly grin. "She did. She went somewhere they were too scared to follow. Believe me, there are some scary places out there. But that's Raven. I don't think she's brave, she's just so single-minded. She believes with every fragment of her being that our people should be free and anyone who doesn't is an enemy. That you should be dead, rather than be a slave. And that's where Payge and Raven don't quite see eye to eye."

"I don't get you. Payge is happy being a slave?"

"He hates it. He loathes it. But he thinks the only way to find another place for us is through a new gate to an empty world. And the only people who can make new gates are the makers. So, he has to stay close to them. Besides, running away isn't an option for him or his clan." Jackdaw wiped at his nose with the back of his hand and grimaced. "Maybe we should get back in. They'll be worried about us, assuming they aren't arguing about something or other."

They shuffled back inside. Payge was rummaging in a locker, and Raven sat at the table, looking worried. She looked up at their approach. "Where have you been?"

"We went for ice cream," Jackdaw said.

"You never thought to tell me?"

"Can you stop being my big sister for one second?"

"No, I can't. I'm always that, more fool me."

Jackdaw sniffed and went to help Payge. Raven called Lottie over. "No chance you brought me one back, is there? I love an ice cream."

"Ah, no," Lottie said. She half sat and half stood, flustered over what to do. "Shall I go and get you one?"

Raven smiled at her. "Can't say I'm not tempted, but no, thank you, not just now. Sit, please, Lottie. I wanted to speak to you." She put a leather bag on to the table and drew a small wooden box and a cloth pouch from it. "I want to try something with you. But only if you agree."

Lottie watched her undo the pouch and shake out some dried seeds.

"Payge told me what you can do. He said you can see the gates. What was it you saw?"

"Lines of light," Lottie said. "A network of them, but they seemed to go in directions I couldn't really look. I know what that sounds like but it's hard to describe it in any other way. Does everyone see them that way?"

"No." Raven fiddled with the drawstring on the pouch. "Yes. Sort of."

"I don't understand."

Raven used her fingertip to shift a couple of stray seeds back into the pile. "Each gate is unique to its maker. I don't know how they're made but it's common knowledge that once made, they can't be moved. They can't be changed. The link they make is fixed. It's said the elder races could do more. Pity none of them are around to ask. A maker being able to see a gate they have made themselves is a rare talent. A rare talent amongst a rare breed. I've never heard of a maker being able to see a gate they haven't made. Then there's closing them. This is where it really starts to get interesting."

Lottie huddled closer to Raven. "I wouldn't be so sure. You had me from the start."

Raven tried to hide her smile before going on. "The only person who can close a gate is the one who made it in the first place. Or so they say. But there's your world, where all the gates closed at once, centuries ago. Or so the story goes. Then, not so long back, a fair number simply reopened. Why would that be?"

"I don't know. A magic reset button?"

"Good an explanation as any." Raven separated one of the seeds from the rest. "Since then, more makers have arisen from your people than anywhere else in this neighbourhood of worlds."

Lottie eyed the seeds with some apprehension. "You're going to ask me to eat them, aren't you?"

Raven nodded. "They contain a psychotropic drug. The makers use it in their training to enhance perception.

133

There's also this." She opened the wooden box and lifted out a flat stone with a hole in the middle, placing it on the table.

Lottie reached for it. Raven stopped her hand. "Not yet. This first." She held up the dried seed.

Lottie glanced at it but couldn't help her gaze falling to the stone. "I feel it," she said. "It's pulling at me. I don't like it. But I want it."

Raven put the stone back in the box. "Better?"

Lottie nodded.

"It's a gate," Raven said. "Like the one you went through to get to Ore. Only much smaller. The makers use them for learning. And amusement. I thought by using the maker's own methods, I could help you understand this a bit more. But only if you want to. So, I'll ask you again, do you want to do this?"

Lottie had to wet her lips before she could speak. "Yes." She looked Raven in the eye. "I want to do this." She held out her hand for the seed. "Can I have a drink of water with it?"

Raven fetched a glass of water, crushed the seed into it and Lottie drank it down. "How long does this take?" she asked.

"Give it perhaps fifteen or twenty minutes."

They chatted on and off for a time, but Lottie found the conversation difficult to follow, Raven's words slipping from her mind as soon as she heard them, but still, she felt warm and fuzzy and protected. "This is nice," she murmured, not sure if Raven had heard her or if she had even said it, only that Raven was looking at her closely. Payge had come over to join her.

"Hello, Payge," Lottie said. "You look very… big." This struck her as the funniest thing, and she broke into a fit of giggles. When she recovered, her head felt so clear. She stared at Raven in rapt attention. "You are so beautiful. I wish I was like you." And watched as Raven dropped her gaze to the tabletop.

A dislocating wrench of vertigo. "Oh," Lottie said. She was looking at herself, as though she was standing some way off from the table. There she was, sitting next to Raven and Payge. She felt calm, in a way that didn't feel right in itself. "This is a bit odd."

"Are you okay?" Raven asked.

Lottie heard the words through two sets of ears, the voice sounding slightly different to each. Because, she realised, she was standing two different distances away. Tapping her hand on the table, one hand felt the wood beneath her fingertips, and the other passed through air. She felt two sets of muscles move the weight of two sets of fingers. Just out of sync with each other, no more than a fraction.

She rubbed her thumb across her fingertips, feeling the minute drag of her fingerprints. And she looked at her other self, who had looked up a fraction slower. She looked into the eyes of her own self, sitting at the table.

What am I thinking? What is she thinking?

It came as a jolt, a sickening stab of fear. She didn't know the person at the table. A stranger sat there with a blank, unknowable face, thinking blank, unknowable thoughts, and she was locked out of those thoughts. And she was getting further away. Away beyond reach. No going back. Lost. Cut off. Severed.

"Lottie!" Raven barked out her name, her concern clear in the way she looked at her.

"I'm fine." She was sitting at the table, looking at the empty space beside the table, expecting to see some pale outline, some ghostly image. There was only empty space. "I feel fine. No worries. Show me the stone."

Jagged anticipation rose in her as Raven slid the box towards her. She fretted when Raven fumbled with the catch. But it melted into warmth when the box was opened. Raven held the stone up so she could see through the hole in the middle, no wider than a fingernail. The stone itself was the size of her palm. Raven took her hand away and the stone hung in the air. Lottie could feel her lips draw back into a huge grin.

Because the stone called out to her, it sang a song of immaculate geometry. She saw it all now, lines and curves of gold and deepest blue. They filled the air around her, passing through the table, the floor, Raven, Payge, herself. Here was an anchor line. She lifted a hand to trace it back to where it was bedded in reality. Here, these ellipses carried forces away, to open up this space, so these lines could... It fell into her mind, like looking at a puzzle for hour on baffling hour, then in one glorious moment it orders itself into a solution, unbidden by any force of will. Lottie saw how the gate worked. She saw through it. To what lay on the other side.

It was huge and cold, the abyssal cold of outer space, but it was aware, and it was trapped behind the gate, where it burnt with malevolent fury and all it wanted was to snuff out her pathetic warmth. "Reach for me," it said to her.

A ringing in her ears, modulating up and down with her breathing. Sharp pain spiking in the base of her skull. Lottie reached out for the stone, frost glittering on her fingers. Her lips parted, skin tearing where the cold had stuck them together. Her thoughts were drawn through into the other place, like sand running through an hourglass, a tiny piece of her at a time, hurtling away at frantic speed. It would take all of her, she knew this with terrible certainty. Every last morsel of heat and life in her until she was nothing.

There was only the geometry of the gate and whatever it was that existed on the other side of it. This was the only portal, and she knew it was a slender rope across a pitiless chasm. Cut the rope and there was nothing but gravity and the fall.

She reached for one of the anchor lines. Heat was leaching out of her innermost self; she could feel her blood slowing in her body. The cold, the other place, screamed when her hand found the anchor line but still it kept pulling her in, atom by atom, even as it pleaded with her. For mercy, for understanding, for another chance. She crushed the anchor line in her frigid hand, twisted and pulled and it gave way. The entire structure of the gate began to unravel, and Lottie wept at its loss.

She heard the thump of a stone hitting wood, but the sound meant nothing to her. Panic took her as she swept her gaze round the room. "Where is this place?" she asked. "I don't know this." There was the smell of oil, and there were people she didn't know. And a struggle for the last thing she could remember. A rain-washed street, a bus home from the library. The stranger following her. *He's brought me here.* Her fear held an edge as keen as splintered glass. *He has friends and now they're going to—*

Her name was being called, over and over. A face loomed at her, an inhuman thing with the teeth of a predator. Lottie screamed and tried to stand up, only her legs lacked the strength to hold her, and she fell, pushing her way along the floor as the thing came over the table at her. She kicked at it, catching it in the stomach. "Get away from me, you little monster!"

Her head felt as if it might split open, a high-pitched whine in her ears. For one awful second, she did not know who she was. She wanted to cry in terror when a huge figure leant over her. She cowered from it until her thoughts cleared for an instant and she saw him. "Payge," she pleaded. "Help." She lifted a hand to him; the world shrank to a dot in a blinding white space and then she knew nothing.

⁓

"Do you think she's going to be alright?" Jackdaw asked.

Raven only looked at him before she turned back to where they had made Lottie as comfortable as they could on the concrete floor. "I don't know." She studied the girl's open, unmoving eyes. "This wasn't supposed to happen."

Payge laid down Lottie's hand. "Her pulse and breathing are fine."

"Should we try to get her to someone?" Jackdaw said. "Someone who can help with this kind of thing."

Payge shook his head. "No. We wait for now. She might come round."

"She might not," Raven said. "I shouldn't have pushed her."

"It was a risk," Payge said. The three of them fell to silence and waiting.

⤮

At some timeless point, Lottie knew she had left the white space. It was an abstract thought that flowed through her dreaming, a message from herself. Maybe not warm and comfortable, but she was with her friends. She was safe. She slept.

⤮

"Lottie. Can you hear me? Can you open your eyes? It's time to wake up."

She struggled to reach wakefulness, the soothing embrace of deep sleep not wanting to let her go. There was some soft resistance covering her and she mumbled something she didn't understand, while she pushed against it. Then opened her eyes and stopped fighting the tartan blanket that lay on top of her. "I'm up, I'm up." Propping herself up on one hand, rubbing at her face with the other. "You can stop going on at me now."

"I didn't say anything." Payge was sitting alone at the table, watching over her.

"Didn't you just call on me?"

"No."

Puzzling at his reply, Lottie looked around. "You let me sleep on the floor?"

"There was nowhere else to put you."

Her joints sent out a litany of protest as she shifted her position. "I feel awful. I've slept in these clothes twice now." Pulled the neck of her top out, she stuck her nose in the opening. "I smell."

Payge smiled at her. "You always smell. It's just the intensity that varies. Here, let me help you."

With his aid, she hobbled over to the table and eased herself into a chair, moving with care, exploring the multiple places her body was telling her were not happy.

"Tea?"

"Yes, please. I'd love a cup."

"Do you remember anything? From earlier?" He wiped inside a mug with a dish towel as dirty as the floor, then put a teabag in it.

"That better not be mine," Lottie said. As Payge sighed and found another mug, she thought about his question. "Yes, I remember." Her gaze fell on the flat stone with the hole in it, lying on the table. She jerked away, her chair scraping on the floor.

Payge came over and set the mugs of tea down. "It's just a stone now, Lottie. You closed the gate. Go on, pick it up."

She looked at the stone but held her hand back. "I did, didn't I? I destroyed it." Her face creased into a frown. "There was something on the other side of the gate. A monster." She glanced up, afraid he would be smiling at what she had said. Payge nodded back, his look serious. "It was trapped," she said. "It's trapped forever now, isn't it? Why would anyone make something so horrible?"

"Who knows?" Payge settled in the chair opposite her. "Some of the makers have only a nodding acquaintance with sanity. And reality." He picked up the stone and rolled it edge-on between his thumb and forefinger. "They do it because they can. Because they want to." Setting the stone down, he sighed. "Selfishness and cruelty are not unique to your people. Not by any measure. You need to understand how much danger this... talent... of yours, puts you in. Not just from Steals, from all of the makers." He poked at the stone with one finger. "If you can do the same to any other gate, you're a direct threat to them. Or a valuable asset. One they don't want their rivals to have. Better to not have you around at all."

Lottie clutched her mug of tea, staring at the stone. "I don't know how I did it. I just reacted." She looked up at him. "What should I do?"

"Tell no one. Don't do it again. And hope it stays secret."

"But it's only you three who know."

"Three too many. Secrets have a way of getting themselves found out."

"You mean I can't trust you?"

"Of course you can trust me. But Raven will use any weapon she can against the makers. And Jackdaw, though I trust him with my life, if it came to it, would likely side with her. She's his blood-sister and blood ties run too strong in our people for him to do anything else."

"Why don't you trade me to Steals for your freedom?" The question came from nowhere and it was out of her before she had time to think about it.

Payge looked at her. Lottie shifted in her chair. His unwavering stare mellowed into an understanding nod. "A good question and one that needs answering, though the answer is simple enough. Why would the master negotiate with his slave when he can just take what he wants? If I went to Steals to talk about a deal, he would simply force the truth from me. Then, in all likelihood, have me killed."

"But that doesn't make any sense. He's only setting you free, one person. And he gets me." Lottie paused. "I can't believe I'm having this discussion. A few days ago, I was worrying about exams."

"Steals would be seen to be weak if he negotiated with me and the story got out. He's not the most powerful of the makers, so if he did get his hands on you, it might worsen his position. The makers favour stability. They know if one gains too much of an edge, the rest will join together to pull them down. It's equilibrium of paranoia. That's why you can trust me. I can't gain anything from you. You have no value to me."

"It sounds horrible, what goes on between these makers."

Payge spread his hands out on the table. "It is, but the worst of it falls on the likes of us. I can help you escape it. We know another maker has moved against Steals. He's probably preoccupied dealing with that. Which gives us a chance to work out this pattern you're in and end it for you. After that? It's a big world. You can disappear into it.

Take your secret with you. Get on with your life. Hard as it might be, it's your best shot at putting all this behind you. But you need to finish the pattern."

"I think I got that bit," Lottie said.

Payge ran a hand over his head and drew a long breath. "You never asked for any of this. And I've seen so many people broken by the makers. I'd like to see one of them walk away untouched for once."

"I think I'm a fair distance away from being untouched by all this. I'm not sure I've got any kind of life to go back to."

Payge rose and began to clear the table. "You're alive. That's a great starting point. Now we need to get ready. We need to help Elizabeth. Where will she be tonight?"

"What day is it? Saturday? She'll be at the student union."

"Then that's where we'll be." Payge carried on his work, humming to himself as he went.

⁓

Later in the evening, Lottie sat at the table, finishing the fish and chips that Payge had brought in for her. The others moved around the garage, busying themselves with bits and pieces of equipment. Mostly weapons, it seemed. She stopped licking her fingers when Jackdaw laid a webbing belt and holster on the table. Her eyes widened. "Is that a real gun?"

Jackdaw slid the weapon out of its holster. "Sure is. Nineteen eleven Model Colt 45. If someone's coming at you and you want them to stop, then this is your go-to guy." The gun looked the size of a cannon in Jackdaw's small hand.

"Can I have a go? I've never held a gun before." She expected Jackdaw to say no.

He slid the magazine out with practised ease and checked the chamber was clear. "Sure thing. Knock yourself out."

It was heavy and smelt of machine oil. Lottie turned it over in her hands.

"This, on the other hand, is mine." Jackdaw hefted a revolver. "Webley 38. Good British gun, this."

"We're not actually planning on shooting anyone tonight, are we? I mean, it's a student union."

"No, we're not," Payge said. He reached over to snatch the weapon from her hand. "Don't give her these, please." He directed this at Jackdaw, who was now laying out knives of various lengths on the table. "She doesn't get a knife either. Probably end up stabbing herself."

Raven came over, adjusting a harness that secured a pair of knives under her arms. "Finish your meal, Lottie."

"Speak softly and carry a big stick," Jackdaw said, stealing a chip from her. "And a knife or two, in case you lose your stick. And a gun. For back-up. Just to be on the safe side." He began threading a khaki-coloured belt around his waist. Lottie thought he looked like a boy getting ready to play at soldiers, but she thought it was better not to say. "What's the plan, boss?" he asked.

Payge looked up from packing a rucksack. "Lottie goes in alone. I'll be with her up to the front door. Once

144

she finds Elizabeth, she gets in touch." He indicated four mobile phones on the table. "You stay with your friend the whole time. You do not act if anything happens. Stay safe. Understand?" He waited for Lottie to nod her assent. "By the time you find Elizabeth, Raven and Jackdaw will be in the building. They'll let me in through a fire exit. I'll meet you and get you out. Now have you finished your meal?"

Lottie crumpled up the greasy wrapping in front of her. "Why don't you just walk in with me?"

"I want whoever is watching you to think you're taking a stupid risk. It might make them less cautious and show themselves sooner."

He turned away, busying himself with his own weapons. Jackdaw slid a small sheath knife across the table to her. "In your pocket with it, quick now."

Lottie slid it off the table in a heartbeat. Raven leant down to whisper in her ear. "Use it only if you need to. Otherwise, keep it hidden. Look after yourself." She patted Lottie on the shoulder, then she too moved off.

"We're not going to walk all the way there, are we?" Lottie said.

Jackdaw answered her. "Nope. We'll take the car."

"I didn't know you had one."

"We don't. Until we steal one."

"Terrific. I can just imagine being stopped by the police in a stolen car, loaded with weapons and inhuman people."

"I know. Great, isn't it? This is what I call a night out."

❧

Payge hunched over the steering wheel as the car wheezed up a hill.

"So why couldn't we have taken the Mercedes instead of this shit heap?" Jackdaw said.

"Will you shut up?"

"It smells like dogs back here. Dead ones at that."

"Well, in that case…" Payge swerved the car into the kerb and ratcheted the handbrake on. "We can walk from here." The engine rattled to a halt. "Out. All of you."

"It might rain," Jackdaw said.

Payge ignored him, climbing out and slamming his door. Jackdaw and Raven flipped up their hoods, and they all followed him onto the deserted street. Looking around, Payge grunted in satisfaction. "Good enough. It's about a mile. The pair of you stay behind Lottie and me."

They walked in silence until they were within sight of the student union building. Payge had them wait as he watched the flow of people coming and going through its doors. After some minutes, he spoke. "Time to get this done."

Raven and Jackdaw nodded their understanding and walked off, looking like two kids out on a Saturday evening. They split up, disappearing into the dark spaces between the student union and the office blocks to either side of it.

"Your turn," Payge said. "Stay safe."

Lottie walked alone towards the union building. Something she had done so many times. Other students walked beside her and past her, talking and laughing, carefree. She felt like a phantom moving amongst the living. Then she was through the doors, moving into the main hall, an airy space that pulsed with the thump of dance beats and the raucous sound of a multitude of voices in pursuit of the heart of Saturday night.

Lottie stood at the threshold, heedless of the people behind her and their need to skirt around her. She caught the backward glances and looked down at herself. At the clothes she had been wearing for two days, creased and dirty. Not Saturday night clothes. Not bright and full of life clothes. She bit at her lip and wondered if she might cry, but there were no tears. Only a feeling of loss and sadness and a growing resentment at these innocents. She tried to shake it away. *Find Liz. Get her out of here. After that I can think about what next.*

Staying close to the wall, she made a circuit of the dance floor, threading through the crowd, checking out the tables tucked into corners. No sign of Liz. Forcing down a growing unease, she left the hall to check the adjoining bar.

No dance music in the bar but the place was packed. The sound of voices, a dull roar. She squeezed between bodies, sometimes saying excuse me, sometimes not. Trying to navigate the room, she began to excuse herself less and shove more. Elbowing between two guys in rugby shirts, to whom she thought she might actually be invisible, she found herself facing a table in the furthest corner.

"Lottie!"

Liz screamed at her, launching herself out of her seat, bouncing off the table as she went. Bottles clattered, drinks wobbled and slopped. Liz ignored them, sweeping Lottie up, wrapping her in a huge embrace. "Where have you been? I was so worried."

Liz held her out at arm's length, and Lottie saw how deeply drunk her friend was. With a soppy grin, Liz hugged her once more. "What are you like?" Her breath was sharp with vodka and sweet with lemonade. "C'mere." Bundling back into the corner, they cosied up to a good-looking young man with a bemused smile on his face.

"This," Liz said, "is Ben. Ben, be a dear and fetch Lottie a drink. What do you fancy?"

"I'll have what you're having."

"Good girl. Same again, please, love. Twice."

Ben smiled back and without a word, snaked his way into the crowd.

Liz pulled Lottie close. "Tell me what's been happening."

"When did you meet him?" Lottie nodded in the direction of the bar.

"About an hour ago. He's gorgeous, isn't he? And he's buying all the drinks."

"About an hour ago." Lottie continued to stare in the direction Ben had taken. Into the crowd but not towards the bar. "How did you meet him?"

Liz gave her a fuzzy look. "He just came up and started talking to me."

"Don't you think that's a bit odd?"

"A good-looking girl like me, on her own on a Saturday night? It would be odd if he didn't. Anyway, what about you? What was all that about last night? And where have you been since, another planet or something? Did you really break into Andrea's dad's place? What for? I don't mind if you did. I just can't see you as the criminal type."

"Slow down. Slow down." Lottie looked at her friend, eagerly awaiting her story. She wondered what she could say. Nothing seemed quite up to the task. "It's been a bit crazy. Yes, I did break in."

Liz's eyes widened with surprise. Her hand flew to her mouth as she began to shake with giggles. "You never did? Go, girl."

"It's not funny."

"It is."

They looked at each other, and Lottie bathed in the warmth of affection for her friend. It was a moment she longed to hang on to, a moment of sunlight in a dark season. "Liz, I'm in a bit of trouble." She stopped to consider. "A lot, actually. But the thing is—"

"Ladies. Here you go." Ben clunked down two glasses. "I got you doubles. Thought it would save time."

"Aw," Liz said. "See? You got to love him. Here." She patted the seat beside herself, and Ben squeezed in.

"What are you doing?" Lottie asked him.

His pleasant face creased in puzzlement. "What do you mean?"

"What are you studying?"

He smiled at her in a sly way, his voice rising as he answered. "Uh, history."

"What year?"

His smile widened. "Lots of them."

Lottie didn't smile. "No, I mean, what year are you in?"

There was a heartbeat before he answered. "First year."

She turned her attention back to Liz. "I need to—" Stopping herself, she tipped her head towards the door. "I need to go… you know." She stood. "Don't move from that seat." Liz looked back at her with drunk incomprehension. In her head, Lottie saw herself coming back to find an empty chair. Two empty chairs. She flailed around for a hook. Something to make her friend stay put.

Sorry, Andrea.

"I'll tell you what Andrea's dad and his assistant were up to." Now that she had Liz's attention, she was out of her seat, backing into the crowd. "One minute." She held up a finger. "Stay there." The crowd closed in, blocking her view of Liz. She wriggled through the press of bodies, digging her phone out as she went. In the corridor outside, she selected Payge from the three names in the phone's menu. It rang once.

"Lottie," Payge said.

"I found her."

"Good. Are you with her now?"

"No."

"Why not?"

"There was someone with her already. I, uh, I got a bad feeling about him. I didn't want to talk to you in front of him. Did I make a mistake? Should I have stayed?"

"No. You did the right thing. Tell me where you are."

"We're in the bar just off the main hall. You'll see the sign for it." She pushed her way back into the bar, ignoring all pretence of politeness. Sliding between the last screen of drinkers and the table in the corner felt like emerging from the undergrowth in a forest. The seats at the table were empty. As were the glasses. All except two. Hers and Ben's. The phone was still pressed to her ear.

"She's gone," Lottie said.

"Think," Payge snapped. "Where?"

Her fear, bright and numbing, didn't want her to think. She forced past it. "The main hall. They need to go through there to get out. I'll go after them from here."

She could barely hear his reply. "Do not go after them. Lottie—"

She hung up, and with desperate speed, made her way back to the hall. Trying to look everywhere at once, she scanned the dance floor. Flashing lights blinded her, shifting dancers blocked her view. The music drowned out all sound. Her feet wanted her to run into the crowd, to dash around in search of Liz. She bid them be still. She held back. She watched. And caught sight of Liz, swaying to the beat, her hands raised above her head, her eyes nearly closed. A clumsy side-step and she fell, a slow process that began at her ankles and knees and spread up her body, leaving her puddled on the floor. Near her, Ben looked on, doing nothing. Lottie moved, driving past the people in her way.

Ben saw her and lunged forward to crouch over Liz, his face razored with shadow and light. Lottie rushed towards him, and as she reached to help her friend, he drove his fist into her stomach.

It was an awkward blow, but it still left her on her knees, doubled over, gagging for breath and fighting the flare of pain that exploded in her belly. Dancers skirted around her, some bumping into her. She got one foot out from under herself and tried to stand. The crowd parted before one of the security staff. Ben lifted his hands in a placatory gesture towards the burly man in the hi-vis jacket.

"My girlfriend's had too much to drink." Ben laid a protective hand on Liz's shoulder. "She attacked her." An accusing finger was stabbed at Lottie.

The security man moved fast, slipping behind her, scooping his hands under her arms, pulling her backwards. "Come on, love. Enough for tonight. Time to go."

Lottie reacted without thinking. Bracing her feet, she backpedalled hard and fast, pushing herself into the man restraining her. They travelled together, two, three, four paces, picking up speed, losing balance, until they tipped to the floor, and she slid out of his grip.

Ben had Liz on her feet, his arm around her waist, her arm draped over his shoulder. Lottie launched herself at them. Ben let Liz go and straight-armed his open palm into Lottie's forehead.

She was on the floor again, stunned, watching while Ben hauled Liz up again. She scrambled after them on her hands and knees. Behind her, the security man cursed. In front, Ben was struggling to get Liz moving. Her slouched form kept slipping from his grasp.

She was gaining on them. They were no more than a few paces away. Getting her feet under her, Lottie pawed the knife Raven had given her from her pocket. The security man grabbed the waistband of her trousers and pulled her backwards.

"No!" A shout of despair, as her balance went. She landed hard, pain lancing up her pelvis and spine, her fall breaking the man's grip. Twisting back on to hands and knees, she scuttled towards Ben as he half-carried, half-dragged Liz to the exit.

Reaching Ben before he reached the doors, she took a clumsy swipe at his legs with the knife. She missed, doing no more than letting Ben know she was there. He turned and kicked at her face. Made awkward by his burden, he only clipped her, making her head snap round. The knife slipped from her grasp and Ben kicked it away.

Before Lottie could gather herself, an arm crooked round her throat, pulling her up into a chokehold. The security man had caught up with her. A second member of security, a woman this time, hurried over. "Call the police," the man shouted. "There's a knife. Find it." The arm around her neck drew tighter. Her arm was forced up her back, painfully far, and she let out a ratcheting gasp.

"You need to let her go."

Payge stood in front of her, looking past her, staring down the security man holding her.

"Mate, can you go away?" the security man said. He motioned to his colleague. "Can you get him out of here?"

The woman nodded and approached Payge. "Let's just see you to the door, sir." She walked forward, one hand held up in front of her. "This is nothing to do with you."

Payge looked at the hand and then at the woman's face beyond it. "Wrong," he said. He stepped forward, slapped the hand out of his path, slipped one leg behind the woman and tripped her over it with a single push. With the woman laid out at his feet, he stamped on her stomach, then her face.

Turning back to Lottie and her captor, he moved to within touching distance of them. "Let her go," he said. "You're hurting her." The security man shifted his gaze left and right. Payge leant in. "No one is coming to help you." He reached forward and grabbed the arm around Lottie's neck.

Lottie winced at the yelp of hurt and surprise, so close to her ear. The pressure round her throat was gone. Payge was twisting the security man's arm into odd angles. She was free, sliding past Payge, ignoring his call for her to stop. Dashing to where she could see Ben. Outside now, still clutching Liz, who walked with heavy footsteps, her head slumped forward.

Too scared of losing sight of them, breaking into a wild charge to catch up with them, Lottie collided with the first person who stepped into her path. Curses and beer flew through the air. Hands grabbed for her. She dodged around them and ran.

Through the doors, into the street, crying out in frustration. Liz was gone. The street was empty. Forcing down her panic, she looked around. *Where? Where could they disappear to the quickest?*

She sprinted to where the student union building, and its neighbour, shielded a side street. Where she saw Ben, Liz still clamped to his side. And a van parked a short distance away. Two people climbed from the van.

"Leave her alone." Lottie's shout did nothing to slow Ben down. The two people who had emerged from the van were walking towards her. A man and a woman, both dressed in dark clothing. "Leave her alone," Lottie said again, quieter this time.

Ben called to the two people from the van. "This is the other one." The woman nodded her understanding.

Lottie took a hesitant step forward. She froze when the woman drew a knife. The oily sheen on the long blade gleamed in the streetlights. Her companion produced a handgun from a coat pocket.

"Get her inside," the woman said. "I'll deal with this one."

"Leave my friend alone." The words floated out of Lottie, fear stealing away any strength they might have had.

"I won't hurt you," the woman said. "If you come with us, you can be with your friend."

"Stay where you are, Lottie." Payge's voice came from behind her, steady and calm.

She saw the startled look on the woman's face, then the line of her mouth hardening as she called back to him. "You've done your part, Payge. Leave now and Steals doesn't need to know you were here."

Lottie spun round. "They're with you?" Payge looked back at her, his face unreadable. She pleaded. "We need to get Liz." She watched him do nothing. "Help me," she urged.

"Lottie…" he said.

For a fleeting moment, they locked eyes. Then Payge dropped his gaze to the ground.

"Fine," Lottie breathed. Her hands clenched into fists, she bit her bottom lip, and knowing she would never make it, she ran at Ben. She knew that if she did make it, she had no way of beating three opponents. She ran anyway.

The noise came from behind her. Two sharp barks, one after the other. The woman in front of her dropped into a crouch, fumbling inside her jacket. At the same time, her companion jerked once, twice, before dropping his gun and slumping to his knees. He pitched forward, making no effort to break his fall, his skull impacting the road with a sickening thump.

Payge was shouting at her to get down. The woman had drawn a handgun and Lottie faltered at the sight of it pointed at her. The muzzle of it lit up. There was that same flat barking noise. In her head, the mad thought circled round that guns didn't sound like that in the movies. Ben was dragging Liz through a sliding door on the side of the van. Lottie ran faster. Only yards away now. The woman had retreated to the driver's door, ignoring her, firing at Payge.

Lottie reached the side door, where Liz's feet were disappearing inside. She dived after them, slamming into Ben. The three of them went down, Lottie's wrist screaming at her in outrage, bent too far back where it took the weight of her landing. Ignoring it, she levered herself up and laid into Ben's back with clumsy blows of her fists.

Ben took the hits, pulled himself clear, rolled over and kicked her in the chest. Moving fast, he was up on his haunches, pushing her over as she tried to struggle up. He straddled her, using his weight to hold her down. A knee pinned her left arm, a hand clamped her right wrist, his free hand digging into her neck. Lottie choked and gagged; she could hear more shots being fired but they seemed far away. Her whole world shrank to the dwindling supply of air she was trying to drag down her constricted throat.

The woman climbed into the driver's seat and pulled the door shut. "Finish it," she spat at Ben. A bullet hammered through the side of the van, deafening in the enclosed space. Lottie barely registered it, panic leaping in her as she suffocated.

The van's engine turned over and shivered into life. Payge's fist rammed through the driver's window, scattering chips of glass. Grabbing the woman by her hair, he yanked her towards him. Her head smacked against the window surround, and she shrieked when her scalp was dragged across the jagged remains of the window. Letting go of her hair, Payge pulled the door open and dragged her out. Forcing her head down, he drove his knee into her face and threw her out of the way. Leaning inside the van, he shot Ben in the back twice before putting a single bullet into the woman at his feet.

Ben slumped on top of Lottie, a long breath leaking from him. She tried to push him aside, but it was like moving a sack of sand. Grunting and heaving, she slid out from under him, her hands coated in his blood. The rear door of the van opened, and Raven leapt inside. Jackdaw followed, landing on top of his sister, who swore and pushed him away. Payge slid into the driver's seat.

"Go," Raven said.

The engine over-revved and tyres squealed as Payge threw the van into a tight circle. The back became a mass of rolling bodies.

"Doors," Payge said over his shoulder. "Get them shut."

Lottie turned, shifted and tried to disentangle her legs while Raven pulled the side door closed and Jackdaw leant out to grab the rear door.

"Closed," Raven said.

They turned a corner onto a main road. Payge slowed down, stopping at traffic lights. Two police cars screamed past them, lights and sirens cutting the night to pieces.

"Are you okay?" Raven said.

Lottie nodded. "Check Liz first. He did something to her." She looked round at Ben. "Is he…?"

"Deader than shit," Jackdaw said.

Lottie turned this idea over in her head, then dismissed it in favour of Liz. "How is she?"

"She's out," Raven said. "Looks like they might have given her something. We can only wait until she comes around. How are you?"

"He kicked me in the boobs," Lottie said. "It really hurt. Why do people keep hitting me? I was never in a fight in my life until a few days ago."

"Comes with the job," Jackdaw said.

Lottie ignored him. "You." She rounded on Payge. "You knew." The van swerved when she thumped her fist into the back of his head. "You lied to me. You knew what they were going to do, and you lied."

"Lottie." Raven laid her hand on her shoulder.

Lottie shrugged it off. "I want him to say it. No, forget it. Pull over. I want out of this. Right now."

Payge drove on, heedless to her protests.

"Pull over." Lottie smacked him on the back of the head a second time, then was thrown forward, as the van screeched to a halt.

Payge twisted in his seat to face her. "Yes, I lied. You don't have to like it, but you should at least try to understand it."

"They were going to kill me."

"I know that now," Payge said. "Steals didn't choose to share that with me at the outset. Only about Elizabeth."

"Oh, and you just have to do everything he says, do you?"

Payge shrugged. "No choice really."

"Liar. You must have a choice."

"Least worst choice. Save as many as I can. Me included."

"What's that supposed to mean?"

Payge stared at her with eyes like broken glass. "I don't have to explain myself to you."

He held her gaze until she had to look away. She glanced at Ben's corpse, puzzled that she felt so unconcerned about the death of another human being. They drove in silence until Payge stopped some distance away from his lock-up. "There," he said.

Raven moved up to peer through the windscreen. "What am I looking at?"

"Those two cars. They don't belong here. I'm guessing Steals knows about this place. He's maybe known about it all along. How, I don't know. Another mistake on my part. They're waiting for us." He started the engine, turned the van around and drove off. Raven returned to her place in the back of the van. Jackdaw slumped down, using Ben's body as a cushion.

"Are we just going to drive around until we run out of petrol?" Lottie asked.

"No. We need to get away from here," Payge said. "Ore's not safe for us. The only other gate near here is the one to Syre. That's where we go."

"Seriously?" Jackdaw said.

"What's wrong with this Syre place?" Lottie asked, picking up on Jackdaw's tone.

"They don't like visitors," Payge said.

Lottie looked to her friend, still out cold on the floor. "What do we do with Liz?"

Raven shrugged. "Take her back home. Leave her there."

"Will she be safe?"

"Of course."

"You said that very quickly. What about the pattern? Isn't that still going?"

Raven said nothing.

"So she won't be safe," Lottie said.

Raven sighed. "I don't know."

"I'm going with her then."

Payge spoke over his shoulder. "An obvious solution presents itself."

"No," Raven said. "You don't get to do that."

"What do you mean?" Lottie asked.

Jackdaw picked at the covering on the van's floor. "He means we leave Liz here. Raven can watch over her. Us three go to Syre. We go where nobody will want to follow. It's the best move."

Raven glared at her brother. "Don't you dare side with him."

"It's the choice that gives us the best chance of success," Payge said. "I can't protect Lottie here." He caught Lottie's eye as he went on. "Yes, I still want you to get through this alive." Looking away, he rubbed at his temple with slow, tired strokes. "And your friend. All of you. We're done with

Steals now, but he won't be done with us. He will come after us. After me, most likely. And there's still someone out there who wants you killed. Without the resources Steals provides, it's more difficult to protect you. I've got no identity here. No money. No shelter. If we go to Syre, it's different. I can do what I need to, if it comes down to it. We have to narrow the options of our enemies."

"You won't come out of Syre if you're caught," Raven said. "Lottie needs to come with me. You can look after this one." She gave Liz a nudge with her toe. A sleep-drenched murmur came from her.

"What about what Lottie might want?" Payge asked.

"What she wants—"

"Let her speak for herself, Raven."

It took Lottie a moment before she could bring herself to speak. "I want Liz to be safe." She tried to be angry at Raven, but she couldn't sustain it. She was too soaked in weariness and despair. "I want this to end."

"There are three of us and two of you," Payge said. "One of us has to stay here with your friend." He glanced at Lottie as he spoke. "The other two need to get you away." Now he looked to Raven. "Steals doesn't know about your involvement. That gives you the advantage here."

"Liz. Her name is Liz," Lottie said. "Can't you say it?"

Payge nodded. "Steals's pattern might be played out to his liking. Liz might be in no further danger. The only thing I'm sure of is that if I stay around her, she will be in danger when Steals comes after me."

"What does the pattern look like now?" Lottie said. "Maybe we can figure out the best thing to do from it?"

"Smart thinking," Payge said. He dug the laptop from his backpack and passed it to Lottie. "Take a look."

When she opened it, the screen was blank. "Nothing. It's gone. What does that mean?"

"Could be it's over. More likely we're locked out of it. They were waiting for us back at the garage. Steals is already moving against us."

No one spoke further. Lottie breathed in air made humid by the press of bodies in the back. Her feet rested against Ben's corpse, whose blood added to the thick scent in the enclosed space. When she couldn't take the silence anymore, she spoke up.

"I'll go with Payge." She kept her gaze fixed on the floor, not wanting to look Raven in the eye. "I know you don't want me to, but I think it's for the best. If you could take care of Liz for me, I promise I'll come to you when this is done."

Raven reached for her, took her hand. The touch was kindness but when Lottie lifted her head, the look Raven sent her way was hard and judgemental. "If it's what you want."

"It is."

Raven drew her hand back. When she spoke, it was to Payge. "You heard what she said. Drive the bloody van."

9

SYRE

"Can't we put her inside?" Lottie said.

Payge looked up from his task of setting Liz down outside the door of her flat. "And risk waking your other friend?"

"But we can't just leave her in the corridor." After winning the battle over not leaving Liz in the street, she felt she should press home her victory.

Payge stood and regarded Liz's slumped form. Quiet snores escaped her lips. "She's sleeping normally now. She'll wake up cold and sore soon enough. Raven will be watching the building the whole time. She's as safe as we can make her."

"We could just shove her inside the door and run for it."

Payge laid a gentle hand on her arm. "Let's not push our luck any further."

Lottie pressed her lips together and blew a breath out through her nose. "Okay."

While Payge walked away, Lottie knelt beside Liz and brushed straggles of hair away from her face. "Be safe, kiddo. I'm sorry. I have to go."

With a last look at her friend, she got to her feet and rushed to catch up.

"Why did you do it?" She dogged Payge's heels as he tramped down the corridor, drawing up beside him when they reached the stairs. Her words echoed around the concrete well of the stairway. "When they tried to kidnap Liz. I asked you to help me and you didn't. Then you did help. Why?"

Payge sighed. "I said I would protect you."

"You said Steals told you to protect me."

"Fair point. Somewhere along the way, I changed my mind. It's a thing people do from time to time when circumstances change."

"When did this happen?"

"I think you know. You're very important." He paused for a moment, as if weighing his words. "To me. I've come to think of you as a friend."

"You've a real way of putting things." She got a grunt for a reply.

Outside the building, Payge exchanged a final few words with Raven before he strode away with Jackdaw by his side. Lottie hung back for a moment. "Please look after her for me."

"I will," Raven said. She gazed at Lottie, searching her face, before seeming to come to some conclusion. "Don't trust Payge. He isn't finished with Steals." Without another word, she too walked away.

Payge looked round when Lottie ran up with him. "What did Raven say to you?"

"Oh. Ah… just to be careful, you know?"

"Uh-huh." Payge stared at her long enough to make her feel uncomfortable before he spoke again. "Worth keeping in mind. Best we get on then."

∽

He drove to a twenty-four-hour supermarket, where Lottie followed him round as he picked up backpacks, spare clothes, bottles of water and some provisions. Then they drove out of the city, threading through country lanes, bumping down a farm track to a dead end, the van's headlights illuminating a dense screen of trees in front of them. Payge killed the engine and climbed out. "I'll go for a look round. You stay here."

A quarter of an hour later, he returned. "No sign anyone's been here recently."

"You think maybe they won't reckon on us trying to reach Syre?" Jackdaw said.

Payge scrubbed at his chin. "Steals is careful. He wouldn't dismiss it. But his lieutenants have got to get word to him first, then wait for word back. Unless they act on their own. Doubtful, but they might. I think we can risk a couple of hours' rest. We'll need it for later."

Lottie tucked her hands into her armpits, shivering in the dark of the early morning. "I'll need it, you mean. You two could probably walk to the ends of the earth without a rest."

Payge gave her a smile. "Exactly. So, back in the van with you. See if you can get your head down for a spell."

Glad to be out of the cold, making herself as comfortable as she could, she thought she would never get to sleep next to a corpse. Then Jackdaw was shaking her awake. "Time to go," he said. "Hurry."

She stretched and yawned, stiff from lying on the unyielding floor, wishing she might get a few hours' sleep in a real bed sometime soon. And caught sight of Ben's body, shoved against the wall of the van. She stared at it, feeling she needed to say something about it. Jackdaw paid the body no more attention than a discarded bag. Grabbing her hand, he pulled her towards the rear doors.

In the pre-dawn light, she could see they were parked next to a sprawling wood. Looking round, she saw the headlights of another vehicle some way off, travelling the same road they had. It stopped at the head of the track that led to the wood, then turned into it. She watched the vehicle's lights as it bounced and jounced along the track. "The local farmer?" she asked.

Payge stood beside her, looking the same way. "If it is, he likes to drive fast." He passed her a backpack and took hold of her hand. "This way."

He led her past scattered stands of hawthorn and gorse, going deeper into the wood. After some minutes, Payge stopped and hushed Lottie into silence. She listened but could only hear bird song, rising with the morning light, and the wind moving through leaves.

The terrain became more difficult, fallen trees blocked their path, a stream had to be crossed. Lottie cried out when her leg went knee-deep into a gully choked with dead wood. The three of them froze. Distinct over the woodland noise, they heard a shout.

"Not far now," Payge said. He leant in, offering a hand to pull her out. "Keep moving."

They came to an overgrown trail, following it to where a derelict cottage stood in a clearing. Thickets of thorn grew around its walls. Snapped timbers, like broken bones, showed through holes in the roof.

"Inside," Payge said.

Lottie eyed the screen of spiky growth that encircled the ruin. Jackdaw drew a revolver from under his jacket. "I'll get your backs."

Payge pushed into the thorns, using his body as a wedge. Lottie hung in close behind him, but branches still snapped and slapped at her, leaving red scratches on exposed skin. She could only imagine what Payge was feeling. Other than an occasional grunt, no sound came from him.

They reached a window that had long since lost its glass. Shouts now came from behind them, and a single shot was fired. Payge turned around and grabbed her, hoisting her through the window in one sweeping movement. She caught a flash of Jackdaw sprinting towards them, then she was rolling across splintery floorboards. Jackdaw leapt through after her. While she sprawled on the floor, wondering what to do, he was on his feet, bracing his hands against the windowsill, sighting on some target she couldn't see. He fired four times, the shots painfully loud in the confines of the small room they were in.

Payge boosted himself through the window. Jackdaw's gun clicked on an empty chamber. Part of the window frame exploded in fragments. Jackdaw swore and ducked, cracking his weapon open, empty cartridges clattering to the ground. Shots smacked into the wall opposite the window, plaster jetting out from the impacts.

"Up." Payge was beside her, pulling her towards the room's only door. Jackdaw poked his head over the sill, to fire off another volley before running after them. In the next room, a confusion of broken boards and joists disappeared into a large hole in the floor. Light shone in through a hole in the roof as big as the one in the floor. Payge led Lottie to the edge of the pit. "Jump," he said.

"In there?" Lottie quailed at him. "How far down is it?"

"Not far. You're landing on dirt. You'll be fine."

Lottie saw herself impaled on a snapped timber. "I don't – ahk!" Payge grabbed the back of her jacket in two hands, swung her over the opening and dropped her in. She fell in a heap, cushioned on soft earth. Payge thumped down beside her in a crouch, one hand down for support. Jackdaw flew through the air, landed on Payge's shoulders and jumped to the ground.

"This way." Payge crawled into a narrow opening made by two angled beams of wood. Lottie hesitated to follow.

Jackdaw shoved her backside. "Move."

She followed Payge's example, crawling through the opening, into a tunnel so low, she was forced from all fours down onto her belly. She tasted dirt, spat it out and pulled herself forward on elbows and knees, ignoring the stones digging into her. The darkness of the tunnel was split by a muzzle flash, Jackdaw firing back the way they had come. Lottie crawled with frantic haste, the tunnel roof no more than inches above her, sensed rather than seen.

"They're still on us." Jackdaw's voice.

The meagre light faded to absolute black. She kept crawling, the change in the sound of her own movements making her aware that she had moved into a far bigger space. A hand on her shoulder made her start.

"It's me." Payge's voice. Close to her. He guided her up. She could see nothing of him, the warmth of his hands holding hers was her only anchor. Lines of light surrounded her, threads of blue and gold making a complex lattice that stretched to places her sight struggled to follow. "I see it," she whispered. "All of it."

"Good for you." He tugged on her hands, pulling her through the lines. An instant of disorientation, a frightening feeling of her mind losing contact with her body. The air smelt different. Fresher, free of dust. The geometry of the gate faded away. She could see Payge again, a dark shape in the gloom. Then Jackdaw, who slipped out of the darkness behind her, as if through a curtain.

"Still with us," he said. "They're not stopping."

"I can close it," Lottie said.

Payge looked at her, mystified.

"The gate. I did it before. With Raven. The little one?"

"Then do it."

Lottie closed her eyes, letting the architecture of the gate grow in her vision. She reached out to one line of it, a thick cord that vanished where the ground would be. Her hand closed over it. No feeling of contact on her skin but a white streak of pain flashed from her skull, down the nerves of her arm, into her hand. A connection made between her and the gate. She held on to it, tried to move it, grunting with the effort, pain drilling into her head, coursing down her arm. She cried out as she put everything she had into bending the ray of light. Nothing happened.

Far away, Payge was telling her to hurry. His hand was on her wrist, pulling at her. But with her other hand touching the gate, it felt like an infant clutching an adult's finger. She was steel. She was iron. But the gate's anchor line was stronger. *You don't undo a knot by trying to snap the rope it's tied with. I need to pull on the right thread.*

She reached, manipulated, working her way into the complexity of the gate. The bones of her hand were twisted and pushed in ways they didn't want to go. She stretched further and turned, held, pulled. Now her hand was caught, trapped in a web of lines, no wriggling free. *Here and here. Gather, bend.*

A blunt-nosed bullet droned past her nose, its lazy progress giving her time to look at it in cross-eyed wonder. Her hand convulsed and was free, leaving behind a strand of light that blurred like a plucked wire. The fuzziness spread further, one line infecting the next, until the whole gate had grown indistinct, the brightness fading from it.

She was flying through the air, crashing into Payge, the pair of them tumbling to the ground in a tangle of arms and legs.

Payge pushed himself free. "What was that?"

Lottie sat up and moaned, cradling her shoulder with

one hand. "That was my sore arm. Bad enough one of those stalker things tried to pull it off. Now you as well?"

"This is some weird shit," Jackdaw said. He pressed his hand against the stone slab behind them. "We walked through that a second ago."

"You closed it?" Payge asked.

Lottie looked around at rock walls and an earth floor. Sunlight shone in through a narrow cleft at the far end of the cave the gate had brought them to. "I must have."

Payge looked at her longer and longer until she grew uncomfortable. Finally, he blew out a deep breath and shook his head. They gathered themselves up and walked towards the sunlight, emerging past a tumble of boulders, into a forest glade.

"Well," Jackdaw said.

Lottie stared. "It's beautiful." She breathed air that held the green scent of living things and the damp odour of fertile earth. Trees with leaves that shimmered pale grey underneath and vibrant green on top, crowded around them. Swooping whistles sounded from dark shapes darting between branches. Spears of brightness were dotted around, where a shaft of sunlight made it through the leaf canopy. She turned a complete circle. The trees loomed all around. A continuous vista that offered no way forward. No points of reference. "Actually, it's quite scary," she said. "You'd get lost in here in no time."

"We won't get lost," Payge said. "There's another gate perhaps two days' walk from here. We'll find it."

"Which direction?"

"Southwest."

"How will we know which way is southwest?"

Payge reached into a pocket, pulled out a field compass and shook it at her.

Lottie blushed. "Stupid," she snapped at herself.

Jackdaw looked up from loading his revolver. "Easy mistake to make, love."

"I need to be smarter than that. Stupid thinking will get us in trouble."

Payge came over to her. "What you did in there with the gate. I'm not going to ask how you did it. It's beyond me. But you did the smart thing. Stop feeling angry at yourself. And sorry for yourself. It's doing you no good."

He crouched down to open his backpack. She stared over the top of him, into the trees. The three people seemed to appear from nowhere. One second, she was looking at the tree line. Two seconds, they stepped out of the trees and into the clearing. She thought it was like an optical illusion, where the image flips to something else if you stare at it just so…

All three of them were tall, they wore camouflage smocks that mimicked the colour of the trees, the pattern on the fabric shifting and blending with their surroundings. Their faces were covered by masks and hoods of the same material. But she recognised their weapons from any number of news reports on television. Unmistakable. AK-47s. "Uh, guys?" she said. At the edge of her vision, she saw Payge and Jackdaw moving, shifting their stance, getting leverage, getting ready to attack.

One of the figures spoke. She couldn't tell which one, the sound of it just seemed to be all around her, sweet and clear. "On the ground, hands behind you."

Payge threw his backpack at them. It spun through the air. Heads turned to track it; weapons tilted towards it. Jackdaw took off, vanishing into the trees. One of the three broke off from the group and ran after him, moving with a bare whisper of sound.

The remaining two came forward, weapons pointed. Copying Payge, Lottie sank to her knees, then lay face down. Her wrists were bound together, and she was lifted to her feet. Her captor led her over to Payge. She was about to speak, but Payge shook his head, the warning in his eyes enough to make her keep her mouth shut. Single gunshots sounded from the trees, followed by a burst of fire. Lottie looked at Payge, fearful this time. Again, he shook his head.

Their captors flipped back their hoods and pulled down their masks. A woman and a man. Each had the same golden hair, the same high cheek bones. Their lips curved in a good-natured way, a natural half-smile. Slanted eyes of sea green sparkled with life. They might have been brother and sister, and they were two of the most beautiful people Lottie had ever seen.

The female spoke in halting words. "Follow. Do not speak." She started for the tree line. The male motioned with the barrel of his weapon and fell in behind them as they followed the woman. They had gone perhaps twenty paces and Lottie couldn't hold herself back any longer. She whispered it. "They're elves."

Payge whispered back. "Shut up."

Lottie never had a chance to reply. A rifle butt slammed into her back, making her stagger and cry out. She got the message. She shut up.

They walked from the time the sun was at its zenith until it was low in the sky. The trees thinned out into more open ground. They reached a community, a scatter of lodges built of wood and roofed with turf. People moving between the lodges, going about their business. Each had the same mesmeric beauty as their captors.

A gaggle of children ran up, staring in silence as they walked past. Lottie smiled at them, miniature versions of the adults. If anything, even more entrancing. One of them spat at her, the warm gob landing on her cheek, trickling down to catch in the corner of her mouth. With her hands bound behind her back, there was nothing she could do to wipe it away.

The children scampered off, silver peals of happy laughter ringing in the air. And all around her, she heard those magical voices, speaking, calling to each other, singing for the joy of it. Heartbreaking in their beauty. Wherever she looked, she saw weapons. Guns and knives. Men and women greeting each other before exchanging weapons for tools or infants, switching from guard duty to childcare to work tasks and back again, in a seamless changing of roles.

Their captors took them to the edge of the settlement, to where it bordered open moorland that swept away to the horizon in undulating mounds. The forest was a vast crescent, dwindling into the distance. With that vista of freedom in sight, they were led to a cluster of cages, large enough to walk around in, not tall enough to stand upright in.

Forced to the ground inside one, Lottie stayed that way until she heard the lock snap closed. Sitting up and rubbing at the chafed skin on her wrists, she looked across to where Payge sat in his own prison, a few yards away.

"This isn't so good, is it?"

Payge gave a grim laugh. "That about sums it up."

"Do you think Jackdaw got away? Is there any chance he can get us out?"

The pain on Payge's face was clear to see. "These bastards are fast. They hunt. They're very good at it."

"Jackdaw's fast. I've seen him."

Payge shrugged. "He'll be okay, I'm sure."

"Why did they hit me when I called them elves?"

Payge looked as if he had tasted something foul. "They consider it an act of aggression for anyone to call them by anything other than their race name. They loathe anyone other than themselves using their race name. They think no act is unreasonable in preventing corruption of their ways. I wouldn't waste my time on trying to understand them. I'd suggest you do the same."

Lottie's reply was hesitant. "That's a bit extreme. If they don't like company, why don't they just block up the gate?"

Payge wiped at his brow, then looked at his hand. "I'm sorry for snapping at you. You're only asking. I understand. They don't block up the gates because the makers wouldn't like it. And they aren't ready to get the makers angry at them. Besides, didn't you see the Kalashnikovs?"

"I did wonder about them."

"They like guns. Guns beat swords and arrows every time. And because they have a gate to your world, they can get them." He stopped talking for a moment, looking at her, considering. "Your world. Separated for so long.

Now connected again. In all that time, the other worlds have seen little in the way of change. Small kingdoms and fiefdoms. A complex picture but a stable one. Now that stability is slipping away. In no small part due to people running guns out of your world. Some, like these bastards, are taking advantage of that. So, like all zealots everywhere, they either tie themselves in knots to justify the break with their dogma or they just ignore the difficult areas." He laid his hands in his lap. "I'd put them all out of my misery if I could. Every last one of them. Men, women and children."

"You're not in any kind of grey area on this, then? Any room for debate?"

Payge smiled at her. "Am I being a bit too heavy?"

She smiled back. "Just a bit."

"They murdered an entire clan of my people. Refugees who were fleeing the plague on our world. They killed them all. Without compunction. To send a message to anyone else who might think about stepping on their territory. Too heavy?"

"No, not at all."

♾

The soft light of evening seemed to last forever. Lottie lay on the grass, listening to her body, letting it relax. She drifted into sleep, only to be awoken by the rattle of the gate. A tray of food was pushed under it. The scent of cooked meat and fresh bread reached her, and she hurried over.

Picking up the hunk of bread first, she tore at it, feeding herself chunks of it. It only made her hunger grow.

Abandoning the bread, she turned to the meat, a small roasted bird of some kind. She picked it up and bit into it. Savoury juice flooded her tongue. As she chewed, she caught Payge watching her. He had no tray of food. She saw him run the tip of his tongue over his top lip.

"Do me a favour," he said. "Eat that as far away from me as you can?"

She nodded, her cheeks stuffed. Getting to her knees, she lifted the tray. It slipped through her greasy fingers, the food cascading to the ground. She looked at it, crestfallen.

"Pick it up," Payge said. "Don't waste it. You'll need your strength." With that, he walked to the furthest corner of his cage and turned his back on her.

౾

The evening grew darker, and the air grew cooler. Lottie curled up on the ground and shivered through a broken sleep. Come the dawn, she awoke to find herself huddled into a tight ball. She struggled up, unwilling to stretch out and lose the meagre heat her close-clutched limbs had managed to conserve during the night. A guard moved soundlessly to her cage, placing a tray of food under the gate before walking off.

"Eat your breakfast," Payge called to her. He sat cross-legged in the middle of his own cage.

She slumped down on to the grass. "I feel so bloody useless."

"Then listen. These bastards, I won't show them the respect of calling them by their true name, they don't see us as people. To them, we're less than animals. They're actually quite keen on animals. Our lives don't mean anything to them because they don't believe we are truly alive. They believe it is only themselves who are alive."

"That's barking mad."

"No more than any other belief system. The only thing we can do to help ourselves right now is to stay strong. Now eat. Drink too. You'll get dehydrated if you don't."

Walking hunched over, she reached the gate and eyed the breakfast tray. "Fruit." She held up an apple. A wedge of something white and squishy. "Cheese, I think." She sniffed at a cup. "Eugh. Don't know what that is."

"Fermented milk, probably."

"Cold meat." She waved what she thought might be a leg of chicken in the air. Payge followed the movement of it like a hunting cat, watching with rapt attention while she ate.

"Why aren't they feeding you?"

"I don't know."

"Yes, you do. You're just not telling me. I know that voice by now."

To her surprise, Payge laughed, a good, honest sound. "You really hate not knowing, don't you?"

"I like to know what's going on. That doesn't make me a bad person."

"No, it doesn't. Why do you need to know?"

"I get… uncomfortable not knowing."

"You mean scared?"

Lottie looked down at her breakfast. "No, not scared. Just… unsettled." She lifted her head to look at him. "There was never anyone there for me. When I was a kid. When I was a teenager. I went from one care home to the next and the next, until one day I was eighteen and then it was the front door they showed me."

"I couldn't imagine not knowing who my blood-kin were. I don't think I could face that every waking moment."

Silence lay between them.

"We're in a lot of trouble here, aren't we?" Lottie said.

"That we are."

"Are they going to let us go?"

"No. That much I'm sure of."

"They're going to kill us?"

"Likely."

"What chance do we have?"

Payge drew a breath. "Two only. The fact that you closed a gate might mean something to them. They would be more than happy for Syre to become a sundered realm. They might want your help with that. But our best chance is Jackdaw. If he's alive. So, for his sake, we need to be patient and be ready. Now finish your breakfast."

It began to rain, making them retreat to what shelter they had. Lottie hunched up against the cold and damp and grew tired and miserable and bored. The only respite was mealtimes, when hot flavoursome food drove away the misery. The rain let up as darkness fell and she settled in as best she could, shivering her way through the night on the wet ground.

The morning sun brought some warmth, her breakfast tray was waiting for her, and the cage opposite was empty. While she ate, she looked through the walls of her prison to the open land beyond. She could see nothing that had been made by a pair of hands. The landscape was pristine and wild. *It's beautiful. They don't deserve this. Or maybe they do because they've kept it that way. I'm going to be killed by a bunch of tree-hugging fascist elves.* She lay on the ground and tried not to think any more.

Sometime in the afternoon, she heard the rattle of chains. Payge was led back to his pen, manacles on his wrists, an iron collar around his neck with chains looped through rings on its front and rear, the chains held fast by four guards. Lottie winced when he was forced to the ground by blows to his head and the back of his knees. A knife was held to his temple while his bonds were removed.

When the guards were gone, Lottie called to him. He struggled to his feet, looking weary, favouring his left leg, bleeding from cuts to his face and hands.

"What did they do to you?"

He licked at cracked lips. "Damn, but I'm thirsty. I was fighting."

"Fighting? Who with?"

"Not who, what." Payge shook his head at her unasked question. "Doesn't matter. Lottie, I think I know…"

Two guards approached Lottie's cage. The gate was unlocked. "Speak when told," she was instructed.

They took her to a lodge in the centre of the village. The interior was a single room that combined kitchen, living space and sleeping area. Wooden beams, woven rugs, stitched blankets. Homely and comfortable. Weapons mounted on racks on the walls.

Sitting at the table in the kitchen area was one of the elves. This one was different from the others. She looked older. Lottie's guards marched her to the table, then moved to flank her. The older female studied her for some time before speaking. "Your name for me will be Cisiphane. This is not my true name." She stopped, as if to emphasise her point or to allow Lottie time to understand it. "Your companion. The troll. He is no more than what we expected. Their race has been slaves for too long. They lack all wisdom. How was the gate closed?"

She drew a short knife from her sleeve. The guards grabbed Lottie and pulled her forward. She struggled against them, afraid of what was to come. They were too strong. Her hand was forced flat on the tabletop. Cisiphane set her blade over the first joint on Lottie's thumb. The keen edge slit the top layer of her skin, stinging, drawing blood. "Speak true."

Lottie couldn't draw her gaze away from the knife or keep the tremor from her voice. "I did it."

"You lie."

The pressure on the blade increased. She felt it cut through her flesh. Blood welled up around the knife's edge. Burning pain flared, making her shake her head in frantic terror. "I did. I did it. It was me." The blade was pushed down harder. She was sure she could feel it pressing on bone. She promised herself she would not scream until it became unbearable.

Cisiphane lifted the knife and folded it away into her sleeve. "How?"

"I don't know."

The knife reappeared.

"Please, I'm telling you the truth. I don't know how I can do these things, I just can. Up until a little while ago I didn't even know what these gates were. I'm sorry. I don't know any more." Tears dripped down her cheeks and fell away, unwiped. Her chin trembled; her lips closed into a tight pocket. "Please?"

Cisiphane tested the edge of her blade with her thumb. "Only a maker can close a gate. You are not any kind of maker. This changes nothing."

❧

Back in her cage, Lottie nursed her bleeding thumb as best she could, pressing against the cut to stem the flow. Payge was asleep in a corner of his cage. She looked up from her injury. Payge stood so close to the walls of his cage that the steel bars pressed into his face. He was as close to her as he could possibly get. She hadn't heard his approach. Not a sound. His gaze was fixed on her injured hand.

"Uh, Payge? You're drooling."

He smeared the slick of saliva away without taking his eyes off her hand.

"Payge? Are you okay? Only you don't seem okay." She covered her wound with her good hand. "Payge?" she pleaded.

He looked like a man coming out of a deep slumber. His eyes focussed on her in slow increments. Realisation, then worry, creased his features. With care, he sat down to face her. "I'm hungry, Lottie. Really hungry."

"I know. I'm sorry. I wish I could…"

Payge gave her a small smile. "And I know you would. Even if you were starving." He rubbed at his eyes, the manacles on his wrists clinking in time to his movements. "I never thought it would come to this."

"Come to what? Why are they doing this? Feeding me and not you? Is this meant to be some kind of psychological thing?"

"No, it's nothing like that."

"They know about the gate. They questioned me about it."

"Really?" Payge sat up straighter. "Tell me." An energy was in him that hadn't been there a moment before. She recounted her questioning, what little there was to tell.

"Does that help us?"

"It might. They always guard the gate. Maybe they were waiting for us because they were told to. I don't know. I can't think straight." He made a rumbling growl in his throat. "Lottie, I need to tell you something. It's about me. My people. We were infected with a plague."

"I know."

Payge looked at her, worried, confused, a little lost. "How could you know?"

"Jackdaw told me a while back."

"Oh." The lost look on his face made her want to reach out to him. "I didn't know that." He looked away for some moments, brow knitted in concentration. He began to speak without looking at her, annunciating each word with care. "It started out as a rare disease amongst our people. Until some maker decided to turn it into a weapon. Make it more infectious. Make it hereditary. It has a broad range of symptoms and effects. I've got the more common ones. High pain threshold. Increased muscle and bone density. An enhanced metabolism. Makes me stronger and faster than I should be. And creates better conditions in me for the disease to flourish. I need to feed it. If I don't, my higher brain functions start to erode. My metabolism speeds up more as the disease tries to get me to eat more. Eat anything."

"The old folk tales," Lottie said. "Trolls and ogres. They were always man-eaters."

Payge nodded.

"You're winding me up."

"I wish I was."

"Why are they starving you?"

"So I end up in that state."

"Doesn't that make you more, uh, dangerous?"

"Yes."

Lottie didn't ask her next question. Payge answered it anyway. "They enjoy hunting."

ॐ

Early the next morning, Lottie was woken by a kick. A party of elves, laden with camping gear and weapons, led them into the forest. For hours, she tramped behind Payge until they reached a wide clearing. In the middle of the clearing stood two hutches, each big enough to hold a person. They were led to them and pushed inside.

Sitting on the grass, hunched forward to avoid striking her head on the wooden poles that formed the roof of her prison, Lottie stared through the thick wire at the activity around her. Tents were pitched, campfires were lit, and meat was set roasting over the open flames.

She tried to get Payge's attention, but he sat with his back to her, unmoving and unresponsive. A platter of meat was brought over for her. She ate it mechanically, not looking up from her plate.

"Lottie." Payge spoke in a whisper just loud enough for her to hear. His words came out in splintered bursts. "I'm too hungry. Can't think. When it happens. Remember. It is not me."

"When what happens?" Lottie asked. She felt cold now. She knew.

The words stuttered out of him, his body making small rocking movements as he spoke. "They hunt me. You run. I hunt. I hunt you."

"Payge, no. No, you won't. You promised to look after me."

He made a bitter noise. "I did."

Then he crept away and lay down, silent to any prompt she made. Lottie lay down too, crying tears of sullen anger. When her tears did nothing to help her, she wiped them away, curled up and waited.

◠

Movement and voices roused her. Around the camp there was lively chatter. Laughter. Someone broke into song and two or three others joined in. The words were meaningless, but Lottie listened still, unable to deny the beauty of it.

Weapons were sharpened and made ready, short lances and knives. The chatter took on a high, excited tone. A group of three broke away from the preparations to make their way to her cage. Lottie recognised Cisiphane at the head of the group. The cage door was unlocked, and she was bundled out.

"Please don't do this."

Her plea was ignored. Her hand was grasped and spread. Cisiphane drew her knife, and Lottie squealed when a gash was carved across her open palm. She curled her hand into a fist over the wound. Drips of scarlet leaked between her fingers.

"Go," Cisiphane said. "You have a thousand counts until we open the other cage. We will not harm you while the troll lives."

With that, she walked away. The clearing emptied, the elves vanishing into the woods, leaving Lottie alone with Payge. She walked over to his cage. The lock on it had been removed, the door held fast by a heavy bolt, needing only to be lifted and slid.

"Payge?" she said.

He stayed seated in the middle of his cage, head down, eyes closed. His breathing came in short bursts. Lottie reached out to the bolt. Too stiff to move with one hand, she lifted her wounded hand to it as well. Metal scraped on metal. Payge's head flicked up at the sound. Her blood dripped on the bars of the cage.

He shuffled over to the gate. Bringing his head level with the bolt, he laced his fingers through the wire mesh and pulled his upper body and face into it, pulled until the mesh was pressing into his skin. His tongue flicked through a gap near the bolt, where her hand still rested. She jerked her hand away, clutching it to her chest. Payge's tongue licked at the spots of her blood on the metal. He raised his eyes to meet her horrified gaze. She saw the last light of humanity in them dwindling away. His voice was a hoarse whisper. "Run, Lottie." The light faded and she was staring at the blank eyes of a starving predator. She ran.

She ran until her legs and her lungs could take her no further. She made herself rest. Then she ran again. She ran until she had to stop to vomit up the last meal she had eaten. She ran again. She squeezed her cut hand and knew that anything she did would be hopeless, but she still ran.

The sound was faint, coming and going on the breeze. Crouched against a tree, heaving in huge gulps of air, she strained to hear it. When her breathing was more under her control, she took a few steps in what she thought was the right direction, then stopped to listen. Nothing. The urge to run was so strong. Standing still, she felt naked. She made to move off. And caught the sound again. The sound of running water.

She headed towards it. The pitch of the ground changed to a gentle downward slope, and she picked up her pace. It was unmistakable now, the gurgle and chuckle of a river flowing over stones. An idea came to her, not much of one, but better than nothing. Maybe a way to break her trail.

The slope became steeper, carrying her along until she burst through a screen of foliage onto a stone shelf overhanging a river. Beneath the shelf, the river flowed in brown swirls and sleek motion, hemmed in by sheer rock walls. Lottie peered over the edge of her platform, the drop to the swift current giving her pause.

A faint sound, the barest rustle of leaves, came from behind her. She spun round. Payge faced her across the bare span of rock. Holding up her hands, realising she had no place to step back to, she begged him. "Payge, please? It's me. You—"

He sprang forward. She jumped backwards, an action without thought. She felt his fingertips snag her sleeve then there was the shock of hitting cold water. Pushing through a storm of bubbles, she broke the surface, spitting and wiping at her eyes. Payge remained on the rock overhang and for one cold moment Lottie thought he was going to follow her. Then he turned and was gone.

A few strokes took her to the middle of the river, where she angled her body into the line of the flow. The current caught her and carried her. The river widened. She struck out for the opposite bank, but as soon as she turned into the current, it pushed against her, forcing her away. She tried again, throwing herself into the effort. But the river fought back harder, the bank got no nearer.

Her fingers and toes were growing numb, the cold crept up her limbs and the river sucked the heat away from her core. An eddy swiped at her, swirling her round, pulling her under. She surfaced, coughing out water, paddling her hands to right herself.

The river granted her a concession. The flow of water smoothed out and she was able to grasp a brief respite, bobbing head and shoulders above the surface, still moving fast. Turning herself to get a better look round, she caught sight of a huge branch knifing through the water towards her, its splintered end aimed at her head. Kicking out and digging in with her hands, she tried to get clear. Not fast enough. It was almost on top of her.

She ducked under the surface. The branch scraped over her back, snagging on her clothes. When she lifted her head to reach the surface, the branch stopped her. The river burbled and swished in her ears while she clawed and wriggled and pushed against the stubborn tree branch. She stayed hooked to it as her lungs burnt and she grew frantic, the terror of drowning made real by how little breath she had left.

The branch hammered into an outcrop of rock, the impact making it tumble, flipping Lottie out of the water, where she inhaled once before she was drawn under again. Face up, she was looking at blue sky smeared by a thin film of water. All that stood between her and the air. Craning her neck, pulling against her stretched and tangled clothing, her nose and lips just broke the surface. When she tried to breathe, wavelets slopped over her, making her gag. She tried again, winning a full breath, giving her strength enough to hook an arm over the branch and drag her head above the surface.

She shifted her arm to firm up her grip on the branch. It rolled under her weight, threatening to tip her under. Clutching it tighter, she willed it to stay stable and true. The riverbank was close. The current felt slacker, but she was wed to her branch, her clothing still caught up in it, the arm holding her above water tiring fast.

Under water. You've got to go under water and slip out

of your top. Her teeth chattered; shivers ripped through her. *You are not getting out of this any other way. Do it or wait until you've not the strength to hang on.*

Her fear wouldn't let her. Not while there was still air to breathe. The river carried on its procession, swift and uncaring. It swept round a wide curve. Lottie felt her toes dragging through mud or sand, pulling her legs back, threatening her precarious balance. Her forward progress slowed as her feet dug into the sandbar her toes had found. Fresh hope kindled in her.

I am not going to be killed by a bloody stick.

Taking a deep breath, she ducked her head under the surface. With the sandbar under her, she pushed her back against the branch, plodding with awkward steps. The fabric of her top loosened but refused to give up its grip on the branch despite her tugging. The sandbar dropped away, and her legs thrashed in empty water.

This is it. The thought flashed through her head. *I've nothing left.*

She heard a muted twang as her top released its hold on the branch. Floating free, she collided with the sandbar where it rose up again. Her head broke the surface. Using her hands and feet, she climbed up the sloped edge of the sandbar, staggering and slipping when the loose material gave way beneath her, splashing back into the water, coughing and choking, until she was standing knee-deep in the river, the bank not two yards away.

Her gaze went downstream to where the branch rolled in the current, a limb lifting in farewell to its fellow traveller.

You can sod off.

A hysterical laugh jumped out of her, transmuted into racking sobs. Covering her face with her hands, she let them come. *You're still standing in a river*, part of her said after the fifth or sixth sob. She drew a big breath and waded to the bank.

Water streamed off her. The breeze caught her, chilling her further. She recalled something she'd seen about survival that involved fire, dry clothes and body heat. Looking down at herself, she supposed that wringing out her sopping clothes would have to do. The sun on her bare skin put some warmth back into her and that made putting her damp gear back on feel all the worse. The fabric clung to her, cold and clammy. With a sigh, she started away from the river.

Blood leaked from the cut on her hand. Too worn down to care, she trudged along, flanking the tree line that paralleled the course of the river, sure that she was safe.

Safe for now. Because they couldn't have crossed the river. Safe. Just walk. Put distance between us. Worry about the night when it is the night. Worry about food when I'm hungry.

Her hand throbbed.

Worry about infection when my hand drops off. One thing at a time. Distance first.

So, she walked.

She stuck to the open ground between the river and the trees. Walking warmed her up enough for her to lift her head and begin to look round. The breeze shifted the leaves, creating random patterns of green and shadow all along the edge of the forest. A sudden gust moved branches, allowing her a deeper glimpse into the trees. She thought she saw a dark shape moving in there. She kept walking, picking up her pace.

The wood began to thin out, sunlit clearings opening up between the ranks of trees. A look round and she saw Payge shadowing her, matching her pace, making no attempt at stealth. Lottie stopped and stared at him. Hoping that maybe…

He broke towards her, and she began her own desperate run. She flew over the ground, but she didn't fly fast enough. The muffled thud of his encroaching footfalls, his breath coming in rasping barks, so near.

Don't do this, don't do this, please don't do this. The rhythm of her thoughts beat in time to her footfalls, a plea to her pursuer that was as futile as her running. A rising snarl told her the moment was almost here.

The snarl turned into a howl of frustration as Lottie heard a thump and a scuffle of noises, the sound of a body tumbling and falling in the grass. Not risking a look round, she veered hard towards the tree line, sprinting for the depths of the wood. She chanced a look back. Seeing no pursuit, she slowed to a walking pace, thinking stealth might be preferable to speed. Her sides ached, and her legs dragged. Black despair wanted to take hold of her but she pushed it back. *Please don't let it be the last thing I ever feel.* It felt like a prayer, but she didn't know who it was to.

The woods were quiet around her. Restful. She stood for a moment. The blackness wasn't far away. She sniffed and wiped at her eyes. Lifting her head up, she walked on.

"Bloody hell!"

A camouflaged figure stepped out in front of her, making her jump. Lottie raised her hands, backing away from the hunting lance that was pointed at her middle. The figure drew off its hood and mask. Cisiphane shook out her hair; the lance she held in one hand never wavered. Lottie eyed the lance's leaf-shaped blade. It looked horribly sharp. "What, ah, what happens now?"

Cisiphane raised the lance and considered its point. "Arkwright set us to look for a human woman. It might be you. It might not be you. This spoils our hunt." She lifted the lance level with Lottie's throat.

"Drop the pig sticker, elf bastard." The voice came from over Lottie's shoulder. Jackdaw's voice. She saw Cisiphane look past her, her expression locked between cold anger and bitter calculation. Jackdaw called again. "Move away, Lottie. She won't hurt you. Not if she wants to live."

Lottie stepped back until she could just see Jackdaw from the corner of her eye. Cisiphane lowered her lance and raised one hand in surrender. Jackdaw shot her.

Cisiphane staggered back a step, dropping her lance, clutching a hand to where the bullet had gouged a bloody furrow in her ribs. Jackdaw pulled the trigger again, and the revolver clicked uselessly. Drawing a knife, Cisiphane rushed him, sweeping the blade in a wide arc, forcing Jackdaw to retreat. Giving him no time to recover, she lunged forward, slashing in a counterstroke. Jackdaw jumped back and landed off balance, giving Cisiphane the instant she needed. Swinging her arm back round, clubbing Jackdaw with the butt of the knife, she sent him spinning to the ground.

Lottie snatched up the fallen lance as Cisiphane turned to face her. Pointing the lance towards the woman, she took a step forward. The tip of the lance trembled. She tightened her grip on the shaft and still it trembled in her hands. Cisiphane held her knife out at arm's length, crouched over, one hand still clasped to her wounded flank. Lottie realised that Cisiphane would have to step into the lance to get to her. Its length gave her the advantage she needed. All she had to do was drive it into Cisiphane's body. She would have to stab another person.

"Drop the knife." She made a jab at Cisiphane, a half-hearted gesture.

Cisiphane raised her hand, took a step back and let the knife fall to the ground. Lottie licked at her lips and looked round for Jackdaw. Batting the lance to one side with the flat of her hand, Cisiphane stepped into the space she had made and backhanded her fist into Lottie's face. Lottie reeled back, one hand going to her nose, losing her grip on the lance. It swung down, tangling her legs, making her trip. A wild grab to stop herself falling. She caught hold of Cisiphane, dragging the woman down with her.

Cisiphane wriggled and squirmed to free herself from under Lottie's body, her efforts becoming frantic as her gaze fixed on something over and past Lottie's shoulder. A hand closed over Lottie's ankle, and she was pulled backwards, belly down. Twisting round to find Payge hauling her away. She shrieked at him, kicked at his hand, tried to stop him by digging the heel of her free leg into the ground. It did no good. Her leg was wrenched up and she was sliding backwards over the grass.

Jackdaw ran up behind Payge, swinging the revolver to clout him on the head. The big man grunted, staggered and released his grip on Lottie's ankle.

"Up," Jackdaw said.

She scrambled to her feet, Jackdaw was pulling her hand, and they were running. He let go of her but pushed her on. She took a few more steps before coming to a halt.

"Get to cover," Jackdaw snapped at her. Turning round, he moved into a shooter's stance, his revolver pointed at Payge.

"You can't," Lottie cried.

"Only if I have to," he said.

Lottie opened her mouth, to tell him the gun had already misfired once, and how did he know it wouldn't do it again on the next round. Payge took cautious steps towards them. Jackdaw pulled back the hammer on his weapon. It clicked into place. He dipped his head to sight his target and then he was utterly still. Payge had also stopped, his gaze fixed on Jackdaw.

When it came, it was fast. Payge spun round and sprinted away, tracking towards where Cisiphane had vanished into the trees. With deliberate care, Jackdaw uncocked and lowered his gun. He blew out a breath. "I really thought I was going to have to shoot him there."

Lottie dared to move. She ran at him and was down on her knees, hugging him for all she was worth. "I thought you were dead." She forced the words out through her tears, pulling him tighter to her. He smelt musty, overlaid with the scent of dirt and the woods. "I thought you were dead."

Breaking her embrace, she sat back on her heels so she could wipe at her eyes. Her cheeks were soaked, and her nose was streaming. "Look at the state of me." A weak laugh escaped her. "I don't suppose you've got a tissue?"

Jackdaw gave her a smile instead. "I'm all out of paper products. It's a good day if I can find a leaf that doesn't have rough bits on it, to take care of business."

She laughed at that and felt good about it. "You're disgusting."

"All part of my natural charm."

"How did you know where we were? And how did you escape?"

"I was never that far away, but I couldn't get close enough to do anything to help. Too many guards. Sorry." He looked at her, and she waved it away. "Second question. I escaped by being faster and better at hiding than these bastards are at catching. It wasn't easy, though. They kept after me for days. And they're good. Just not as good as me—"

A shriek of pain cut through the air. They both looked in the direction of the cry.

"Is that…?" Lottie asked.

"I think he just caught her," Jackdaw said.

"What will he do to her?"

"He'll feed."

"Will he come back to us?"

"In a little while, he will." He considered for a moment. "It's probably best if you stop here. Hide yourself. They're still after us and there's some of them around here. I'll see to Payge."

"I think he fought it, Jackdaw. I think he fought it as hard as he could. For me."

Jackdaw nodded his understanding. "Aye, he would. He would do that for his friends."

They stood for a moment, silence hanging between them. Jackdaw cleared his throat. "Here." He dug in his backpack and pulled out one of the camouflaged smocks worn by her captors. Lottie unravelled it and turned it over in her hands. Dried blood stained a large portion of the front of it.

"Sorry about the mess on it. Its former owner had no use for it, and it seemed a shame to leave it. Stick it on." Jackdaw watched her with a critical eye as she tried to get it over her head without it touching her hair. "It won't bite you. And I imagine you're freezing after your swim."

"You saw that?" Lottie asked. Realisation clicked in. "And you left me in there?"

"I saw you and Payge. I saw you jump in. Nothing I could do at the time. I was on the opposite bank. I had to draw away two of our friends with the spears. And I don't swim too great." Jackdaw gave her an apologetic shrug. "It was a good call on your part though."

"I nearly drowned."

He grinned at her. "But you didn't."

"Would Payge really have attacked me?"

"Not him, just what was left behind."

She shuddered. "Are you all like that? Are you like that?"

"I'm not. Nor my kin and clan but too many of us are."

"I think I need to talk to him about that."

"Now is most definitely not the time. I need you hidden. Go on now. Over there."

Jackdaw pointed to a stand of trees grown close together. Lottie made her way over and settled herself in the space between them. Twigs and stones dug into her. She shifted around to escape their torment but only found more to sit on. Insects buzzed around and she let them. A beetle the size of her thumb, with an iridescent green carapace, trundled across the leaf litter. She watched it until it was out of sight. She kept still and stayed put until she heard Jackdaw call her name.

Jackdaw and Payge were making their way towards her, Payge carrying some object suspended from his fist by a multitude of threads. It swung in short arcs as he strode along, then it caught his leg, spun and turned, and Lottie was looking at Cisiphane's slack-jawed features.

Her hand went to her mouth. "Oh," she said. She had to drag her gaze from the severed head to Payge's face. His mouth was slathered with gore, his eyes were hard and sharp and knowing. He picked up the fallen lance and stuck the haft of it into the ground.

Jackdaw walked over to her as she watched Payge with sick fascination. "What is he doing?" she asked.

Using both hands, Payge lifted Cisiphane's head up before plunging it onto the point of the lance. The meaty sound of impact made Lottie look away. Payge turned from his labour and walked past them without saying a word.

"Sending a message," Jackdaw said. He seemed about to elaborate then he shrugged. "Come on, we've got some walking to do." Taking her hand, he led her after Payge.

They travelled quickly, Payge to her left, Jackdaw to her right, herself in the middle. When they stopped to rest, Jackdaw broke the silence that had stood between them since they set off. "You reckon they'll keep after us?"

"They will," Payge said. He stretched himself out on the grass. "Rest for a while."

Lottie plonked herself cross-legged on the grass beside him. He was streaked with dirt and his mouth crusted with dried blood. A couple of gobbets of flesh clung to his clothes. But his face shone with intelligence. "You've got... uhm... stuff." She circled the air around her own lips with one finger. "And there and there." She pointed to his clothes.

Payge brushed at them in an absent way. "You know it wasn't me. Back there."

"I know. It was done to you."

"Good. It's good that you see it."

She wanted to ask him what it was like but thought maybe now wasn't the time. She thought she should ask him if mutilating bodies was not him either, but she held back.

"What's the plan?" Jackdaw said. "Head for the nearest gate?"

Payge sucked in his cheeks. "They'll be waiting for us. If they don't catch us before."

"We could go to ground. Hide out and wait for things to settle a bit."

"We could, but we've nothing other than what's in your pack."

"We've lived off less."

"True. But it's no country for hiding out in. Give me some hills and I'd say yes. But this?" He gestured round. "Either it's flat and open or it's trees. Their country, not ours."

They sat in silence for a time.

"There's been something on my mind," Lottie said. "What I've been thinking about is…" She stopped, unsure how to go on. "I never asked you. While we were locked up. And there was never the chance before that. And…" She picked at the grass, pulling out blade after blade until she held a small bunch of stems between her fingers. She let them drop as she addressed Payge. "Where are you taking me? I mean, after here? You could have left me at home. Let me disappear. You said so yourself. It's a big world. Easy to get lost in. And I have no value to you. You said that as well." There. It was said. It couldn't be unsaid. Lottie pressed her teeth into her lower lip and waited.

Payge answered in his mild way. "Why didn't you ask me this before?"

"I, uh, I thought that maybe we needed to be there for each other. You know, strong? When we were locked up. So, I didn't want us to argue?"

"And what about now? We don't need to be strong for each other now?"

"Well, yes, we do, I suppose. But it's different now."

"Different, how?" Payge pressed her, his words still mild, his gaze like flint.

"We're free."

Payge looked away. "We've swapped a small prison for a larger one. I thought by now you would see that. I was wrong. Now can we get on with what we need to do?"

Lottie picked furiously at the grass, not answering, not looking at him. "You and that sodding book." Pick, pick, pick at the grass. "I would never have—" She sniffed to clear her clotted throat, then wiped at her eyes.

"What book?" Payge asked.

"The book in your shop. The stupid book in your stupid shop. If you hadn't given it to me, none of this would have happened. I nearly drowned. And nearly had my thumb cut off. And, and… all the other stuff. Because of that stupid book. I'm a medical student. I want to graduate and go and work in a hospital somewhere and have friends and colleagues around me." She spread out the crushed and broken blades of grass between her fingers. "I've lied to my friends and left them behind. And all I've got in the world now is you two."

"That book?" Payge said. "As I recall, you came into the shop, and you took it from me."

"Did I? Did I really? Just by sheer chance? Or was I steered there?"

"Were you? Do you think you were? Did it feel like it?"

"You keep answering questions with more questions. It isn't fair. You always do that."

He snapped back at her. "To make you think."

She rubbed at her nose, leaving glistening trails on the back of her hand. "So where are we going? After here?"

Payge nodded to himself, as though coming to some conclusion. He shrugged. "I was going to take you to Steals. Though I doubt it makes any odds now. Like as not, we'll die here."

Lottie rounded on him. "You what?"

"You heard."

"You were—" Lottie stopped, open-mouthed. "Did you know?" She shot this at Jackdaw, who shook his head. "You were going to hand me over?" She turned the idea over in her head, trying to get a handle on it. "Why? Don't I mean anything to you…" She trailed off. "I thought you were my friend?"

He drew a breath, held it, then let it leak out. "I had planned to use you to buy some of my clan their freedom. The ones that Steals owns. Once it became clear what you could do. He might have been able to keep you safe and hidden from the other makers. So you would get some benefit from the deal. I'm done with being Steals's dog." He turned his gaze on Jackdaw. "About that much, your sister had the right of it."

"You told me Steals wouldn't treat with you," Lottie said.

"Perhaps I did. It was what you needed to hear at the time. But he'll listen to me."

"You lied to me." Lottie found the surprise had robbed her of all anger. "What do I do? I'm stuck here with you. Am I just supposed to let you take me to him?"

"You'd suppose right. Not that we're getting there. Or anywhere."

"I'm not happy with this," Jackdaw said.

"I don't care," Payge said.

"You utter bastard!" Lottie's anger came screaming back at her. She sprang up, launching herself at him. He swatted her away, sending her tumbling into the grass. She rolled and came back at him again. This time, his slap was hard. Hard enough to stun her. Gathering herself up on to her hands and knees, she glared at him, panting, rage burning to her core. With a low growl, she ran at him once more. She knew it was coming but she didn't care; the urge to hurt was too strong.

She was looking up at the sky, the taste of blood in the back of her throat, her head spinning. She touched her fingers to her nose. They came away bloody. Struggling up to a crouch, wobbling and catching herself, she fixed her gaze on Payge. Taking deep breaths to stop her vision swaying, she tensed up to spring.

"Lottie, don't." It was Jackdaw who said it.

"No. Let her." Payge.

She ran at him again. Her world exploded into light, then darkness.

It came back in muggy strands of grey. Grass pressed against her cheek. Her head hurt with a savage, stabbing ache. She heard voices but her brain stubbornly refused to resolve them into any meaningful words. Raising herself up on to one arm, the world swam around her, and she collapsed back to the grass with a moan. The voices stopped. Lottie waited until the world's rotational velocity slowed, then tried again. This time, her arm held its own against the world. She spat, a weak gesture that produced a red splat on the grass in front of her.

"Are you done?" Payge said.

"No." Lottie shook her head, and a wave of nausea assaulted her, but she crawled on her hands and knees towards his voice. A firm shove tumbled her over again.

"Bastard," she mumbled from her place on the ground, kicking in the direction the shove had come from. Her kick passed through empty air.

"Now are you done?"

"Fuck off." Lottie shifted onto her side, away from the hateful voice.

"I'm going now. You can come with me or wait here for them to find you."

The sound of footsteps through grass.

"That took some stones." Jackdaw's voice. "And was pretty dumb." He walked into her line of vision and squatted down to peer at her. "I think he went easy on you."

Lottie lifted herself into a sitting position.

"Ready to walk?" Jackdaw said.

"No." She stared at the ground. Tears weren't far away but were forced back. A welter of emotions were crushed down. Only anger remained, because it felt good.

"We need to move."

"Give me a minute."

"Half a minute. No more."

Lottie tried to push herself up, then sat back down. "I can't." Those tears were creeping back.

"Here, take my hand." Fingers like a child's closed her wrist in a steel grip and pulled her up. "Lean on me."

She did, the difference in height between them making her feel awkward. "I can walk."

"I knew you could."

10

ANOTHER GIRL FROM ANOTHER PLANET

Lottie was struggling to make the pace and she knew it. She knew it from the way Jackdaw hovered near her, always trying to be ready with a steadying hand. From the way Payge shot mean looks back at her from his place in the lead. The two of them flowed through the terrain like water over stones. Lottie stumbled and tripped, veered and crashed. She fought the terrain, and it fought back better and harder.

They skirted the edge of the forest, staying just inside the tree line. She tried to convince herself the going would be easiest here, but brambles and thorns thought otherwise. With the sun just dipping to the horizon, Payge called a halt. Once they shared out the water and some scraps of dried meat that Jackdaw offered, he moved off to sit on his own.

"I don't know if this will agree with you, if you get my meaning." Jackdaw inspected the brown strip of flesh he held in his hand. "Me and Payge, we can eat pretty much anything." Hunching his shoulders, he passed it to her. "Give it a try. You have to eat something."

Lottie put it in her mouth and chewed and chomped on it. It was tough, stringy and bitter. She thought that ingesting something so alien might not be such a good idea but then it occurred to her she had no idea what she had been eating when she was a prisoner, so she attacked it with as much enthusiasm as she could muster.

"Good girl," Jackdaw said. "You need to keep your strength up."

"Are we carrying on in the dark?"

"'Fraid so. It might be the only chance we get to put some distance between us and them."

"I'm finding it difficult now. I don't think I can do this at night."

"I'll guide you. It doesn't matter if we don't move fast. As long as we keep moving."

Lottie chewed her strip of dinner a bit more. "I think I'd get more nourishment from eating a twig."

"Mm."

"I still have trouble with all this."

"All what?"

She waved a hand in the air. "This. This other planet. This other universe. It feels like it should be different, but it looks so much like home. And there's so much that doesn't make sense."

"Like what?" Jackdaw lay back in the grass.

"Like we can breathe the air. And gravity feels the same. And there's grass and trees. And people that look pretty much like people."

"I don't look like people. I look like something from your Halloween." He paused for a second before carrying on. "Besides, we're the people. It's all the rest of you that look odd."

Lottie smiled. "You know what I mean. How is everything so the same?"

"It's not all like this. I've seen some stuff, I can tell you. And I've heard of places…"

Lottie leant forward. "Like what? You're not getting away with leaving it there."

Jackdaw continued to stare at the sky, but he pointed a finger at her. "No dragons, before you ask. That's what you lot always ask about first. Bloody obsessed with them, you are. No, no dragons. But there's strangeness out there. And monsters." He stopped to consider. "But I can see where you're coming from." Propping himself up on one elbow, he studied her. "Tell you what, if we get out of this, I'll take you to my favourite tavern. You buy every round and I'll talk until you're too drunk to listen or I'm too drunk to talk. How does that sound?"

"It sounds good. But how come we can understand each other?"

"The air is filled with a magical ether that translates everything that's said."

"Really?"

Jackdaw grinned at her, showing all his pointed teeth. "You are so gullible. You learn new languages, you dope." He flopped back to the ground. "Hence, you tend to limit yourself to worlds where there are others who communicate by making sounds with their mouths and using gestures."

As Jackdaw finished speaking, Payge stood and made ready to leave.

"What about him?" Lottie asked. "What happens when we get to some point that doesn't just involve running away? Are we going to not speak our way through any problems we have?"

Jackdaw rubbed at the corner of one eye. "I dunno. I've never seen him like this. It's worrying me."

"You're worried? About him? Well, thank you very much."

"Sorry." Jackdaw followed Lottie as she strode off. "Of course I'm worried about him. And I'm really worried about you. So now I've got the pair of you to worry about. That's not two worries but one big, tied-together worry, so when I say I'm worried about him, I'm worried about you too. The only person I'm not worried about is me because I've not got the time to worry about me."

"Now I'm sorry," Lottie said. "We can both be worried and sorry together."

"Seems fair. Let's give him the night and come the morning we can maybe sort things out."

"I'm being taken to be sold and there's not a damn thing I can do about it. I can't see what there is to sort out."

Jackdaw laid a hand on her arm to slow her down. The distance between them and Payge increased. When it seemed to Lottie that Payge was a ridiculous distance ahead, Jackdaw spoke without looking at her. "If it comes to it, I'll do all I can for you."

Lottie nodded in reply. "Thank you. That… can't be easy for you."

Jackdaw looked sad and weary. "There's nothing good about this. Nothing at all."

Lottie didn't know how to reply. The pair of them hurried into the growing darkness to catch up to Payge.

༄

No moon. Not a proper one, like my own moon.

Lottie sat in the darkness of the forest and watched the two small pebbles this world had for moons. She remembered as a girl, looking at the moon through binoculars, fascinated by its landscape. Fascinated by a place she could never go to but could see in such detail.

The moon rabbit. Up there on his own small world.

She had read and loved the story of the moon rabbit. The girl who looked at the moon's meteor-scarred terrain and knew it was an airless desert. The girl who knew the moon rabbit lived up there. *Which was impossible. Like portals between worlds are impossible. And those worlds themselves are impossible, populated by people who are impossible.*

She huffed out a breath. Closing her eyes, she settled herself into a more comfortable position. *Just breath. Relax. Need to relax.*

The night-time sounds of the forest faded into a murmur. She occupied her own inner world and nowhere else. Only… something. Pulling. Pulling at her. A subtle feeling acting on a sense she couldn't identify. It felt like touch, but not physical. It felt like yearning for a place she didn't know. It felt like… over there.

Lottie snapped open her eyes. She climbed to her feet, her thoughts came tumbling back and the feeling slipped away. She stilled her mind again, relaxing herself and to her delight, the feeling ghosted back. Turning herself around, it faded. When she completed a full circle, it grew again. *I'm like a compass. Seeking a pole.* And she knew. It was a gate.

How can I sense a gate? Maybe like feeling temperature, like heat and cold. Maybe I'm sensing something that the gate gives off. Like radiation. That gave her a shiver.

With a narrowing of her eyes, she began to experiment. Talking to herself, humming, running songs through her head. And after each, she would quiet her mind and turn to face the direction from which the gate called to her. When she was satisfied, she trotted over to where Payge and Jackdaw sat too far apart to be considered in company. She didn't fancy it up. "I know where the nearest gate is. I don't know how. I just do."

They both stared at her. Payge rose to his feet. "When did this happen?"

"Just now. It happened just now. I was sitting, thinking. No, not thinking, and I could feel it. Like turning your face to the sun and feeling its warmth."

He studied her, his expression unreadable before it slipped into curiosity and puzzlement. "I've never heard of such. Not from anyone."

"Does this change anything?" she asked.

Payge worked at his bottom lip with his teeth. "Tell me if anything else happens. We should be going."

They left the shelter of the forest and started across open ground. To Lottie, it didn't make much difference. The moons had both set, taking their faint light with them. She could see so little in the darkness, she had to rely on Jackdaw leading her. "Can you see where you're going in this?" she asked.

"Sure can," he said. "Mind that—"

"Ow!"

"Rock, there."

They trudged on for what felt like an eternity until Jackdaw helped her up a steep bank, the top of which seemed more even under her feet. "What's this?" she asked.

"A green lane," Jackdaw said.

"Lottie." Payge's voice cut through the darkness. She could barely see him. But the harsh note in the way he spoke since he came back was gone. "Can you show me the direction you think the gate's in?"

Lottie lifted her hand and pointed to where her sense told her the gate lay.

"Straight down the road," Jackdaw said. "Do we risk it?"

"We risk it."

As they resumed walking, Lottie felt some small relief that Payge was at least talking to them. And troubled that she should feel relieved at all. The slow realisation that she could make out the arrow-straight track told her the dawn couldn't be far off. Her yawns began to string together,

her legs ached with the dull intensity of overwork and any worry she had seemed small next to her tiredness.

"We'll stop here," Payge said. "Lay up for a while and get some rest."

Some distance away, they found a shallow depression in the ground, screened from the track by a tangle of thorn bushes. Jackdaw surveyed the area with a critical eye. "It's not great but it'll have to do."

Sinking down, Lottie could have cried with the pleasure of taking the weight off her feet. Breathing in the clean scent of dry earth and plant resin, she stretched with delicious abandon. "I could sleep for a week."

Jackdaw set up his rucksack as a pillow for her. "Get to it then."

❧

The sun was well above the horizon when Jackdaw shook her awake. "Come on, sleepy-head. You've been laid there long enough."

Back on the grassy roadway, Lottie enjoyed the feeling of warming up and stretching out the stiffness in her legs. Her stomach grumbled at her, and she tried to tell it to shut up. As she fell into the rhythm of walking, she felt for the gate. Nothing. Nothing there at all. She called out to Payge, walking ahead of her. "I can't feel it now. The gate, I mean."

He slowed his pace until she drew level with him. "Tell me."

She could only give a helpless shrug in reply. "It's gone."

"Or was never there at all. We stay with the track. It's taking us in the right direction."

They moved through a landscape of unrelenting sameness, the ground rising and falling in gentle swells of brown and ochre, broken only by small pools of water and thickets of thorn bushes. With only her footfalls and the unchanging scenery to keep her occupied, Lottie began counting her steps. Her counting faded away, as the distance they covered grew, and there was only the swing of her legs and swish of her feet through the grass and the cycle of her breathing.

And a faint tugging at her mind. She shook her head, muttered to herself. *You're imagining it. Because you want it to be there. Day time now. No time for phantoms or imagination.*

Her ankle went over in a rut, making her stumble, then stop. The direction of the gate in her mind, sure and certain knowledge, glowing like a beacon against the sky. She watched the backs of her two companions. "Arkwright," she called out to them. The name came to her from nowhere. Pulled into her head by a string of association that leapt from one thought to the next, like an electric current seeking earth. "Arkwright," she said again, wondering at it.

"What?" Payge spoke with some irritation, turning to the sound of her call.

"The woman. The elf woman. The one that you... you know." Lottie bit her lip, thinking hard. "She mentioned a name. Arkwright or the Arkwright. I can't remember which. It's the name of the person who wanted me killed. Sorry. I should have remembered, shouldn't I? And the gate is that way." She pointed well off the track. "It's not far away. If we keep going this way, we'll miss it."

Payge stalked back to where she stood, Jackdaw trailing behind him.

"Arkwright?" he said. "That was the name she gave?"

"Yes. Who is he?" Lottie said. "Or she? Or it?"

Payge looked thoughtful, his expression open. Lottie felt a wound inside her start to heal a little. "She," he said. "She's a maker. The youngest. The most recent to emerge. One of your people. Aggressive. Ambitious. And unorthodox. Not given to acts of kindness. And now she's moved against Steals."

"Does it help us? Maybe change things for us?"

"You're saying the gate's this way?" He nodded in the direction she had pointed.

"You believe me now?" Lottie couldn't stop her mouth setting itself in a pout.

Payge grunted a reply. He looked along the track in the direction they had been walking. "I'm willing to entertain the idea," he said. With that, he struck off the path, going in the direction Lottie had shown him.

11

TOWER AND GATE

"It's in there?" Jackdaw flopped onto his back with a groan. "We are so done for. We might as well pick a spot and build a house because we're going to be here forever."

Lottie crawled forward on her stomach to peer through the tumble of boulders they were sheltering behind. On the other side of them, a gentle slope led down to the floor of a shallow valley, where a squat tower stood. The tower lacked windows and doors. A rope ladder strung down one wall was the only concession to access she could see. Guards with automatic rifles stood on the roof and patrolled the surroundings.

Payge shifted closer to her, to look through the same gap in the boulders. "There must be a trapdoor in the roof," he said. Turning on his side, he spoke to Jackdaw. "Can you climb the wall to get to it?"

"I can climb it. Provided nobody is shooting at me. But what if this trapdoor of yours is locked?"

"Aren't you a thief?"

"Yes, but…"

"There you go then. That's your job."

"So, what's yours?"

"I'll take care of the guards."

"What about the ones on the roof?"

"Fair point. That is a problem." Payge rubbed at his face.

"And the ones on the ground?" Jackdaw said. "How are you going to deal with them? Sneak up on them one by one?"

"We've got your revolver and a knife."

"There are two bullets left in it. Fat lot of good that is against an AK-47. You might get one. Two, if you're really lucky. You won't get all of them. Like as not, there's more in that hut over there. Or inside the tower."

"If I can get one guard, get his weapon, I can deal with the rest."

"And the ones on the roof?"

"I'll keep their heads down while you make the climb. You take the revolver. Once you get up there, sort out the ones on the roof. You can hold off any on the inside who try to come out."

"And as soon as I appear over the edge, one of them will shoot me. We cannot win this." Jackdaw stabbed a finger into the ground to drive his point home.

Payge didn't answer him at first. He shuffled away from their vantage point, took a seat on the grass and stared back at them. "I am not staying in this place. I'd rather die here, trying to escape, than live as a prisoner. Not that we will live long, if we're caught."

"There are no other gates we could go to?" Lottie said.

Jackdaw pulled a sour face. "None. This is it."

Lottie drew a breath. "I don't want to stay either. I'll do what I can to help."

"I feel better about this already," Payge said. He ignored Lottie's narrowed eyes and pressed together lips. "We'll move on them at dusk. You'll hang back until we come for you."

She went right on glaring at him. "I said I wanted to help."

"And I heard you. You can help by not getting in the way."

"What if you two get in trouble? What if you get killed? What do I do then?"

"That's up to you."

"If it's up to me, I want to come with you. I can at least draw their fire away from you."

"Draw their fire?" Payge blew out a disgusted breath. "You are unbelievable. You do know most people who get shot don't die right away? If you're wounded, we either have to leave you here or come back, find you, and carry you away. Likely killing us all."

"So leave me, if it's what needs to be done." Lottie didn't want to dwell on the hard truth of what her simple statement actually meant. She forced herself on. "I'll come after you when you leave me here. You can't stop me."

Payge rubbed at his face with both hands. "Fine," he said. "Whatever. We might as well die in the way of our own choosing."

Jackdaw and Payge left her alone, crawling away to take up positions where they could observe the movements of the tower guards. Lottie took herself further away, finding a more comfortable spot to pass the time as they waited for the light to fail. With nothing to do but fidget, her nerves stretched tighter and tighter, drawn on the rack of her own thoughts. When Jackdaw came by to check on her, he looked at her for the longest time. "How are you holding up?" he asked.

"I'm scared." She gave him a shaky grin. "Scared for all of us. I, uh, I don't have many friends." Her fingers began to pick at the fabric of her trousers. She sank her hand into the grass and her fingers began to pluck at that instead. "People think I'm annoying. I rabbit on too much about what's in my head. I ask dumb questions that embarrass people. Or make them angry. I don't realise I'm doing it. I don't know why they get angry. It's only a question, isn't it? Now I'm doing it to you."

She sniffed and wiped at her eyes. "See what I mean. I can't stop myself. I'm stupid that way. Inept. That's a good word, isn't it? I'm inept. I can't do all the stuff that you two can. I can't do all the stuff I was supposed to do as a student. I can't even be good at being bad at something. Like Liz. Everybody likes Liz. She's like a friend to the world. I can't do that. I want to, but it's… Sorry. I'm boring you, aren't I?"

Jackdaw stretched out on the ground, his hands clasped behind his head. "No. I've heard a lot worse from men and women waiting to go into a fight." He shifted so that he was propped up on one elbow. "Yes, you are a pain in the backside. Sometimes. Yes, you are my friend. And yes, it's okay to be scared. Better now?"

"No." She smiled to herself. "Yes. A little bit."

"Good."

"I don't want anything to happen to us. Any of us."

"It won't. We'll all be fine."

"You're just saying that to make me feel better."

"Of course I am. But you didn't need to point it out."

"See what I mean?" She stared at the ground. "I can't help myself."

"It doesn't make you a bad person. Now, I'm off for another look round."

He moved away, leaving Lottie to carry on doing nothing but wait. She stared at the sky, watching it darken. Closed her eyes and tried to not think about anything. Spectral lines of blue and gold crept into her inner vision, appearing like frost on a window. She let them come, enthralled as they grew in complexity. Shuffling round, drawn by the same feeling that had guided them here, only stronger now, growing with each passing moment, she faced a nexus of glowing lines, a radiant core, centred on where she knew the tower lay, but stretching out to the surrounding landscape, huge and inextricably bound to it.

One line passed near her, within arm's length. She reached for it, touched it. The pain was a shard of glass driven into her head. Her hand jerked back, as if from an electric shock. She stared, wide-eyed, gasping in fright and hurt. The structure of the gate faded. The pain slipped away. "Ouch." She spoke quietly to herself, rubbing at her temple. Her hand tingled with pins and needles. "Not good. Not good at all."

"Talking to yourself is a bad sign." Jackdaw had stolen up behind her, unheard. "Shows you're away with the fairies."

"Says the guy with the green skin."

"I didn't mean it literally. That would be plain daft. Anyway, time to go."

Jackdaw walked away a few paces. Lottie stood up, her gaze shifting to the top of the ridge and the nest of boulders. She could see Payge laid out behind them, watching the tower. Her feet suddenly seemed reluctant to do her bidding. "We're really going to do this?"

Jackdaw turned around at the sound of her voice. "Aye." He spoke softly. "We are."

Fidgeting with her hands, rubbing her thumbs over her fingertips, she tried to work up some spit. Her throat clicked as she dry-swallowed. "Have you and Payge… have you done this kind of thing often?"

Jackdaw made a face. "Assault a well-fortified position defended by a superior force? Not so much. You won't find a chapter on it in a military 'How To' manual. Probably for a very good reason. On the bright side, we are attacking downhill. It could be worse."

"How?"

"It could be snowing."

"You're not making me feel any better."

"C'mere." Jackdaw held out his arm for her. Lottie walked towards him, and he slipped his arm around her waist. She put her arm around his shoulders, grateful for the touch of another person. Together they stepped up the slope to join Payge.

"Get your hand off my butt, Jackdaw."

"It's to bring me luck. An old custom of our people."

"Yeah, right," Lottie said. But she didn't make him shift his hand until they had to break apart and crawl up to the edge of the valley.

∽

They lay in silence, watching the movements of the guards around the tower. As darkness set in, logs were lit in fire-baskets set on tall poles spread around the tower. The guards moved out beyond the edge of the light they cast.

"This is about the best chance we're going to get," Payge said. He set his hand on top of Lottie's, while looking her in the eye. "Stay here. Understand?" Then to Jackdaw, "Ready?"

The two of them slithered out of their hiding place, disappearing into the darkness. She watched for as many minutes, seeing nothing of their movements. Shifting to one side, she readied herself to follow them. Then stopped herself. "Don't. Don't do it." A whispered entreaty.

I'll only make things worse. I'll make some dumb mistake.

So, sit here doing nothing. Because doing nothing always works so well. It worked so well that night at the bus stop.

Her lips tightened into a thin line. *I can't make this much worse than it already is.*

She scrambled past the rocks and boulders that had been their cover and started down the side of the valley. A muzzle flash and the bark of gunfire broke the darkness and the quiet. She saw Payge, silhouetted against the firelight, aim a rifle. An AK-47 like the guards carried. He fired once, then went to ground. Return fire drew down on his position. Lottie crawled towards a low mound, where she thought she might get a better vantage point. Gunfire erupted again. Multiple shots. Three people on top of the tower, all aiming at the same point. The point where Payge had last fired from. The shooting from the tower ceased, leaving the quiet and the darkness.

"Crazy," she breathed. "How does anybody know what they're doing?"

She wriggled towards her goal, flattening herself on top of the mossy outcrop that gave her a view of the whole of the valley. Shots broke out from her right, then it seemed, from all directions. A cacophony of staccato barks. Payge was on his feet again, running fast and low, the guards on the tower seeking him out with measured bursts from their weapons. He fired back, his shots sparking off the stone battlements, before he vanished into cover, chased by bullets.

Now she saw Jackdaw slip into the circle of firelight that surrounded the tower, sprinting for the wall. He never made it. Gunfire from above tore the ground around him. He swerved left and right before diving behind the meagre cover of a hump of rock. The rope ladder was slung over the tower's parapet, and one of the guards began to climb down. Shots from the darkness; Payge trying to get a bead on the guard. He failed and was rewarded with return fire from his left and right.

From her viewpoint, Lottie saw how it would end. Jackdaw would be dead in the time it took the guard to reach him. There would be no climbing the wall. They would run from this place. No, she would run from this place. For without Jackdaw to hold them together, there would be no Lottie and Payge. He would stay here to die. She would run on her own. With nowhere to go. Because the only way out was inside the tower.

Inside the tower. The gate is inside the tower. She closed her eyes and the geometry of it crowded into her mind, bright lines vectoring into a burning centre. *Inside. Not where we need it. Why can't it be outside?*

Opening her eyes, she saw the guard reach the end of the ladder and crouch beside it. He began edging away from the wall, seeking a line of sight on Jackdaw.

Outside. Move it outside. Pick up the gate. All of it. Because he only has seconds. She reached and gathered as best she could. Then she pulled. *Oh my. It's heavy. So heavy.* Like trying to move a mountain. Like trying to move the world. She strained and strained, pressing herself into the ground, blood thumping behind her eyes in time to the beat of her heart. *Too heavy for me. Too heavy.*

Lift it, you stupid bitch.

White pain skewered behind her left eye. She tasted blood in the back of her throat.

Heavy. So heavy.

It moved. And once it moved, it was free. But it carried that awful weight with it. Behind her closed eyes, she saw the hot core of the gate moving upwards in a shallow parabolic. It wanted to go its own way, but she pushed it and the pain in her head racked up. She spat out her suffering in animal grunts, in spit and snot. *Move, you bastard. Move.*

It slid through the earth, passed through the wall of the tower, slipped into open air, where its nature changed, the solid core of it opening into a nest of intersecting loops that swirled and orbited around each other. She held it fast, slowed it down and aimed it so it glided past the guard and through the rock where Jackdaw hid. She could see it with her eyes open now. A startling realisation. Lifting it into the air, she let it swing round towards her. It was coming at her, gathering speed, gathering mass. Seeking earth like a lightning bolt. Seeking her. Dizzying potential, growing and growing, needing to find release.

I can't do this much longer. This is killing me. Stop it moving. Push against it. Make. It. Stop.

The effort left her drained and disorientated, but it checked the gate's motion. It hung in the air, teetering and unsteady.

She pushed herself up on to her knees, swaying, shuffling to reach the gate. Her balance failed, and she pitched towards her left-hand side. Her left arm hung useless, unable to break her fall. The impact didn't hurt. Her arm felt like a piece of wood under her. Dull pressure points on her face where something was sticking into her flesh. She knew she should be really worried about the lack of sensation, but her thoughts dripped slow and thick, like molten lead.

Using her right arm, she forced herself on to her knees. *Payge is still out there.* A dark thought followed on the heels of the first. *I could leave him behind.*

She closed her eyes. It would be so easy to slide the gate forward. It wanted to come to her. It had grown smaller, coalesced into a tight ball of woven strands. Inside the weave, a perfect sphere had formed, no bigger than her fist. She could feel the gate becoming lighter, the sphere drawing mass from it. The sphere wasn't a gate. She was certain in a short while there would be no gate.

Do I want to abandon him? She considered her own question with appalled fascination. Her thoughts looped back to the first thing Payge had ever given her. The book, *Anatomy*.

He let me have it, but I opened it. Do I want to leave him to die?

She remembered being cold and alone and terrified on a dark street on a wet night. And he had been there. She opened her eyes. *Where are you, Payge?*

He was nowhere. Struggling to her feet, she started up the valley side, away from the tower and the gate. "Payge?" She called his name as she staggered forward. Her left leg wouldn't do what it was told, her left arm clumsy and burning with pins and needles.

Flashes of light erupted off to one side. The hoarse crack-crack-crack of shots. Another weapon opened up, the bullets shredding the undergrowth no more than a few yards from her. She dropped flat, face down, the fragrant smell of some herb she had crushed under her, sweet and unexpected in her nose. Then silence, and she was crawling onwards, some idiot part of her mind yammering at her that if only she stayed low, she would be fine, they would miss her and—

With a yelp, she tumbled head first into a ditch, the weight of her own body pulling her down, her legs slithering after until she was a tangle of limbs laid in a thin slurry of mud. A hand clapped over her nose and mouth; her arm was gripped in a lock. Kicking and wriggling, she squealed in fright, the sound coming out as a muffled squeak.

"Lottie, hush. It's me. Be quiet or you'll get us shot."

She was released, and she scrunched round. "Did you have to grab me like that? I just about wet myself."

"Quiet." He pressed a big finger to her lips, his face shadowed in the murk. "They're close. What did you do with Jackdaw? I saw him vanish." The finger withdrew.

She breathed out her own reply. "I moved the gate. Over him."

"You moved the gate?"

Lottie gave a nod.

"Where is it now?"

"Down there, towards the tower. Not far from us." She twisted her head round to look, and the pain came back, bright and sharp, stabbing in through her eye and along her optic nerve. She sucked in a breath, pressing fingers to her eye socket.

"Are you hurt?"

"No. Yes. I've done something to myself. Moving the gate." She rubbed at her temple and blinked, feeling the residue of that queer numbness still spotting her face. "The gate. It's…" She looked around with more care. The gate had stayed where she halted it. The sphere inside it was larger now. A good measure larger. "I don't think we've got much time. It's closing. Or doing something. I don't know what."

"I see. Can you move it towards us?"

"I'll try." She closed her eyes and reached for the nest of light. The feel of it stayed her hand. Some vibration off it or the press of it against her mind, the potential it now carried. She bit at her lip before answering. "I can't. I don't think trying to move it would be a good idea. It's changed so much. I think it's beyond moving."

"Can we still get through it?"

"I've no idea."

"Can you run?"

"I can run."

"Which direction is it in? Exactly? Point to it."

Lottie raised her hand, her finger outstretched. The thought occurred to her that Payge had taken her words at face value. He believed what she had said. He trusted her. "That way."

He shifted into a crouch. "We run straight at it, yes? Behind me. Ready?"

"Now?" Lottie asked.

But he was already moving. She hauled herself after him, her left leg lagging a fraction behind where it needed to be, slowing her down. The gap between them grew. "Payge," she cried. "I can't…"

She watched him reach the gate, run into the space it occupied. It was as if he snapped out of existence. She was alone. "No. Please." The gate was so close.

Off to one side, she heard someone running towards her – one of the guards, near enough that he could have cut her down. Not his intent. He was almost on her. So close. Her wayward left leg collapsed under her. As she tried to lift herself up, Payge reappeared, tumbling to the ground in front of her. Grabbing her wrists, he stepped backwards, pulling her along. "Hold on to me. Do not let go."

The transition into the gate was shocking. Lottie felt it first in her arms, then her head and torso. The gate was stretching her. Like gravity had flipped from the vertical to the horizontal. She closed her eyes and saw the sphere directly above her, spinning dizzyingly fast, beginning to flatten and widen into a bloated ellipsoid. Her ankles were gripped by an unseen pair of hands, which began to pull her back. The sphere had taken on a drunken wobble as it flashed round.

"Payge," she shouted. "Pull."

She shot forward a couple of feet, opening her eyes to grey daylight and Jackdaw bending over her. "Hang on," he said.

She peered down her body, to where her legs vanished below the knee. A final pull and her feet appeared with the guard still gripping her ankles. He let go of her and clawed his way forward. There was a comical popping sound. The guard slumped face down. Payge let her go and fell backwards. Jackdaw was at her side. "Are you okay? Can you sit up?"

"I think so," Lottie said. She sat up. "I – oh."

The guard at her feet had been sliced in half, neat as you like, a glut of blood and innards oozing out of his sectioned torso.

"Sorry. Should have said." Jackdaw laid a hand on her arm. "Let's get you away from here."

But Lottie could not drag her gaze away from the butchery, not until Jackdaw pulled her away. They passed

Payge, sitting on the grass, taking deep breaths, his face haggard. She caught the look Jackdaw gave him and the slight nod he gave back. "The gate?" he asked her.

"Gone," she said.

"Good." He got to his feet and followed. All of them, by unspoken mutual agreement, wanting clear of the location of the gate.

The land around them was as drab and featureless as Lottie had ever seen. A faint hint of brine and the rumble and hiss of waves on a shore reached them. Stopping in the lee of a grass-covered mound, Lottie lay down and stared at the blank expanse of the sky, a grey skein from horizon to zenith.

"That went better than I thought it would," Jackdaw said.

She didn't have the strength to lift anything to throw at him.

12

THE LOW COUNTRIES

"What did you say this place was called?" Lottie asked.

"Bad Beag," Payge said.

"Who lives here?"

"Nobody." Payge went on checking through the contents of Jackdaw's backpack. "It's too dangerous."

Lottie gazed round the landscape. The scrubby grass was as tired and washed-out looking as the flat vault of the sky. "It doesn't look dangerous."

Without looking up from his work, Payge asked her a question. "What direction did we come from?"

"Ah… I've no idea. It all looks the same."

"It is all the same. The sky is always like that. There's no sun, no stars, no north, no south. Bad Beag is an inconstant world. The land moves. There are three gates here. The only things on this world that stay put. Until you moved one, that is."

"I was only trying to help."

"I know." He glanced at her, gave her half a smile. "And I'm grateful you did."

She shifted her hips to one side and peered at the ground. "The land moves? So there are earthquakes or landslides and stuff?"

"No, it just moves around."

Lottie looked at him with some doubt. "Ground doesn't do that."

"It does here. Time is just as inconstant as the land. Like I said, a dangerous place."

She searched his face for any hint that he might be messing with her, but he continued with his task, his big fingers cinching the straps on the backpack with the same practised ease he seemed to bring to anything he did. "Has anyone tried to live here?"

"Some," Payge said. "Nobody ever saw them again to ask how it went."

"How can something like this exist?"

"Because somebody made it this way. Perhaps an elder race. Or a maker. There was a time when they could do much more than open up gates and orchestrate conspiracies."

"So, was it a very good idea to send Jackdaw to look for the other two gates?"

"He's very good at finding things."

"How does he do it?"

"He has a skill."

"He's a good man. Imp. Goblin. Whatever he is. He's a good friend to have."

231

"That he is."

"Payge, you have to talk to me." Lottie watched him pick up the backpack and begin to fiddle with the fastenings again. "What happens next? Between us? Are you still going to take me to Steals? After I got you out of there?" She nodded in what she hoped was the direction of the gate they had escaped through.

Payge gave the top of the backpack a thoughtful look. He raised his head to her.

"Found it," Jackdaw called. He trotted up, jerking a thumb behind him. "Over that way, not more than two minutes' walk."

Payge stood up. "Then what are we sitting here for?"

As he walked away, Lottie gave Jackdaw a furious stare. He held up his hands in bewilderment. "What's up with you?" he asked.

"Seems like I'm the only one who didn't escape."

❦

They reached a cobbled path, one of three that radiated from a central point marked by a standing stone. Large cairns of grey rock stood at the end of each of the paths. Payge pointed towards the furthest. "The gate in there will take us to Alt Graad, one of the Low Countries." He favoured Lottie with a glance. "It's a free state. The gate won't be guarded but it will be watched. Nothing we can do about that but there are people in Alt Graad I know and trust. We'll get some help. Get fed, get rested."

Lottie held up her hands, pressing her wrists together.

"Perhaps you should tie me up. I might run away. But where would I go? I don't have any people I trust, do I?"

"Payge…?" Jackdaw said.

"Don't," he replied. "Now get through there." He gestured at the narrow entrance built into the flank of the cairn. Jackdaw gave a resigned shrug and walked through it. Lottie waited, staring at Payge. "I'll carry you through if I need to," he said.

She continued her silent regard. It occurred to her that they might be the only two people on this entire world. "I deserve to know why you're doing this. I've at least earnt that much from saving you."

"You have, and I will tell you. But not here."

Knowing that was as much as he was going to give her, she followed Jackdaw into the cairn. She walked straight forward, seeing the lines of the gate around her, and it guided her better than light ever could. Reaching out to try to touch one, but there was no purchase to be had. It was like trying to grasp wisps of smoke. *Whatever I had, it's spent.*

There was still a prickling of pins and needles in her left side, in her toes and fingers. Still that numb feeling in her face, but fading, like the anaesthetic after a visit to the dentist. She wondered if whatever it was she could do would come back. She thought about how she would feel if it didn't. It troubled her that she didn't have a good answer.

Then she was in a wide corridor, panelled with wood, lit with the steady glow of electric lamps fitted to brass sconces on the walls. Jackdaw was standing before a door at the end of the corridor, waiting on her. Payge appeared behind her, bumping her out of the way, making for the door and pushing it open.

Lottie stared with some amazement at the office the open door revealed. It was empty, save for a single desk and chair. Behind the desk sat a pebble-skinned goblin, no bigger than Jackdaw, dressed in what looked like a military uniform from the age of muskets and powder. Or, she thought, the uniform of a bell boy in a swanky hotel. The goblin peered at them with a mix of suspicion and disbelief. "Welcome to Alt Graad," it said. "State your business."

"Piss off," Payge snapped back.

The gatekeeper, as Lottie assumed it was, seemed to take this without rancour. "Just doing my job," it said.

Jackdaw approached the desk. "Ignore him, he's had a bit of a day. We all have, come to that." He leant close to the gatekeeper and spoke in a low voice. The gatekeeper smiled and nodded, clearly pleased. They carried on their conversation, exchanging knowing laughs. With a final smirk to the gatekeeper, Jackdaw looked up. "We're good to go. Nothing and nobody waiting for us outside. Remember that inn down by the river? The Camps, it was called? We could stop off there. They always looked after you, if you drank plenty."

"Seems fair," Payge said. Wrapping a hand round Lottie's wrist, he steered her to the exit.

Outside, they stopped by the edge of a wide road. Lottie gazed round at the low buildings lining the street, built in a myriad of styles and materials, but all well-appointed and prosperous-looking, ornate with plate-glass windows and gilt signage. Buggies and carts, people and creatures, some walking, some riding, some driving, moved up and down the street with no regard for any kind of rules of traffic. A traction engine rumbled past, hissing and leaking steam, a gang of at least six of Jackdaw's people hanging off it, squabbling, shouting and hitting the metal beast with hammers.

She was shoved from behind. Payge spoke in her ear. "You're staring like a hayseed. Stop it. You'll attract the wrong kind of attention."

He grabbed her collar and pulled her into the flow of foot traffic. As she bumped and "excuse me'd" her way through the crowd, she wondered why he bothered holding on to her. *Where would I run to?*

On the heels of her thought came the hollow ache of loneliness, ever her companion through the years. *Even if I knew how to get out of this place, who would I go to? "Pardon me, I was kidnapped by creatures out of fairy tales." Who would even believe me?* She followed in Payge's wake until they reached the inn by the river and her miserable thoughts trailed after her.

 భ

Alone in her room at the inn, Lottie lay in the bath and let the heat soak through to her bones. She drifted somewhere between waking and sleep. She wasn't sure what the tiny bottle of oil Jackdaw had brought for her to put in the bath water was, but it turned the water milky, eased bruises, numbed cuts and grazes and made her feel, in general, the best she had felt in days.

"You look like you're really enjoying that."

Lottie sat bolt upright at the sound of the voice, slopping water on the floor as she crossed her arms over her breasts. Raven stood by the bathtub, looking down at her, a mischievous smile on her lips.

"How did you get in here? Payge locked the door. How long have you been standing there?"

"Not long." She sat down beside the tub, resting an arm on the edge of it, letting her fingers trail through the water. Lottie shifted more upright, pressing her arms tighter to herself.

"Don't worry," Raven said. "I'm not going to jump in there with you." Her pointed nails drifted over the top of Lottie's thigh. "Unless you ask me to, that is."

Lottie slid down until only her head and knees were above the waterline. She felt her cheeks reddening. "Uh, no, I, uh, I don't. I was just getting out."

"Okay." Raven hopped up and walked to the bed. "I've been watching the gate for days, waiting on you. Followed you here. I met the pair of them downstairs. Excused myself and came up here. My brother isn't the only one who's good at getting through locked doors. I should know. I taught him." She shook out a towel the size of a sail and held it between outstretched hands. Her smile took on a knowing curve as she peeked over the top of the towel. "Come on then, out with you."

"Can you lift that up a bit more?"

Raven tipped her head to one side. "Why would I do that?"

Lottie felt herself blushing again. "Just… you know."

Sighing in mock resignation, Raven lifted the towel until it was above her head. Lottie climbed out of the tub and padded over to her.

"At least let me dry your hair for you," Raven said. She wrapped the towel around Lottie, covering her from head to knee, then began to rub at her scalp, drawing out locks of her hair with gentle motions. Lottie let her, relaxing into it, enjoying the feeling of being wanted and cared for.

"Never be ashamed of what you look like." She scrubbed Lottie's hair more vigorously now. "Not ever. There will always be plenty of men around who'll only be too happy to help you with that. Ignore them. They're full of shit." She stopped her drying and turned Lottie around to look at her. "You got that?"

Lottie gave her a solemn nod. "Never be ashamed. They're full of shit. I got it."

Raven gave her head a final, friendly rub. "My woman. Get dressed. I'll take you downstairs so you can get something to eat, and I can hear what the two idiots have to say to us."

"Can you look away?"

Raven blew out a breath. "Yes, I'll look away."

She dressed herself in the change of clothes that had been left for her, eyeing each functional piece with some reserve. "And here we have the brown collection. Note the extensive use of brown in the making of it." Lastly, she picked up a forest-green jerkin. "Now this I could get to like." She slipped it on and did up the bone buttons, smoothing her hands over the jerkin's supple leather and the curves of her body.

Raven opened the door for her. "Looking good, girl. After you."

Payge and Jackdaw were hunched over clay mugs at a table in the common room. They both looked up as Lottie and Raven approached.

"You've scrubbed up well," Jackdaw said. "What took you so long?"

"Girl talk," Raven said. She walked up behind her little brother. "You know how us girlies are when we get chatting." Drawing back her hand, she landed a slap on the back of his head.

"Ow. What was that for?"

"Because I'm your big sister, that's what for."

Lottie didn't hear them. Her gaze was on the bread, cheese and slices of roast meat that lay on the table. A mug was waiting for her, creamy foam topping over the rim.

"Sit," Payge said. "Please. Help yourself."

She sat and grabbed bread and meat, laying one on the other, taking a huge bite, chewing on too much at once, gulping beer to help swallow.

Jackdaw watched her with a critical eye. "You'll lose a finger, if you're not careful."

Lottie mumbled back and waved a negation. They left her in silence to eat her fill. When she had stopped wolfing down her meal, she looked between her three companions. "What is it?" she asked, speaking around a mouthful of bread, stopping to wipe crumbs off the table with the flat of her hand. "What have I done?"

"Maybe you should finish eating that before you speak again?" Jackdaw said. "Don't answer, just nod. Good. Now,

Payge would like to speak to you. Don't interrupt him, ask questions, pass comment or anything. Just let him say his piece. Can you do that? For the sake of the two hours it's taken to convince him to say this. Time I could have spent drinking or thieving."

Lottie nodded and chewed and waited for Payge. He laced his thick fingers together, concentrating on the battered tabletop. Raven sat back in her chair, looking at him with cool regard. "Say what you have to say, Payge. She's earnt it."

He lifted his head, fixing his gaze on Lottie. "Some of this, I've already told you. Steals holds my blood-kin as slaves. The few that are left. That's his hold on me. Their lives. And I value them over you, Lottie." He looked at his hands for a moment before going on. "You saw what I became back in Syre. I told you about the plague we carry. What I didn't tell you about is how unpredictable the disease is. My symptoms are stable. But tomorrow? I could start to lose my mind. Maybe permanently. My body could warp. I could begin to sicken and die. Steals has the cure. In small enough doses, the cure can keep the symptoms of the disease suppressed but it still lives on inside us. That's the prison he holds us in. That's how he makes us his possessions. He's promised to fully treat us all when some scheme he's working on is complete. What that scheme is and when it will be, he hasn't told us. In the meantime, my people are dying. So, I hoped to trade you for them and for the cure."

His fingers touched the mug in front of him, moving it a fraction to one side. "What afflicts my kin and clan is a variant of the plague that infected our whole race. Jackdaw told you about that. But somebody, some maker, took the original strain and remade it."

His eyes shifted to look down at the tabletop again. "They keep doing it. The makers. Jackdaw and his clan are fortunate. They were only susceptible to the original strain. So far. Other clans are gone now. Wiped out. Some maker is still working with that plague, and my fear is that eventually, either by accident or intent, they'll make one that will kill us all. I think you would be worth more to Steals than all of my blood-kin. But you got us out of Syre, and I have to consider that."

"I'd say you need to do more than consider it," Raven said.

Lottie scowled at her while she thought about what she might say. "That's awful," she said. It sounded inadequate, even to her own ears. Her fingers found a leftover crust of bread. She dug her thumbnail into it, staring at her hand as she ground the crust into pieces. "I've no family to know what it would feel like to lose them all. I've only got my friends. The ones I have back home." She looked round the faces sharing the table with her. "The ones I have here. I don't want to lose any of them. I don't have enough of them that I can afford to do that." Wiping nascent tears from her eyes left specks of bread on her cheeks. She rubbed them away with the heel of her hand, sniffing deeply as she did so.

Payge spoke to her. "Lottie, look at me."

She shook her head, unable to look up, unable to wipe the tears quickly enough to stop them all.

Payge reached across the table, lifting her chin, making her look at him. He spoke again. "Look at me."

She did, though she had to sniff more – her nose was running; she couldn't see properly through her tears.

"I would ask you to forgive me," Payge said. "As a friend."

She nodded her head, not trusting herself to speak. Nodded again and again, in quick motions. And she held back the sobs that wanted to come. She swallowed and held them back and scrubbed at her soaked cheeks and drew a breath and knew she would be alright.

Raven's hand found hers and held it tight. Jackdaw reached across to give her other hand a squeeze. "I don't suppose anyone has a tissue?" she asked.

They sat around the table and talked and ate and drank. Raven told them all that had happened since they had last seen each other.

"Is Liz okay? And Andrea? Are they both okay?" Lottie looked to Raven for an answer.

"They're fine," Raven said. "Worried, though. Worried about you. Worried sick. They think you've run away because of the break-in."

"I'd like to go home. Can I?" She looked from Raven to Payge.

"Any sign of Steals or his crew around Lottie's friends?" Payge asked.

Raven shook her head. "Nothing. Not a thing. It may be that Steals has gotten what he wanted, and the pattern is ended." She looked up at Lottie. "Or he could be waiting for you to reappear."

"That's your way of saying I can't go home, isn't it?"

Raven favoured her with a brief smile. "I don't think it's safe for you yet. Not with everything that's happened."

"When will it be safe, do you think?"

Neither Payge nor Jackdaw paid her question any attention. They weren't looking at her. They were looking behind her. Raven twisted round to see. Lottie did the same.

Five people stood in a rough semi-circle across the width of the room, hemming them in. One of the five wasn't human – a cliff face of bone and muscle, hunched over to avoid hitting the ceiling. Three were men, armed with blades and guns and the easy stance of those who knew how to use them. In the middle stood a woman, her hair plaited with beads, her skin as dark as charcoal, her hands stuffed in the pockets of a riding coat that draped to her ankles. She nodded to them in a companionable way. "I'm Arkwright," she said. "We should have a talk."

Lottie switched back round. She took in the little shake of the head that Payge gave Jackdaw and Raven. Keeping one hand on the table, he held out his other to an empty chair. "Please," he said. "Join us."

"Don't mind if I do." The woman gave them all a warm smile and sat down. The leather of her jacket creaked as she stretched across for the mug of ale in front of Payge. "You mind?" She took her time drinking before setting down the mug, wiping her lips and letting out a small burp. "Not bad."

"So, talk," Payge said.

Arkwright pursed her lips for a moment. "Here's the thing. Word reaches me that the gate from Bad Beag to Syre is gone. Vanished, like it never was."

"I can't speak of things I know nothing of," Payge said.

Arkwright tapped at her bottom lip with her thumb. "A very poor lie. Disappointing. What do you say to that?"

Payge shifted in his seat but said nothing.

"Why are you trying to kill me?" Lottie said. A dig in her arm from Raven did nothing to shut her up. "What did I ever do to you?"

A tweak of puzzlement crossed Arkwright's face. "Oh, that? Nothing personal, really. Just taking care of business. Anyway, I stopped that some time ago."

"You did? When was that?"

"When you escaped to Syre. Yes, that would be it. Things changed after that. Markedly. Became far more interesting." Arkwright studied the fingertips of her left hand, then shifted her gaze to Lottie. "Like when the gate from our world to Syre disappeared for a few hours. All of a sudden, pop! It's back. And you three were the last through it Her look stayed fixed on Lottie. "Or more specifically, you were."

"So, you don't want me dead?"

"No." Arkwright gave her an impish smile. "Not anymore. You're far more useful the way you are now."

"But what about the elves? One of them said you wanted me dead. They were going to do it too."

Arkwright's eyes widened. "You didn't call them that to their faces, did you? Never mind. Good on you, if you did. You know what they're like. No changing their minds once they're set on something. I did try, though."

"It didn't work," Lottie said.

"Couldn't get the message through to them."

"You were just going to let us die?"

"It wouldn't have been the worst thing to happen."

Lottie gave her a dubious look. "I'd beg to differ on that one."

"I pretty much run this place, you know," Arkwright said, gesturing around at the walls.

"What, this inn?" Lottie said.

Arkwright pealed out a merry laugh. "Oh, I do like you." Her smile turned feral. "No. I run this world. Such as it is." Her voice grew hard. "The same as Steals runs his little patch. But you get to the point where your little patch just isn't big enough anymore."

"A whole world isn't big enough for you?"

Arkwright shrugged. "It isn't much of a world. It's small. Most of it is empty. What people there are wouldn't fill up a small city back home."

Lottie stared at her. "And you're what? The queen? The president?"

"Not as such," Arkwright said. "It's more like other people run it for my benefit. We makers like to stay in the shadows. We're a shifty lot." She gave Lottie a sly grin. "But the people that run things here know who they work for. Not bad for a little girl from a broken home in a sink estate, now, is it?"

"And here's the thing." Arkwright reached across to take Lottie's hand, drawing it across the table towards her. "Humans are far and away the best makers. What takes other races years to learn, we pick up instinctively. Intuitively. Like we were born to it." She turned Lottie's hand palm up and began to trace the lines on it with her finger. "Since the gates to our world reopened, we've carved quite the little empire out of other people's territory. We can do things others can't. And that's started to cause some degree of worry in certain circles that have had it their own way for a long time. Too long a time."

Letting go of Lottie's hand, she carried on speaking, brisk and businesslike. "I've been told Steals has access to elder race knowledge. Or even that he is in contact with one of the elder races." She stopped to look at her own hand for a moment. "He's a crafty old sod, I'll grant him that much. Still, it begs the question, how far can we go? Bodies are in motion. Change is in the air. And all this before the gates to Syre. What did you do there? How did you do it?"

"I didn't do anything," Lottie said.

Arkwright gave her a knowing look. "Clearly."

Payge set his elbows on the table and leant close to Arkwright. "You're not with Steals on this," he said. "Who are you with? You're not doing this on your own."

There was a light in the Arkwright's eyes that Lottie classified as slightly manic. "No. I'm not." Digging into an inside pocket in her coat, she drew out a small bottle filled with a straw-coloured liquid. "Know what this is?"

Lottie shook her head.

"The cure. For Payge and his clan."

Payge grew perfectly still, his entire focus on the woman.

"I bought it from Steals. I own it now. I bought your kin at the same time."

"Why would you do that, and why should I believe you," Payge said.

Arkwright flipped the bottle into the air, catching it on its descent with a swipe of her left hand. She flipped it up again. "To make him think all is well and the worlds continue to spin as they should. I have papers and such, if you want to see them. Bills of sale. All stamped and certified and done proper."

"And the cure works? You know it's genuine?"

"I witnessed Steals giving it to a clan-sister of yours. I took her in, starved her for a couple of weeks and she was none the worse for it."

Arkwright threw the bottle high, her hand out to catch it. Payge moved faster than Lottie would have thought possible, the bottle snatched from the air above Arkwright's open palm. Arkwright's men moved in. She held up her hands to placate them. "Your kin-sister is one of my army now. A trusted lieutenant, free to leave whenever she chooses. Though I have to say, she chooses to stay." She held out her hand to Payge. "I can take you to her, if that would help. And you can have what's in that bottle."

"What do you want for it?" Payge asked.

"A simple enough job. Kill Steals for me. I'd do it but you know how it is. Why have a dog and bark yourself. What do you say?"

Payge opened his hand and passed the vial to Arkwright, who took it with a look of growing delight. "And I'll have Lottie as well. She's too precious to lose to Steals."

"Don't I get a say in this?" Lottie said.

"Do any of us?" Payge looked at Arkwright, his gaze searching. "I know what happens to people who kill makers. I've hunted them down before."

"I have friends in high places," Arkwright said. "Actually, I have only one friend in a low place. He's a very old and very great friend. There'll be no comeback from the other makers."

Payge answered her in a flat voice. "I'll do your bidding for you." He looked to Lottie. "This is the best I can do. At least you'll be safe."

Lottie stood up, her chair scraping back on the flagstone floor.

"Sit down," Arkwright snapped at her.

One of Arkwright's men made to move towards the table. Lottie sat back down.

"Good," Arkwright said. She sat back with the air of a job well done. "Let's discuss the details."

The discussion began, and wound on for some time, as plans and arrangements were made. Lottie, excluded from it by unspoken consent, stared past everyone, fixing her gaze on the wall opposite her.

"Uhm, what's that?" she asked no one in particular and no one paid her any heed, but at the far end of the room, a complex pattern of lines had begun to appear. Brilliant white, they tracked through the floor, the ceiling, the furniture. Faster and faster, burning like meteor trails. Lottie felt their pull, a subtle gravity that snared her in. In the scant second it took her to ask her question, the pattern completed itself. "Guys…?" she said, reaching out to grab Payge's sleeve.

Three people, appearing through the lattice of white lines, charged into the common room. Three very big and well-armed people. Lottie tried to stand. Payge pulled her back down, pushing Arkwright at the same time, sending the woman tumbling backwards. Snatching the edge of the table, he tipped it onto its side. His hand on the top of her head, pushing her down until she was behind the overturned table. "Stay down," he said.

"Intend to," she gasped back.

The room was a riot of sound. Lottie could see nothing of it. Only Payge, Raven and Jackdaw. Payge hiked a thumb over his shoulder, towards the back of the room. "Find us a way out."

As Jackdaw and Raven scooted off, a body sailed over the table, landing and rolling in a mess of limbs and bloody clothing. Payge pulled Lottie close, tucking one arm over her shoulders. "When I say—"

The table was lifted and thrown through the air. Lottie caught a brief impression of the thrower. He looked like Payge, only bigger and stronger and meaner. Much bigger. Much stronger. Payge was on him fast, they were grappling, then they were on the ground, the bigger man's fists breaking through Payge's desperate blocks, landing solid blows on his head and face.

No more than seconds had gone by. Lottie could only stare, feeling frozen out of the mayhem around her. Until she was grabbed and lifted clear of the ground, wriggling and lashing out helplessly. Her captor grinned at her. "Quit squirming, girlie, or it's a slap you'll get." He slapped her anyway, a casual back-hand flick that made the room spin. She had a vertiginous snatch of a bloodied Payge, laid out on the floor. Of Arkwright backing away, one hand to her mouth, the other sweeping a handgun from one target to the next. A scatter of broken bodies. Then she was being carried through what she knew must be a gate. That had appeared from nowhere.

13

PERSUASION AND SANDWICHES

The quality of the light changed, the daylight of the room at the inn became the mellow shine of lamplight. Lottie smelt stone and earth mixed with the oily scent of the lamps that hung round a rock-walled chamber. Her captor set her on the ground. Narrow eyes with huge pupils regarded her from under the bony ridge of a brow. A hand the size of a shovel blade, with skin as rough as tree bark, motioned her up. "Come, Lottie. I won't ask again."

She stood and took a hesitant step back. "Who are you? Are you going to hurt me?"

Something that might have been a smile revealed teeth that she would have preferred not to see. "It's right, what I was told about you. I'll give you my name. After that I will break one of your fingers every time you ask me something. Understand?" He waited until she gave him a fast nod. "You can call me Tawse."

"Do—"

"Uh-uh." He waved a finger at her. "Remember? Now we need to be away." His hand closed over hers, swallowing it entirely.

"Wait," she said, "And that wasn't a question." She closed her eyes and turned to where she knew the gate lay. "Oh my." Its complexity dazzled her. Glimmering white in the darkness, it moved, its lines flowing over each other with organic grace. The other gates she had seen were simple melodies compared to the symphony that hung before her. Then it faded and was gone.

A none-too-gentle tug on her wrist yanked her back. Tawse led her to an open-topped cage suspended on a chain. As they climbed into the cage, Lottie peered up the line of the chain, up and up, into a shaft cut in the roof of the chamber, a shaft that ended in a small circle of light above them. Tawse yanked a handle attached to a wire that ran alongside the chain. Slowly, the cage began to ascend, swaying and lurching, creaking and clanking.

They had gone perhaps a third of the way up when Lottie spoke. "I don't feel so good." Clammy sweat coated her face. She clung to the side of the cage and tried to swallow down her rising nausea. "That was a statement, by the way."

Tawse laughed and handed her a flask. "Drink. And if you have to do it, do it over the side, not over me."

Lottie opened the flask and took a mouthful. It wasn't water but it tasted light and sweet and good. "What is this?" she asked. The flask froze on its second journey to her lips. "Oh shit," she said.

"I'll let you have that, for it's a fair question to ask. It's a cordial. It won't do you any harm." He grinned at her. "You want to ask something, don't you?"

Lottie nodded.

"Too bad. Mr Steals is waiting for you." He regarded her for some moments.

"What?" Lottie said. She burped, tasted acid and put a hand over her mouth. When she trusted her stomach enough to open her mouth again, she spoke. "That wasn't a question."

"Of course it was a question."

"You were staring at me. I've a right to know why."

"No, you don't. You don't have a right to know anything. The things you know need to be earnt, they're not gifts. You were being petulant. Now you're going to regret it."

Lottie swallowed, shifting under his gaze. "You're really going to break my finger? Do I get to pick which one?"

Tawse gave her a wry smile. "That's three fingers."

"Oh shit," Lottie said. She waited.

Tawse slapped her on the upper arm, knocking her into the side of the cage. His fearsome grin split his lips wide. "Your fingers are safe. Ask anything else and I'll belt you on the back of the head."

Lottie kept her own counsel until the cage broached the top of the shaft and halted beside a wooden pier jutting out from the edge of the shaft. The pier shifted under their feet as they crossed, making her acutely aware there was nothing like a handrail between her and the drop to the bottom. They stepped on to solid ground, Tawse leading her through a door to a huge room that appeared to be part workshop and part library. There were book-lined shelves, tables crowded with apparatus and drawings, blackboards scrawled with symbols and diagrams. A tall clock ticked and tocked the time away in deep notes.

In the midst of it all stood a modest desk of plain wood. The bespectacled man in rolled-up shirt sleeves who sat behind it rose and walked around to meet them. "Lottie, so good to see you at last." He took off his glasses and peered at her before hooking them back over his ears. "Thank you, Tawse. I appreciate this." He paused, inspecting Tawse's face and body. "You are injured?"

Tawse shrugged. "My vest took a bullet. No harm done."

"Your two companions?"

Tawse shook his head.

"Damn," Steals said. "I'm sorry. She is worth their sacrifice, believe me."

Tawse stalked over and sat in one of the two mismatched chairs in front of the desk. The chair gave an ominous creak as it took his weight. Stretching out his legs, he let out a sigh of pleasure. "We do what we have to do, boss. The greater good."

Steals shook his head. "Tawse," he said. Then he said no more. Only smiled before turning to Lottie. "Can I get you something to drink? Some wine, perhaps?"

"No," Lottie said, "but thank you anyway." She looked around, unsure what to do next.

"I'll have one of those, if you're offering," Tawse said.

"Of course." Steals wandered back to his own side of the desk and lifted up a wine bottle, showing it to Lottie. "Sure?" She shook her head. "Sit then, at least. Please." Steals motioned to the second chair.

Lottie sat down, her legs tucked under, her fingers knotted together in her lap. Beside her, Tawse lolled in his seat. He drained the glass Steals passed to him, before reaching for a refill.

Steals returned to his own chair, picking up his glass and swirling his wine. "Here's the thing, Lottie," he said. "The gate from Earth to Syre. The gate you closed for a time. With no knowledge, with no training as a maker. Despite the fact – the immutable fact, mind – that only a gate's builder can close it." He pressed his attention on Tawse. "Quite remarkable, wouldn't you agree?"

Tawse shifted in his seat, making it groan in protest. "As you say, boss. Remarkable."

"Then the gate from Syre to Bad Beag. Who knows what happened there?" Steals took a sip of his wine. All his attention turned to Lottie. "You know, don't you?" He sipped again. "And I would like to know too. Very much indeed." His gaze was steady and unflinching. "I prefer mysteries when they're solved."

"I… uh…"

"Yes?" Steals said.

"I… um… I don't know anything about it." Lottie hunched herself tighter into her chair, readying herself for the onslaught. There was silence but for the hypnotic tick-tock of the clock. It ticked and it tocked and Lottie wound her fingers evermore tightly together.

"Of course you don't," Steals said.

"Huh?"

"How could you? You're just a girl. Caught up with a bad crowd." Steals leant back and drank his wine. "Wouldn't you agree, Tawse?"

"A bad crowd, as you say, boss."

"There's no cure, you know," Steals said.

"What?"

"For the plague that afflicts Payge's people. What do you make of my gate downstairs?"

"Eh? Oh, it's different from the others, much more intricate. More complicated. And it was white. Though I don't know if the colour makes any odds."

"You can see them?" There was wonder in Steals's voice. "See the gates?"

"No, I—" Lottie drew in a breath. "Yes. I can."

"Absolutely amazing." Steals reached for the wine, pouring himself another glassful. "I don't know about anybody else, but I need a drink after that one."

"What did you mean about Payge?"

"What I said. There is no cure."

"Then why is he sure there is?"

Steals sighed. "Because he needs to believe in something. He's very single-minded."

"I noticed," Lottie said.

"But not very flexible in his thinking."

"The woman, Arkwright. She said she bought Payge's people from you. Along with the cure. Did she?"

"Yes, to the people, no to the cure."

"That's obscene."

255

Steals leant forward, catching her in his gaze. "It is, but that's the way things still work here. And you have to go with it before you can change it. We're not exactly shining examples ourselves, given the millions back home who live such desperate lives."

"I meant the cure," Lottie said. "But the slavery thing. That too."

"Of course you did." Steals sat back. "Arkwright lied about the cure. It's a palliative, no more. It merely suppresses symptoms. And, I suspect, becomes less effective with time. It was the best I could do." He looked at his hands before he spoke again. "It's beyond my skills to make a cure."

"But Payge said you had it. That was your hold over him."

"I may have led him to believe that. I needed him, but I knew he wouldn't work for me willingly. I don't make any claim to be a decent person, Lottie."

"Does anyone work for you willingly? Does he?" She nodded towards Tawse, who was reaching for the wine bottle again.

"I'll ask him, shall I? Tawse, do you work for me willingly?"

Tawse set the bottle on the table and eased back into his chair. "When you aren't being a horse's arse, I'd say I do."

"See?" Steals said. "Same as most of my people."

"You could have ordered him to say that."

Steals laughed and pointed to Tawse. "Hear that? An intelligent voice. Why can't you be more like her?"

Tawse stuck his nose in his wine glass and inhaled. "Not part of my skill set."

"Will you let me go?" Lottie said. "I want to go home."

Steals's voice was loaded with sympathy. "Not possible just yet, I'm afraid. For now, I can offer you protection."

Lottie folded her arms. "Seems like most people want to do that. Forgive me for being sceptical about it."

"Understandable view, after what you've been through."

"That you caused. You did this to me. Your sodding bookshop. You targeted me and my friends. You made me lie to them and you tore us apart. There were things trying to kill me because of you." Her anger broke on his placid demeanour. The silence stretched out. Feeling faintly ridiculous, she sat back in her chair.

"You're right. It was terrible what I did to you. But it needed to be done. On the plus side, it did turn out well. Your friends are alive and safe for now. Although Elizabeth badly needs help with her drinking. And Andrea needs to sort out her personal life, but her father has been pushed in the right direction, which was the whole point. Thank you for that."

"What do you mean by safe for now?"

"I have someone keeping an eye on them, but Arkwright may still move against them."

"Move against them?" She watched the smallest of grimaces cross Steals's face.

"Kill them, I suppose I should say. Why gild the truth? Only a possibility but Arkwright can be a bit impulsive. Never use a scalpel when you can use a sledgehammer, is often her way."

Lottie chewed at her lip. "I need to help them."

"No, you don't. There's nothing you could do. And besides, Andrew Ross is going through a very dark period right now, worrying about his daughter's safety. Just the thing he needs as a goad for his ambition. Andrea's dad is right where I want him. I can't have that put at risk by you popping up and blabbing about his grubby affairs."

"Why? Why do you need that?"

"It won't hurt for you to know. I'm pleased the book attracted you. I did take a bit of a risk with that. It's not always reliable. Remarkable how it does work though."

"Answer the question," Lottie said.

"Oh-ho. You hear that, Tawse? She has learnt a thing or two from Payge. Good for you, Lottie. You've come a long way from that miserable student flat." He rose from his chair and paced the floor for a time before stopping to sit on the edge of the desk. "Why is my gate buried so deep?"

"Shielding, I expect," Lottie said. "Against interference. From what, I don't know. Your gate is deep down, so needs a lot of it. Meaning, it's more vulnerable than most, maybe more fragile? That's telling me it's either more complicated or it's something different."

Steals slapped the desk before reaching for his glass to take a quick gulp. "Damn, but she's good. Eh, Tawse?"

"I have a terrible habit of judging people only by their actions, not their words," Tawse said.

"You're as bad as Payge. You are the most pig-headed people I've ever known."

Tawse grunted and helped himself to the bottle. Steals turned back to Lottie. "So what's your next question?"

Lottie watched as Tawse lifted an empty glass, impossibly delicate in his huge fingers. He poured some wine and offered it to her. Letting out a breath, she accepted it. "Thank you," she said. The wine tasted exceptional. "What does your gate do?"

Steals gave her a pleased look. "Think of the other gates you've been through as like a lens, changing the light that goes through it, but fixed in its output. They can only do one thing. You see?" He waited for her to nod her understanding before going on. "Using the same analogy, I've made something more akin to a telescope."

"A gate you can focus?" Lottie said. "Adjust its output? You're saying you can go anywhere with it?"

"Mm-hm, that's the general idea."

"Why?"

"Always the best question." He looked at her over the top of his wine glass. "History first. What do you know about the gates on our world?"

"Um, I was told they all vanished centuries ago. Nobody knows how or why. Then they reappeared sometime in the last century. Nobody has the answer for that one either."

"A fair summary," Steals said. "Only, our world changed significantly in the time we were cut off from everywhere else. A revolution happened. Now we're a high-tech world. Much more so than the others in this neighbourhood. Or perhaps anywhere, come to that. And there are an awful lot of us humans. Nowhere I've seen is so heavily populated. Have you ever studied what happens when technologically advanced people come in contact with stable, low-tech cultures? Empires, Lottie. Empires are built."

"So this is all about power. All these people being hurt so you can lord it over them."

Steals studied the contents of his glass. "I think we could do with some more of this. Tawse, could you oblige?"

"Sure thing, boss." Tawse levered himself up and clumped away.

Steals watched him go. "Did you ever wonder why the book worked the way it did?"

"How do you mean?"

"No need to be coy. Or ashamed. It called to you, didn't it? You couldn't resist it."

"I did think it was a bit… odd, I suppose. I thought it was just me." She took a sip and then a gulp. "You're saying it wasn't me? The book was actually doing something to me?"

"That's exactly what I'm saying. In a much earlier age, you'd have said it cast a glamour on you."

"Not possible. It was only a book."

"Don't close your mind so quickly. It'll become a bad habit. Possibly a fatal habit. Yes, it was only a book. I travel all over, looking for the strange and the unique. Bit of a hobby of mine." His eyes twinkled at her. "Who hasn't wanted to own a quaint bookshop in the old town, eh?"

"Makes a nice change from ruining people's lives, does it?"

Steals laughed. "I do like you, Lottie. You're honest. A rare commodity. But back to the book. In my travels, I happened upon a world one of the elder races had occupied. Looked like they had just stood up and left, but once I got over the strangeness of it, there was treasure everywhere."

Lottie found she couldn't help herself. "Payge mentioned the elder races. Who were they?"

"Difficult to say since there's no one around that's ever met them, and by all accounts they were notoriously stand-offish when they were here. What we do know – sorry, what I know, is that their knowledge has a common root. The gates, the patterns; these are what we know how to use. The thing with the books. That's something I developed myself. But they all draw on the same base techniques and learning."

"How does it work then?" She was being drawn in. She knew it, and she knew she shouldn't, but it was irresistible.

Steals flicked his hand in the air in a negligent gesture. "Quantum manipulation? Using consciousness to collapse probabilities to desired states? Magic? I don't know. Not yet anyway. There's a huge amount to find out. I can't do it alone. It's too much. I need people around me. Smart, open-minded people who want to learn."

Lottie gave him a wary look. "You want me to work for you? After what you did to me? Seriously?"

"Work with me. There's a difference. And really, you need to put all that behind you. Holding on to the past will only hold you back."

"Does that mean abandoning my friends when they need me?"

"I told you your flatmates were okay for now."

"No, you didn't, and I have other friends."

"You think Payge and his obnoxious sidekick are your friends?"

"Payge is…" She huffed out a breath. "We've been through a lot. He's… he's serious with me. He cares."

"He was doing what I told him to do."

"Forced to help build your little empire, you mean."

Steals bobbed his head, not agreeing or disagreeing. "Empires. They get a bad name. Slavery. Repression. Genocide. Horrible, horrible things. But if you can put them to one side… Empires are levers that can shift worlds. And where I want to go, I need that lever. The more we search, the more worlds we find. Many are inhospitable, some few are not. Of the few that are not, none are empty. Except for the one I've found. And us humans live on a very crowded planet. Now, any more questions?"

"Could I have some more of that wine?"

"Of course." Steals gave a jovial laugh. "I was hoping for something a bit deeper but it's a start."

Lottie stood, pushing her chair back with her calves, hands clenched into fists by her sides. Steals reached for the wine bottle. "You should sit back down."

"Maybe I shouldn't." She began to back away from the desk.

"You really don't want to run." He poured the last of the wine into his glass.

Lottie went on backing away until she bumped into something solid. Then she bolted for the door. She almost made it. The door swung open, and Tawse stepped through. "Going somewhere?" he said. He held a plate in one hand and a bottle in the other.

She slumped to a stop. "No. Going nowhere. Apparently."

Tawse proffered up the plate. "I brought a bite to eat. Want some?"

"What's on the sandwiches?" Steals asked.

"Corned beef and mustard."

"Oh, excellent. French or English?"

"English, of course."

"Better still. Bring 'em over then. Now, Lottie. Sit. Have a drink and eat something." Steals picked up a sandwich and took a huge bite. "Tell you what, since I've been so utterly horrible to you, I'll make you a deal." He pointed at her with the corner of his sandwich. "You come with me. I want to show you something. After you've seen it, you can leave if you want. But I've a hunch you'll want to stay. Deal?"

"You're lying."

"Of course I am. But I still think you'll want to stay when you see it."

14

ELDER

"So," Steals said, "what do you think?"

A sound came out of Lottie's mouth. She heard it. It sounded like, "Uhk".

He led her to the very edge of the platform. Beyond it, the landscape stretched away to hills made grey and indistinct by distance. Between their viewpoint and these hills, the ground was flat and level in all directions, inlaid with pathways of burnished bronze that formed lines and loops, curls and whorls, like a language written in the earth. Between the pathways, plants and trees grew in lush profusion.

Struggling with the scale of it, Lottie realised the pathways might be as broad as a football field. "It's…" She looked at Steals as she pointed. "Those things, those pillars, are floating?"

He grinned at her. "Just like the one you're standing in now."

She turned again to goggle at the white columns suspended in the air above the bronze paths. Columns that stretched to the height of skyscrapers. Some taller than that. Some that disappeared upwards into the haze of the sky. There were dozens of them scattered over the landscape, all the same colour, marbled in shades of white. All of them moving, drifting above the bronze paths in a stately dance of epic proportions.

"What is this?" she said.

Steals lifted his hand towards the view. "What I told you about. It's an elder world. Or was. Now it's empty."

"The people who lived here, they just left all this behind?"

"Seems so."

A legion of questions danced in Lottie's mind. One of the foremost was that if they were standing in a column the size of a building that was floating in the air, then what exactly was making it do that and would it carry on doing it for as long as she was standing in it. "Is this safe?" she said.

Steals stamped his foot on the floor a few times. "Seems to be solid enough."

"You don't sound too sure about anything."

"I'm not." He walked away from the edge and Lottie followed. Steals turned around on the spot, looking up at the ceiling. "As I said before, there's still quite a bit to find out yet."

"I imagine there is." She walked to the lip of the balcony again, heedless of the lack of any kind of barrier between her and the open air. The vista beyond called to be looked at and any sense of caution was a meagre rein on that call. She watched the procession of the columns for some time. Steals came over and stood beside her, sometimes watching her, sometimes watching what lay beyond.

Movement off to one side caught her eye. She leant out over the edge of the platform for a peek. "There's another column heading towards us. It looks like it's going to be awfully close."

"Mm-hm," Steals said. He rocked back on his heels, hands in his pockets.

"Shouldn't we do something?" Lottie poked her head out again for a second look. "Get away, maybe?"

Steals examined a fingernail. "We could."

The encroaching column was crossing their path now, moving in front of the scallop-shaped space they stood in, its progress utterly silent as it occluded their view of the elder world. Their own column was still heading directly for it. Lottie wondered if the feeling of impending, unavoidable dread that gripped her was the way sailors felt immediately before a collision at sea. The movement of the two columns went on and on; they drew ever closer. Lottie looked to Steals, hoping he might do something. He watched the column passing them with some interest.

"Notice how the marbling effect on them moves around?" he said. "It's very subtle. You only really get to see it when you're this close up."

Lottie didn't want to look at it. She looked instead at the vertical slice of landscape she could see emerging to one side of the column crossing their path. Judging speed and distances, the hope grew in her that they might not collide. She waited, gnawing at her bottom lip, watching the pale pillars making their relentless progress. Then the way ahead of them was clear and the great dance went on.

"Do they ever stop moving?" she asked.

"No. I've measured them. They move at that same speed all the time. About a fast-walking pace. Uncannily precise. And there is a pattern to their movements."

She looked at him, but he shook his head. "I haven't been able to figure out what it means. They never speed up, they never slow down, even when they go round corners. I've no idea what kind of physics governs them but it's not the physics of our world. I don't know what holds them up. You can walk under them if you like." He grinned at her. "And if you're brave enough."

Lottie found her gaze drawn back to the vista before them and the hypnotic grace of the movement of the columns. "What are they? Is the whole world like this?"

Steals gave her a bemused look. "Give me a chance, Lottie. I haven't been able to look everywhere yet. As to what they are, this is the part you're going to like the most." He beamed a smile at her. "This is a library."

Lottie craned her head upwards and around, following the curved lines of the space they stood in. The wall around her was the same white marble colour as the outside of the columns. The floor was devoid of any feature but for a slender rod in its centre, which rose to waist height. "It doesn't look like any library I've ever seen."

Steals nodded. "Me neither, but that's what it is."

"I'm assuming these things aren't packed full of books."

"No books. What we have instead… well, come over here and I'll show you."

Steals led her over to the rod and pointed to a bronze plate on its top. "I've called this the touchstone, for want of a better name. You touch it, it tells you things." He caught her look. "I know, I've a tendency to be too literal-minded. Give it a try."

Lottie spread her fingers above the plate. She held her hand there. "Have you tried it?"

"Of course."

"And you were okay after it?"

"Yes." Steals smiled at her. "I think everything that the elder race knew is stored in these structures. But it's only information, Lottie. What harm can it do?"

Lottie dropped her hand to her side and shook her head. "Bad experience with trying new things recently. I got to see this little gate. And what was on the other side of it."

"You mentioned you can see the gates. I find this quite fascinating. What do you see when you look at them?"

Lottie turned her attention back to the touchstone, shying away from his intense look. "Geometry," she said. "Lines, like a structure. Some of them are anchors, they disappear into whatever is around the gate. Others are weird. It hurts to look at them. They go in directions that aren't there." She stopped herself. "That doesn't make sense, does it?"

"It does if your mind is trying to construct a visual representation of something that exists outside the universe you're using as your reference point."

"Oh," Lottie said. She thought for a second. "What do you see?"

"Nothing at all." His face crinkled in amusement at her puzzled look. "Only a few of us can. I mean, we all try, and we train, and we hope we will see what we are making but most never achieve anything of it. The few that do only see vague impressions. Ghosts of things. Except you, it would seem."

"How can you make things you can't see?"

"I can make radio waves, but I can't see them very well."

Lottie stared at her feet. "Now I'm just being thick."

"Not true. You're learning. Always the best part of the day."

She looked up, to consider the touchstone again. "This is a bit like a computer. It's their version of the internet?"

"Better than that. Much better. By a long, long way. The touchstone puts ideas in your head. Knowledge without learning. Mastery without practice. It doesn't last, unfortunately. It fades as soon as you break the connection. But fragments remain, bits and pieces of wisdom we can take away and use. We can improve on that, I'm certain of it. Find ways to fix in our minds the knowledge the touchstone imparts. If we can do that, who knows what we might do? That's its power. Now, are you going to try it?"

Lottie flexed her hand over the touchstone and looked at Steals. He nodded back to her in a reassuring way. Her fingers hovered over it. "Do I have to say or do anything?"

"No. Just touch it."

And she did.

There was an instant of connection, a snap in her head like an electrical circuit being made. And she simply knew. She knew how to navigate the vast cache of information before her. She knew how to do it, the way she knew how to move her own body. Without conscious thought, without mental effort. Everything was here. She only needed to think it and it would be hers.

"Holy shit." Stepping back, she looked at her fingers, as if the knowledge of the elders might be written there.

"You connected with it?" Steals said.

"Connected? It felt like somebody pulled the top off my skull and filled me up with knowing." Lottie looked from her hand to the touchstone, to Steals. "It's still there. I can feel it. I remember." She focussed her puzzlement on Steals. "The people that lived here before, they weren't human, so how can I understand what the touchstone told me?" Her own question made her pause. "I've just touched a stick with a plate on the end and it downloaded information into my head. Why am I even asking that question?"

"Because it's a good one," Steals said. "I've not tested the touchstone extensively, but so far, it has only responded to me. And now, you."

"I'm not sure what that's got to do with it."

"Makers, my dear Lottie. It appears the touchstone only responds to makers. Or whatever makers have that's different from everyone else." He stared at her for a few moments. "You know what that makes us?"

Lottie shook her head.

He winked at her. "It makes us in charge."

"You're saying I'm a maker?"

"No. You're not a maker. Not yet. But you have it in you to be one. I realise that might take a bit of getting used to." He gestured round at the space they were in. "Along with all of this. A lot to take in on one sitting." Cocking his head at her, he smiled. "But you seem to be coping admirably. Now try it again. This time, think of something that interests you. See what it does."

She faced the touchstone, glancing once at Steals before pressing her hand to the bronze plate again. *Okay, what about these gates, then? How do they work?*

It felt like falling. No, it felt like being propelled downwards, driven at some insane speed towards a destination of unfathomable complexity. Back there, way back there, she felt her body responding, her pulse racing, her breathing coming fast and shallow.

So much to know, a vast ocean of knowledge. It was intoxicating. It was dazzling. It pulled at her, at her heart and mind, at her bones, at her womb. She wanted to scream and cry and laugh. She wanted to play. She wanted to build. She wanted to learn. And she did. That ocean tipped and poured and fell on her in a torrent of understanding. It soaked her, it filled her, it would drown her. It was too much. It wasn't enough.

Something slipped past. Some scrap of a dark thing that moved like an eel, which wasn't part of the understanding she wanted. She thought to chase it, catch it, but the understanding still flowed, each new idea a shining bauble of delight and the eel-thing was gone, down into the well of her mind where the torrent now flowed and was contained. A well she had made for herself, and within herself, a well she wanted filled, deep and satisfying to drink from.

"Well?" Steals said.

Lottie stared at her hands as if they were two objects she had never seen before, her mind filled with a pure joy she hadn't known since childhood. She looked up at him. "I can make a gate." Smiled at him. "It's easy. You fold it just so, in the pattern." Her smile faded. Her brows creased. "Or at least I think so." She looked at him again, a worried frown on her face. "I had it a moment ago."

Steals nodded his understanding. "This happened to me. As soon as the connection is broken, you begin to forget what you learnt. I'm sorry, Lottie. It's painful at first. To be given such wisdom, then for it to be taken away. You need to harden yourself against that. Console yourself with whatever fragment you manage to hold on to. Anything we can salvage from the library is a gift." He took her hands in his own, gave them a squeeze, ran his thumbs over her knuckles. "We'll learn to do better. Together."

"No." She bit at her lip, looking from his eyes to their joined hands. She stepped back, pulling her hands away, thinking hard, probing at her own mind. "I haven't forgotten. What I learnt is still with me. I just can't get at it." She clenched her fists, tried to summon an idea, failed, huffed out her frustration.

"Maybe our minds work differently. Maybe you forget in different ways from me. This might be a strength for us."

"I haven't forgotten. Don't you listen?" She turned away from him, chewing at her thumbnail, her arms drawn in tight to her chest.

Steals came up behind her, placing his hands on her shoulders, gently turning her to face him. "I was as upset as you are now, the first time. I stamped around here like a toddler throwing a temper tantrum, shouting and screaming. Bit embarrassing really, for a grown man." His grin was weak and cheesy. "I think we've done enough for one day. We should get back now."

"I do remember it all," Lottie said. "I can see it in my mind. But it's like it's coded and if I had the key, I would understand it. Something is stopping me doing that. I don't have the key."

"Interesting," Steals said. "But we really should go back. There's a matter I need to explain. Then I need to ask you to do a job for me."

Steals took hold of her hand. Lottie didn't notice, didn't respond, lost in her own thoughts. Far in the back of her mind, something slipped and slithered. Some red, eel-like thing.

15

HOW LONG DOES IT TAKE TO COUNT TO A BILLION?

"What have you noticed about the size of the gates?" Steals said. He steered her to a corner of his workshop that was tricked out like a sitting room and placed a mug of tea in front of her. "Sorry, would you have preferred wine?"

Lottie shook her head. She curled up in a big armchair, hugging herself, feeling cold and shivery. "They're different sizes?" It was difficult to think. Difficult to drag answers from her head.

Her answer made him pause. "I forgot. You can see them. How different they must look to you." He studied her, the way an astute uncle might study a particularly talented niece. "The part of each gate that matters, the part that you walk through and gets you where you want to go, is only about the size of a normal door. I've long suspected this is a deliberate limit placed in our knowledge of the workings of the gates. Kind of a design feature, if you like." Steals paced back and forth as he spoke, his hands in his trouser pockets. "Now, how long would it take to get a billion people through a door?"

"Um, that would be… I dunno…?"

"Thirty-two years. Assuming one person through the door every second. One person every second of every minute, of every day. For thirty-two years. And you just know it's going to take longer than one second per person. And supposing we actually want to get about two billion people through the door. Or three even? We could be talking centuries. We don't have that amount of time. Now let's get on, shall we? We need to get to the important bit. The bit where you come in."

Lottie looked up from her tea. "Me? What have I got to do with getting a billion people through a door?"

Steals returned to his chair and raised his own mug to her. "See? I knew you'd come round to my way of thinking."

"I haven't. I'm interested. After what you've shown me. I don't understand about the door. I'm just curious, you know?"

Steals's smile was sly. "Oh, I know."

He carried on smiling at her. For long moments. Until she couldn't stand it anymore. "Are you going to tell me or not?"

"Yes. Of course. There have been three great revolutions in human history."

"What?" Lottie rubbed at one eye and clutched her tea, struggling to work her way through Steals's looping, elliptical conversation.

"Revolutions." He circled his finger in the air. "Three of them. The cognitive revolution, about seventy thousand years ago, when we began to think and communicate in new ways, when we first began to collectively believe in pretend things like gods and money. Then the agricultural revolution, about twelve thousand years ago, when we began to build cities and work together in larger and larger groups. Along comes the scientific revolution, only five hundred years ago, when we began to understand how reality works. Each one coming faster than the last. The next revolution will be the big one, when we become post-human. When we move on to what we will be next. When we become an elder race."

He stopped, looking at her for understanding and when Lottie gave a slight nod, carried on. "I think the gates, or more accurately, the knowledge behind them, is inextricably linked to that event. Only we're not going to make it. We're going to run out of resources, run out of environment. Drag ourselves back into a dark age because we've only got the one planet and we're trashing it. We need more time to let ourselves reach the next milestone. I can't make more time, but I can do something about giving us more resources and I can do something about giving ourselves another world to work with."

"You want us, humankind, to take over that world you just took me to?" She stared at him, struggling to take in the scope of what he was saying.

"Well, nobody else is using it, and it would be rude to colonise one that already has sitting tenants." He gave her a lop-sided grin.

"Is that possible?"

"Just about, but we're going to need a bigger gate. Or a lot of regular-size ones. To get around the billion-people-through-the-door problem. To get enough people to the elder world in a short space of time. To take the pressure off our own world and give everyone a chance at a limitless future. I can't do it alone. It's beyond my ability."

He stopped for a moment and trouble owned his face. "Only a handful of people have been to the elder world. It's a secret for now, but I doubt it will stay that way. Until very recently, matters hung in the balance and the tacit accords between us makers held. I tipped the balance by rescuing you from Arkwright. Using my gate openly like that, it shows my rivals my power. Too much power for their liking, I'd imagine. They'll want to restore the balance. And by restore the balance, I mean they will see me dead. I need to act before that happens. I don't have the forces to defeat Arkwright. I have you. When I found out what you can do, I put everything on the line to get you here."

Lottie shifted in her chair. "What is it you want me to do?"

"What you did to the gates on Syre. I want you to do it again."

Lottie hesitated over her reply. "I'm not sure I could do it again. I don't really know what I did the first time. And the second time... I couldn't walk properly or use my left arm after it. It caused me such pain. I thought it might kill me. I think I was lucky I didn't do myself any permanent damage. Maybe I did but it hasn't shown up yet." She stopped to chew at a nail. "I hadn't thought about that until now."

"What was it you did?"

"I moved the gate from underground—" She bit her lip and looked at him, at his smile of triumph, and she dropped her gaze, hot shame burning her cheeks.

"You moved a gate? That is truly exceptional." Steals tapped his finger on the arm of his chair. "The first gate. The one from Earth to Syre. What did you do to it? You might as well tell me. You've told me most of it anyway."

She dropped her gaze to her hands, forcing her fingers to be still, even as she wanted to twist them together. His voice reached out to her.

"Lottie, I'm sorry you're at the centre of this, you never asked for it. But I don't regret for a single second what I've done to you, because if I hadn't, your unique talent would have gone undiscovered. And believe me, it is unique. I've told you what I want to do. It'll mean revealing all these worlds to the people in power back home. Andrew Ross, your friend Andrea's father, is one of the ways I will begin to do that. Maybe sooner than I had anticipated." He gave a rueful shrug before carrying on.

"Once it's done, once the secret is out, Liz and Andrea will be safe from Arkwright and the other makers. No one will have anything to gain by hurting them. Until then, we're vulnerable and they're vulnerable. Arkwright will have Payge working for her by now and when Arkwright attacks us, Payge will be at the front of it because Arkwright always uses her least trustworthy pawns first. You can stop all that happening, maybe save them all."

He stopped talking and sat in silence, waiting for her to speak. When she did, the words crept out of her. "The first time, I, uh, I just kind of pulled at the fabric of it. I bent it a bit."

Steals rose from his chair. "I see. A distortion of its pattern, disrupting its function. Interesting that it corrected itself. Did it affect you that first time?"

"It was a bit painful but not that bad. The second time, it had more to do with the gate, I think. It felt different, if that makes sense. It looked different."

Steals nodded. "I see. Quite fascinating. The gate from Syre to Bad Beag is far older than the first one. It wasn't made by us or the elder races. Pity we don't have more time. Come over here and look at this."

Steals threaded his way through the workshop to a drawing board with a huge sheet of paper taped to it. Dozens of circles were drawn on it, some large, some small. All interconnected by lines, all neatly labelled. Steals pointed to one of the bigger circles.

"Each main world is connected to three smaller worlds." He gave her a brief smile. "Worldlets, I call them. Each of those are connected to two other worlds. That's the underlying pattern. The whole set up is ancient. It pre-dates even the elder races. The original builders, whoever they were, are unknown. The three gates on each world tend to be close together. But more gates have been added. By the elder races and then by us. Like the one you used to cross from our Earth to Syre. Right now, we're here." He stabbed a finger at a circle marked "Warth".

"Warth is connected to Earth via a gate on Ore, which

Arkwright now controls. Alt Graad, where Arkwright is based, is here." He tapped the paper. "Again, three gates. One to Ore, one to Bad Beag. The third gate on Alt Graad is impractical, the country on the other side of it too hostile. If we can close those two gates out of Alt Graad, it will trap her there and it will send a very clear message to whoever is supporting her."

Lottie looked over the map, taking in the detail of worlds and their connections. "The red circles? They're worlds we can't go to?"

"Correct. Uninhabitable. For us that is."

She counted perhaps a handful of reds amongst the many marked on the paper. "The blue circles?"

"Inhabited worlds. Non-hostile. Generally."

"Black?" There were more of these than the red.

"Definitely hostile. But as you can see, in our neighbourhood, all the worlds are inhabited."

Lottie carried on studying the sheet of paper, reading the names of the worlds. "Your elder world?" she asked, not looking up.

"It's a bit off the grid, to be honest."

"There are more worlds than the ones on here?"

"For sure. I don't know the full extent of the network. When all this is done, I can take you to some of them, show you what's out there. I can teach you. But first, I need you to close those two gates. It's a risk I'd prefer not to take. It's putting you in harm's way. But right now, I don't have any other good choices and we're running out of time. I expect Arkwright will move against me very soon and I don't have enough people or weapons to stop her."

He reached out to lay a hand on her arm. "Do this one thing, then I'll keep you safe. If not, I'll need to keep you here until this is over. Time to choose, Lottie. The greater good, remember."

"I'm not sure what you're doing is right. But…"

"Your friends?"

"Yes. My friends. I have to help them."

"And the rest of it? The new world?"

Lottie dipped her head, not wanting to look at him. "Yes. I want that too."

"We better get on then."

"We're going to do this now?"

"You can think of a better time?"

"I thought there would be plans and briefings and stuff. A good night's sleep. That kind of thing?"

Steals's smile was not unkind. "We could wait a bit." He winked at her. "And we could wake up dead in our beds. It'll take me about an hour to align the gate. Will that do you?"

"How do you align the gate?"

"Complicated sums are required. You don't need to know right now."

Lottie scowled at him. "Now you're starting to sound like Payge."

⁓

An hour later, they took the cage down to the gate. Tawse, and three others so similar to him they could have been brothers, were waiting at the bottom of the shaft.

"We know the gate from Alt Graad to Ore is guarded," Steals said. "But you don't need to get that close, do you? There are fewer guards on the Alt Graad side, so that's where you're going."

He looked at her the way Lottie thought a scientist might look at a newly discovered species, before shaking his head. "We close that gate, Lottie, we really hurt her. I underestimated her, you know." A rueful smile flickered across his face. "Arkwright. She's smart. She took control of Alt Graad in a remarkably short span of time. I thought she was just another small-time crook. A gangster looking to run guns and drugs and carve out a piece of turf. I never figured her for a conqueror. Still…" He lifted his hand, closed it into a fist, then let it drop. "Get this done quickly. Tawse and his people will keep you safe. If you can't close the gate, say so, and he'll get you out of there."

"You already told me all this."

"I know but – I'm scared, Lottie. Scared of what we could lose here."

"She was sending Payge to kill you." It was out of Lottie's mouth before she really thought about what she was saying. "Arkwright, I mean. She was going to keep me."

"I don't doubt it," Steals said. "She gave you no choice, I'll warrant. That's the difference between her and me."

"You never gave Payge any choice."

"No, I didn't. With hindsight, maybe I should have, but when I first started, I took up the same tools and methods as my peers. That's the way we've always done it, as the saying goes. It's difficult to go against orthodoxy when you are learning." A slight shrug of his shoulders. "My mistake. It's done now."

They approached the entrance to the gate.

"Ready?" Tawse said.

Lottie swallowed once and nodded.

16

WEAPON OF CHOICE

She stepped from the dry warmth of the subterranean chamber to the middle of an empty plaza, boxed in on three sides by imposing facades. A burst of vertigo made her sway; Tawse put a hand on her arm to steady her and led her towards the rear of the plaza.

"Are we at the right place?" Lottie asked.

If he opened his mouth to speak, she never knew it. The staccato bark of automatic weapons fire, amplified by the confining walls, shattered the silence. She watched, dumbstruck, as blood exploded from the skull of one of her guards. Another staggered and went to one knee, taking hits to his body.

Tawse shoved her towards a low wall in front of them. "Get behind there. Stay down." He turned to fire his own weapon, emptying the entire magazine in one long, clattering burst.

Lottie threw herself over the wall and flattened herself against the ground. When the firing ceased, she raised her head to have a peek. Tawse was a few yards away, sheltering behind the plinth of a statue. She saw no sign of their attackers. Only the bodies of her escort. One lay where he had fallen. The second lay at the end of a broad smear of blood, where he tried to drag himself back to the gate. The third guard she could see a short way off, sheltered behind the same wall as herself. A hail of fire opened up. Squeaking with fright, she squirmed down, covering her head with her hands as fragments of stone rained down on her.

"Lottie," Tawse called. "Back to the gate. We left a marker where we came through. Look for it. Run when I tell you."

She lifted her head. "You're kidding, right?"

He didn't answer, just swore softly as he looked around the plinth that sheltered him. "They're going for the gate too."

The gunfire was sporadic now, single shots snapping out at irregular intervals, accompanied by the sound of running feet and voices calling.

"Move," Tawse shouted.

Lottie lifted herself up. A glance in the direction of the gate, the air near it distorting into concentric ripples in places. Her thoughts on it were fleeting. *Bullets. Hitting the gate.* Her attention was on the clutch of men directly in front of her. Sprinting towards her.

She looked to Tawse. He was judging the distance between her and the men coming at her. The look on his face told her all she needed to know. He took off for the gate, leaving her behind. She knew she could never make it. Too slow. Too far away. She began to look for another way out.

Behind her, a narrow gap between the two buildings. Hoping it might be an alleyway and not a dead end, she ran for it. It was what she had hoped for. She pelted along the narrow lane. Shouts echoed behind her. Shots were fired. She ran on, heedless of them, until the alleyway opened into a wider street. Not far away, it turned a corner. Running round the corner without slowing, checking behind her, no one in sight. Other streets branched off this one. A chance to lose her pursuer. Closest was a dark opening, no wider than a doorway. She ducked into it.

There wasn't much light in the enclosed walkway she found herself in. Just enough to see that the way out ended in a barred gate. Skirting past stacks of broken boxes, she reached the gate, pulled at it, found it locked. Lottie bit at her lip, pivoted round and saw a figure fly past the entrance to the walkway, calling to those behind. Pressing herself against the wall, sliding down to crouch behind the stacked boxes and crates, keeping as still as she could, she waited and listened.

More running feet going past her hiding place. More shouts, becoming fainter with distance. Then a final set of footsteps, slowing down, petering out. Stopping. Boots gritting on stone, pacing slowly forward. The sound changing as the wearer stepped into the walkway. She could hear his breathing, still fast from his running. He stopped and shifted around. She imagined him looking backwards and forwards. He took another step towards her hiding place. With every muscle in her body tensed, knowing she could not bring herself to move, she squeezed her eyes closed and bowed her head.

In the darkness of her inner vision, a single point of scarlet light grew into a swirling multitude, then coalesced into a red ribbon that twisted and spun in her inner vision.

~Lottie. I can help you. If you let me.

The voice came from nowhere. It was in her head, unspoken and unheard. She bit down to stop herself from speaking out loud in reply. The scarlet ribbon flowed and swam. The voice matched it, rising and falling in low tones of assurance.

~Let me help you.

Footsteps coming towards her, cautious and deliberate, placed one after another. She opened her eyes. Closed them again. The scarlet ribbon remained, moving with the sinuous grace of an eel through water. The voice was a whisper.

~Let me in.

Her nails dug into her palms. Her thighs ached from crouching for so long. Her legs trembled, threatening to spill her forward and out of her hiding. *I'm losing my mind. I'm hearing voices in my head.*

~You are not. We are together. What hurts you, hurts me. Let me help. Let me in.

"How?" She spoke aloud without realising.

~Like this.

An unfolding in her mind, a sliding together of a construct, a pattern. A strange sensation of dislocation, a tiny spark of white appearing. It was a gate, only a speck of a thing. She could feel the pull of it though, minuscule but so familiar. Opening her eyes, she could still see it, a dot of light hanging in the air before her. She followed it as it sank downwards, disappearing into a lump of broken masonry. A pair of boots walked into her field of vision. She lifted her head to peer up at the man who held a gun barrel to her head. The voice in her head spoke again.

~Close your eyes.

She did it without thinking. The red ribbon twisted itself and joined at its ends, becoming like a Mobius strip. Then it flicked open.

It felt like she had been hit on the back of the head with a length of wood. Bright light burst in her vision. A whistle of air going past her face. A meaty splat and a cracking noise. Drops of warm liquid spattered on her cheeks. The loud clatter of something metallic and hefty falling to the ground. She opened her eyes to see the man who had been standing over her. His body slumped against the opposite wall, his ruined face a gory nightmare with the chunk of brick the gate had disappeared into, embedded in it.

"You killed him," she said. The thoughts in her head felt like they were moving at a far slower speed than the rest of the world.

~I said I would help. I did. You don't need to speak out loud.

"Did you have to kill him?"

~No.

"So why did you?"

~

"Answer me. Who are you? What are you? What are you doing inside of me?"

~

288

When she closed her eyes, the scarlet ribbon still spun and twisted and looped round in the darkness. But it looked thinner, less coherent. Weakened.

You don't get to do this to me.

She reached for the eel-thing, as she had reached for the gates. But her head thumped with pain and her hands felt swollen and clumsy. The scarlet ribbon moved in ripples, slinking away into that part of her where the memories from the touchstone were, the place she could not reach. It hid there but she could still feel it, a lurking presence in her thoughts.

Lottie stood and rubbed at her face, looking down at the dead man. *Maybe I killed him. Maybe I'm having some kind of mental breakdown. Maybe I picked up that stone and beat him to death with it.* She looked at her hands, unsoiled by blood, and knew the answer to her question. *It used me. This thing, it used me. Like a tool. Or a weapon.*

Stepping over the body, she made for the entrance to the walkway, only to see it blocked by the silhouette of another person. She stopped, propping one arm against the wall for support, no strength left in her. Her words came out as a low moan. "Please, no more."

"Lottie, it's me."

She lifted her head to squint at the dark figure before her. "Payge?"

He beckoned her forward while he looked up and down the street. "Quickly now. Before they send someone back to check."

She reached him and threw her arms around him.

After a moment, when she didn't let go, he returned her embrace. "Are you okay?" he said.

She pressed her face into his shoulder and spoke into the warm skin of his neck. "No, I'm not okay. I just helped kill a man."

"We can talk about it some other time. We need to be away."

Taking her hand, he led her back the way she had come. A shout from behind alerted them. Payge looked round. "Go," he said.

Still holding hands, they ran for the nearest corner. A single shot chased past them as they rounded it. "Over here." He pulled her across a wide road, through a row of columns in front of an impressive-looking building. The building's door, a slab of wood studded with iron, yielded not an inch when he shoved it.

"Damn," Payge said. Unfastening a holster at his hip, he drew a revolver.

Lottie glanced from the gun to the door. "You're never going to shoot through it with that."

"Didn't intend to." He swivelled to aim at an exquisite painted glass window adjacent to the door.

"You're not!" Lottie said, horrified.

Two shots created an avalanche of broken glass. Kicking away a few long shards that clung on, Payge stepped over the window surround and held out a hand to her. "Now would be a good time."

Lottie swung a leg over the jagged nubs of glass that remained, into the dark interior where shelves lined with books stood row upon row.

"Look for another way out," Payge said.

They ran down the nearest row. Behind them, feet clattered on broken glass. "They're in," she whispered.

Payge spoke normally. "You don't say?"

They reached the end of the row, Lottie pointing out a sign hanging from a bracket. The lettering on it was unreadable but the arrow was unmistakable in its message. "There. That could be an exit."

"Good spot," Payge said.

"Or it could be a toilet."

"Handy if you need to go."

She clapped a hand over her mouth to quiet a burst of manic giggling. The short corridor the sign sent them along ended at a door. Payge held a hand to his lips, gently lifted the bar on the door and slid back its top and bottom bolts. They slipped through, out of the building, into a deserted street. Payge closed the door behind him with the same care he had taken in opening it.

Lottie cast a look up and down the street. "Which way?"

Payge hesitated for a moment before going left. "This way."

The streets grew busier the further they went. Now and then, a wary eye was cast in their direction, but mostly, the sight of a heavily armed man leading a young woman seemed to be no cause for concern. When they reached the edge of a busy market, Payge shucked off his weapons and gear, slinging them behind a row of barrels.

"Won't we maybe need them again at some point?" Lottie asked.

"They're drawing more attention than we can afford

right now. Besides, I have to ask some people for help. They won't give it if I'm armed to the teeth."

"Payge, I need to ask you about something first."

He looked up from re-buckling his belt, then went back to the task as he spoke. "One of the great makers lives here. Called Dorchadas. Maybe the last great maker. He might help us. I worked for him a long time ago. Did some things for him that… well, that earnt me some favour. But first I want to ask around, see if anyone knows where his interests lie, who is working with him. Figure out how best to approach him."

"I wasn't going to ask about that."

"I see. What were you going to ask about? Can it wait?"

"I don't know. Something very odd is happening to me."

Taking Lottie's hand, he threaded his way through the throngs of people, past the traders and their stalls, to an open area in the centre of the market, where a circle of women, men and other creatures sat easy on wooden stools and benches, chatting to each other in amicable tones. In the centre of the circle, a brass kettle hung over a charcoal brazier.

"Payge, I think there's something in my head. Something that shouldn't be there. You're not listening to me, are you?"

He let go of her hand and approached the edge of the circle, where he murmured a few words, touched his forehead with his fingertips and bowed towards the centre. The chatter round the circle ceased. Stares that varied from interested to hostile were directed at him, but one woman motioned him forward. Before he went, he turned to her with the look she had grown to know too well.

"I know. Stay here. Don't speak to anyone. I've got it."

To her surprise, he smiled back at her. "We'll talk when this is done."

"Says you," Lottie whispered under her breath.

With some shuffling and good-natured argument, a space was made for him on a bench, a cup poured and passed over. The chatter broke out again, but Payge didn't seem inclined to join in. His gaze tracked from one speaker to the next. Lottie couldn't follow a single word. Still, she listened, intrigued by the interplay of body language and the tone of the speakers.

Finally, Payge did speak, a casual aside to the man sitting beside him. He pointed to someone across the circle. Laughter followed his comment. Immediately, he was drawn into the conversation and a loud exchange broke out between him and the woman who had invited him in. The exchange ended as abruptly as it had begun. The woman sat down, lifting a steaming cup to her lips. Payge stood up and began to speak.

He spoke as if telling a story, his hands weaving through the air, his face and his body playing their part. When he dropped into more cadenced speech, the talk around the circle died away. All eyes were on him. Heads moved in time to his words, comments were made, fitted with care into the silences between his lines. There was a fire in him that Lottie dearly wanted to warm herself at. More dearly still, she longed to understand what he said.

It's like the thing inside me. I know it's there, but I don't understand it. Maybe it isn't there at all. Maybe I imagined it. Maybe it's me. She shook these thoughts away, not wanting to probe the cold anxiety they brought on. *Okay, let's assume I'm not losing my mind and this thing is real. What is it? Some kind of weird virus?* Thinking she might be infected gave her a shiver. *Can't even sense it now. Maybe it's gone or died or something.*

Closing her eyes, she stilled her thoughts. *Let it come. Let it show itself.* She breathed slow and even. The everyday sounds of the marketplace blended with Payge's voice, lulling her, calming her. She felt at rest. Until something wet and fleshy slithered through her hair.

Letting out a cry of disgust, she ducked down and batted at her head. Moist air, warm and smelling of hay, blew around her neck. She spun round, her anger growing, her fists ready to strike out. Her anger was snuffed out. In its place, wonder and delight.

She stared up at the huge animal in front of her. It had a head like a rhinoceros, only bigger and without the horn. Dark eyes gazed back at her. The beast's sticking-out ears twitched and its soft lips made slapping sounds as it champed its jaw in slow circles. It lifted its long neck until Lottie had to lean back to look up at it. The top of her head barely reached to where its front legs joined the massive barrel of its body.

"Payge!" she squealed. She heard him break off his performance and the irate cries from the circle that followed. She didn't care. She turned to him, unable to stop the smile that spread across her face. "Look at it!"

He glanced from the creature to her, uncomprehending and irked. "It's a bray. So what?"

Lottie pointed up at the beast. "Paraceratherium. The

biggest land animals ever. They're from Earth. Were from Earth. They're extinct. Long time ago. Millions of years. Other kids loved dinosaurs, but I always loved the mega-fauna like these guys." She spoke in a rush, shooing away the beast when it tried to lick her head again. "Isn't it fantastic? How did it get here? People need to know about this."

"They've always been here. Now can I get back to what I was doing? Please?"

"Fine, whatever." Lottie flapped a hand at him before turning back to contemplate the wonder before her. She held her hand up and the creature lowered its head, sniffing at her skin. Bristly hairs on its snout rubbed on her palm and she thought she might just about die with happiness.

A small woman with skin the colour of ochre, hooded and swaddled in baggy robes, approached her and spoke a few words. Lottie shook her head, understanding nothing. The woman said something else, pointing to the beast. Lottie lifted her hands up and let them drop.

Her questioner tapped a short stick on the beast's leg. With stately grace, it started to turn. Lottie stepped back to give it room. The woman let out a yipping cry, slapping her stick twice against her palm. The paraceratherium began to walk away, its tread slow and easy, like it had all the time in the world. The woman spoke again to Lottie before pulling down her hood. Her hair was a mass of curls, like burnished copper, like Lottie's own. She said one more word before turning to follow her animal.

Lottie watched them go, the crowd parting before them and closing behind them. She became aware someone was standing very close behind her, just on the cusp of her peripheral vision. When they spoke, she wasn't sure if it was aimed at her or the departing pair.

"Another people condemned for the sin of being too different."

It was a voice she knew. Raven's voice. She turned, startled and pleased in equal measure. More pleased when Raven wrapped her into a hug. Lottie held her tight in turn, drawing in the scent of her skin, the feel of her hair tickling her nose. "Where have you been?"

Raven held her a moment longer before letting her go.

"You got any more of that for me?" Jackdaw spoke from behind his sister.

"Of course," Lottie said, holding out her arms to him.

"We've been shadowing you and Payge since the plaza," Jackdaw said.

"You can let me go now," Lottie said back.

"Making sure no one got the drop on you."

"You could have done a better job. Someone did get the drop on me. And if your hand goes anywhere further south than it is now, I will pull it clean off your wrist."

Jackdaw let her go and grinned up at her. "Come on. Who doesn't like a big cuddle?"

Raven slapped him on the back of the head, making him wince. "Respect her space."

"I have nothing but the utmost respect for her space." He winked at her, and Raven slapped him again. "What was that for?"

"You know fine well what it was for."

Rubbing at his head, he muttered something indecipherable and wandered over to a street vendor.

"What is going on here?" Lottie asked. She nodded towards Payge, who was now engaged in a debate that flew back and forth across the talking circle.

"He's bargaining for information," Raven said. "Trading on the story he just told. And I have to hand it to him, he is good at it."

"I know. I listened. I couldn't understand but it didn't matter. It was still beautiful."

The two women stood in silence, watching and listening. Raven spoke first. "You should know, the situation has changed considerably since they grabbed you at the inn. Arkwright has moved against Steals. There's fighting in Warth. Here as well. Direct conflict, one maker against another. The peace has ended."

"Wow. A lot can happen in an afternoon."

Raven seemed to consider her next words carefully. "Lottie, they took you two days ago."

"Get real. It's only been a few hours. How can it be two days?"

"Where did Steals take you?"

The question threw Lottie for a moment. "I don't see how that can have anything to do with you thinking I've been gone for two days."

"He must have taken you to another world. Where was it?"

"He called it an elder world. An empty one. Are you sure about the two days?"

"So, the old bastard did find one. The talk was true then. And a much slower temporal environment. That's quite something."

"He wants to use it to help us. Humans, I mean. A place for us to live. Maybe it could help your people as well. I could talk to him. It's a whole empty world after all."

"Yeah, right."

Lottie looked away, unsure how to reply, unsure what to think about the time Raven claimed she had missed. Other questions snagged at her. "How did you know Steals took me? And how did Payge know where we would be when we came back?"

"One of Arkwright's people told us. They have someone very close to Steals."

"A spy?"

"A spy."

"Are you all working for Arkwright now?"

Jackdaw came back over with a bag of roasted nuts. "Want one?" he asked, holding the bag out.

Raven took a couple and popped them in her mouth, crunching away. Lottie held one up and inspected it, then followed Raven's example. When she bit into it, the taste was bitter enough to draw her cheeks in. Leaning over, she spat out the broken remains and wiped her lips.

"Very ladylike," Jackdaw said.

"How can you eat them? They taste awful."

Jackdaw looked in the bag, shrugged and went on feeding himself a steady stream of the nuts. "Taste fine to me."

"Payge and this fool agreed to work for her," Raven said. "I didn't. Though I'd think their agreement is now ended."

Jackdaw looked up from inspecting the inside of the bag of nuts. "Be fair, sis. We only agreed to do it to help find Lottie."

Raven gave him a sour look. "So now we're stuck here on Arkwright's little world with no way out of it. The gates will be guarded. Steals can't use his magic gate to rescue you, if he doesn't know where you are. What did Payge say he was going to do?"

"He said he was going to see if a person called Dorchadas could help us."

Raven stared at her, black eyes searching her face. "Dorchadas? That's what he said?"

Lottie nodded. "I'm sure. Is that bad?"

Raven looked to where Payge was making his way out of the circle. "For him to seek help from Dorchadas? Yes, it's bad."

"Bad, how?"

"Dorchadas is a great collector of things. And a great maker of things. Very small things in particular. Plagues, for instance."

"Payge and Jackdaw both told me about the plague that afflicted your people. Payge said it was a maker who started the whole thing and others have kept it going. I don't understand how people can be so awful to other people."

Raven shook her head. "Me neither, but they are. They always have been. Dorchadas might well have been the one who started it all. I've tried to find out, but he's a difficult person to get close to. Dorchadas, not Payge. Though Payge is difficult enough."

Lottie looked at her. "You're joking, right? I mean, how old would he have to be? You're not joking, are you?"

"No, I'm not."

Silence hung between them. Lottie stared into the

market crowd, trying to work out how to phrase what she wanted to ask. "Speaking of infections, have you ever heard of anything like someone being infected by a memory or an idea of something? I'm only saying because—"

But Raven was walking towards Payge, asking him what he knew, and some impulse stayed Lottie's tongue, stopping her pursuing an answer to her question.

Jackdaw was peering at her, one of the roasted nuts held between his fingers. "Are you feeling okay?"

Lottie nodded but didn't reply. The soundless voice stole into her thoughts, and she knew if she closed her eyes, she would see the scarlet ribbon gliding through her head.

~Not yet, Lottie. It is not yet the time for them to know.

"What are you?" She mouthed it under her breath as she watched Jackdaw walk away, still munching on his snack. The answer she got back was the same.

~Not yet.

Anxiety quickened in her. *This isn't happening. People's minds don't get infected with ideas. They just get ill, mentally ill.* She bit at her lip as her anxiety edged closer to fear. *It just stopped me speaking. Or I stopped myself from speaking. What if going through all those gates has done something to my brain? Changed it somehow? Made me ill?*

Payge called to her, motioning for them to be off. A trembling breath escaped her, then she followed after him.

They left the market square, moving into the maze of streets surrounding it, streets lined with two- and three-storey tenements, all jumbled together. The many shops they passed were small, open-fronted, selling their wares

300

in the street. Overhead, washing hung on criss-cross lines, catching the breeze and the sunshine. People laughed and chatted and went about their business, heedless of the four of them. It struck Lottie as a nice place to live. Until they had to flee along a narrow lane and into a cramped courtyard to avoid a group of armed men searching in shops and questioning people.

"Looking for us, I'd imagine," Payge said. "Jackdaw?"

The small man looked up and nodded before disappearing into the nearest house. Payge checked back the way they had come, then sat on a stone bench, surveying the balconies that overlooked the courtyard.

Lottie followed his scrutiny. She could see nothing but pot plants and colourful blankets hanging out to air. "I could live in one of these. They're a sight better than my own flat." The thought of home and her flatmates drove away the rest of her words.

Payge patted the space on the bench beside him. "Sit for a minute. Rest."

She did, while Raven propped herself against a dry fountain opposite them, closing her eyes and turning her face up to the sun.

Lottie knotted her fingers together and began clicking one thumbnail over the other. "What were you saying to the people when you were in the talking circle?"

Payge shifted himself to a more comfortable position. "If you had listened, instead of spending your time petting a common pack animal…"

"It wasn't a common pack animal, it's an extinct species. That's important."

"You should think about the logic of what you just said."

"You're a really annoying person sometimes."

Payge tipped his head back, resting it against the wall. "You know, people don't value the quiet as much as they used to."

Moments passed in silence.

"Payge?"

"Yes?"

"Steals told me something. Actually, he told me a whole lot of things. But one of the things was about you. I never had a chance to tell you. You were always busy with something. I did think to try, but—"

He sat forward, unfolding his arms and letting his hands drop into his lap. "It's clearly bothering you, so say what's on your mind."

Lottie licked at her lips. Raven had opened her eyes and was watching her with interest. Payge was looking away, checking the entrance to the courtyard.

"He told me there is no cure for what you have. What Arkwright has is only a palliative. He tricked her over it."

"I see," Payge said. He carried on looking round the yard, checking the balconies.

"I thought you might be more…" Lottie stared at her knees. "To be honest, I wasn't sure what I thought you might be when I told you."

"I've had my doubts for some time. But as we do, we hold on to hope. However fragile."

"I'm sorry."

"Don't be. You acted in friendship. Knowing opens up new opportunities."

"I don't get you."

Payge slipped a water bottle from a pouch on his belt, unscrewed the lid and took a sip. He held the bottle out for her. "We'll get back to that. Tell me what else Steals told you."

Lottie took a drink, handed it back. Payge tossed it to Raven, who caught it without looking at it.

"Raven already knows some of this," Lottie said. Payge fixed her with a stare, but her own gaze was on Raven, who nodded back. "We had a chat about it back in the market."

"Did you now?" Payge's regard turned to Raven. "Best you tell me as well then."

She told them both all that had happened to her in the hours she had been with Steals. When she had finished, neither of them spoke. "You look worried."

"He's gone further than I would have guessed he could," Payge said. "Much further."

"I… uh, I don't know quite how you'll take this but I kind of agree with what he's doing." Lottie glanced between Payge and Raven. "It makes sense and he's sincere. Or at least he seems to be. I don't think he's that bad a person. All things considered."

She waited for the outburst. Payge simply bent forward to lean his forearms on his knees. "It did cross your mind he could be lying? Or covering up some other scheme he has in mind? Or that his plans are all some elaborate fantasy?"

"No. He didn't come across that way. Maybe he has done some awful things. I know he has. But then, so have you. But to what end?"

Payge gave her a feral grin. "You've changed quite a bit. You can't make an omelette without breaking a few skulls, eh?"

He stood and dusted himself off as Jackdaw appeared at a doorway. She squinted up, lifting a hand to shade her eyes against the sunlight outlining him. "Are you still going to do what Arkwright wants? Are you still going to try to kill him?"

"I might just kill him for my own satisfaction."

Lottie looked to Raven for help. All she got back was a shrug. "One less maker in the world," Raven said.

"But Steals isn't the problem anymore." Lottie got to her feet and followed Payge across the courtyard to where Jackdaw waited for them. "Arkwright is the problem. If we take out Arkwright, it fixes everything."

"Take out Arkwright?" Payge said. "Are we in a gangster movie now?"

"Stop taking the pee. You know what I mean."

"So what do you mean?"

"We go back to Steals and try again. Do what he asked. Close the gates around Alt Graad. Bottle Arkwright up."

"So that's the plan, is it?" Payge stopped and turned on her. Lottie took a step back, bumping into Raven, who slipped an arm around her waist.

Payge rubbed at his face before speaking again. "There's a war started, Lottie. It's going to be a short, and in all likelihood, brutal one. What blood-kin I have left are with Arkwright. They'll be at the front of this war. If what you say about this cure is true, then there's not much future for us anyway. Me included. What can I do? I'll tell you. I can get even with one of the bastards that caused this misery. I can get to Steals, because he's at his weakest now."

"And how does that solve any of your problems?"

"It doesn't, but it might make me feel better."

"You have to murder someone to feel better about yourself? That makes you worse than they are."

Raven stepped forward, placing herself between them. "The pair of you need to leave this until we're in a safer place. None of this is helping."

Payge drew a breath, then let it out. "You're right." He looked over at Jackdaw. "Show us the way."

Lottie moved around Raven, to catch hold of Payge's sleeve. "I'm asking you to leave Steals alone. Will you do that for a friend?"

Payge looked her in the eye, then down to where she held onto him. "We'll see."

Leaving the courtyard behind, they followed Jackdaw. The doorway he led them through opened into a homely room with low tables and huge cushions scattered on the floor. Jackdaw stopped to lift four pieces of fruit from a bowl.

"Isn't this someone's house?" Lottie said.

Jackdaw passed three of the fruits back and bit into the last one. "Technically, yes. But they're not using it right now, so we should be okay." He took them through to a kitchen, where an iron pot sat on a cooking range. When he paused to sniff the contents, Payge gave him a nudge. Jackdaw's look was resigned as he put the lid back on the pot and guided them outside. Payge stopped a passer-by to ask directions. He thanked the person and pointed along the street. "This way. Not far to go now."

17

RED SHIFT

"This where we find Dorchadas?" Lottie asked. She eyed the windowless structure Payge had brought them to. "It looks like a mausoleum." Walking round it, she found a single iron door was its only feature. When she had completed her circuit, she squinted at Payge. "You're saying this is a shop?"

"Of sorts."

"Not selling much, is he?"

"This is only the door."

"The shop's underground?"

"I've no idea where the shop is. Through the door, down the stairs, there's a gate. The shop is on the other side of it. At least, that's how the folks at the market described it."

Raven came up beside her. "Maybe you can see it. Try for me, would you?"

Lottie nodded. She closed her eyes, fearful of the red

eel appearing, grateful when she felt Raven's hand slip into her own.

When did I start thinking about it as a living thing? She answered her own question. *When you started to deny there's something really wrong with you upstairs.*

The gate lit up in her vision, different again from those she had seen before – an elaborate knot of curves unsupported by any anchoring lines, coloured in hues of yellow and orange.

"I see it. It's quite beautiful."

Raven gave her hand a squeeze and Lottie opened her eyes, asking her question quickly. "Raven, do you know if the gates have ever made anyone ill? Like any kind of physical or mental illness?"

Raven's brow furrowed in puzzlement. "Not that I know of. They do have an effect on matter. Anything you leave in them disintegrates after a while." She smiled at Lottie. "Not a good idea to fall asleep in one. But no, I've never heard of them causing illness. Why do you ask?"

Lottie tried to reply, but as had happened before, her answer would not come. It was infuriating and scary. She knew the words she wanted to say. She simply could not say them. As if some connection in her head had been cut. Like forgetting the name of an old friend. Being able to see their face, knowing their name but unable to access it. "Nothing. Another dumb question that came into my head."

Raven reached to brush the back of her fingers across Lottie's cheek. "You're not telling me something."

"I just worry sometimes. Maybe I worry too much about nothing."

Raven's hand moved up to smooth out a stray lock of Lottie's hair. "Come talk to me when you feel you're able to."

While they spoke, Payge pushed down a handle mounted beside the door. A small panel slid to one side to reveal a circle of glass. Seconds passed. They waited. The click of locks, the sound of metal sliding on metal. The door glided open. "We're in," he said.

They stepped over the threshold. Lottie noticed the door was easily a hand-span thick. It reminded her of the door on a safe. Inside, the building consisted of a single room with a sunken stairway in its centre. With a clunking of gears, the door closed behind them. The sunshine was cut off, the room stayed illuminated by a dull light that came from no obvious source.

Payge walked over to the stairwell and peered into it. "Downstairs it is then."

"I've got a bad feeling about this," Jackdaw said.

Raven gave him an exasperated look and moved to join Payge. A voice rose from the pit at her feet.

"This a'way."

Footsteps padded up the stairs. The creature that appeared was short, barely waist height. Its head emerged from its thick torso with no narrowing to suggest a neck. Dumpy legs gave it a waddling gait. It beckoned them forward with a three-fingered hand. "Come. Come, come."

Payge looked around at each of them in turn and without a word, followed the creature down the stairway. At Jackdaw's invite, Lottie went next, Raven behind her. The stairs took them to another door, looking as thick and heavy as the first. It opened at the creature's touch. Beyond it was a short passage that ended in a blank wall. When Lottie blinked, the gate blazed in her inner sight.

She closed her eyes, taking in the beauty of it, the difference between it and the other gates she had seen. While the others were linear and functional looking in their construction, the one before her spoke of craft, artfulness, the love of creation. She walked forward, bathed in its light, feeling its substance passing through her as she passed through it. The light from it was filling her up, shining under her skin, making her radiant. On the other side of the gate, the voice stole into her head.

~We are not safe here.

The briefest flicker of scarlet in her inner vision. Not a skulking away. The motion of a predator, circling just out of sight. The thin and insubstantial eel-thing was gone. In its place, a creature of power, a shape to be fearful of.

Lottie opened her eyes, half-expecting to see the scarlet creature winding itself around the room she was in. Instead, she saw walls covered with shelves that were partitioned into compartments of varying sizes. Each of these nooks and cubby-holes housed some object. The floor was taken up by tables that stretched the full length of the great room, the space between them only enough for a single person to pass along. Each table was crammed with items of indeterminate origin and unknown function, some in glass cases or under bell jars, some mounted on plinths, some simply laid on the tabletop.

Their escort, the little homunculus, waddled over to a tall pulpit by one wall. Climbing up to the top, it seated itself, picked up a pen, dipped it in an ink bottle and began to write. The only sounds were the muted crackle of a wood fire and the steady scratching of the pen nib on paper.

"What do we do now?" Lottie whispered.

"We wait here," Payge said.

The fire crackled and the pen scritched and scratched without pause. Lottie looked round at the myriad objects in the room until she heard someone speak.

"Payge. Greetings. It's been some time."

The next words that were spoken, she didn't understand. Payge answered in what sounded like the same language. Lottie stepped to one side, to see around Payge, to see who he was speaking to.

The speaker was almost the same height as she was but short-limbed and plump. Thick-necked and square-faced, with eyes set inhumanly far apart. He held a string of amber beads that he rubbed with the three fingers of his hand. Payge carried on speaking; the person she assumed was Dorchadas carried on listening. Payge ended with a gesture towards her, Jackdaw and Raven.

"I see," Dorchadas said. He looked Lottie over with some interest. "Come with me, Payge. We can talk further."

Payge turned to her. "Stay here." His gaze switched to Raven and Jackdaw. "Keep an eye on her."

"Why can't I come with you?" Lottie said.

"Because he says, and I'm not arguing, because I want to get back out of here alive." He paused for a moment, as if about to say more, then shook it away and followed Dorchadas.

When they were gone, Jackdaw wandered along the

length of one of the tables, looking here and there. "He's got a lot of nice stuff here."

"He has," Raven said. She followed in her brother's footsteps. "You should keep your hands in your pockets."

"Sister. It wounds me you could even think that. The thought never crossed my mind."

"Liar," Raven said with a smile.

The two of them carried on browsing, leaving Lottie to herself. She trailed after them, taking her time, enjoying how good she felt after coming through the gate. The first time she had gone through one without feeling ill afterwards.

One item caught her eye, a sculpture fashioned in bright and dark metal, of a tree, and a figure reaching up to a branch, not quite able to pick the fruit from it. She knelt to get a better look. Although no more than the height of her hand, the detail of the piece was breathtaking. She reached out to turn it so she might see the reaching figure's face.

The little homunculus's voice rasped out. "Doan touchat. Iss'ah fragile."

Lottie stood up. "Not touching it." The creature stared at her over the top of its pulpit, its dip pen clutched in its chubby fingers. She backed away with her hands in the air. Raven and Jackdaw were at the opposite end of the room, arguing over the purpose of some object. Lottie walked further, stopping to look at a glass-fronted box. It held a single sheet of yellowed parchment that was covered in writing from top to bottom and edge to edge, without a single break. She leant closer to the glass.

"Doan touchat. Iss'ah, very 'spensive."

"I'm sure." She reached the end of the table, idled there, tempted to run her fingers along its carved edge, just to see what reaction she would get. She stuck a finger out.

"Doan—"

She whipped her finger back in and smiled to herself. Facing her were the rank upon rank of pigeonholes on the back wall. Among the devices, bottles, paintings and books stored there were a few skulls. Some of them looked human.

A flash of brightness from one object caught her eye. Sidled along on tiptoes to get a better look, she found it was a cube of glass about the size of her fist, green, with rounded corners and a grainy texture, like drift glass found on a beach. In the centre of the cube, a spark of light. Her hand reached up for the cube without a single conscious thought.

"Doan touchat," her watcher said. "Iss'ah, mo'ran you lifesworth."

Lottie dropped her arm to her side but carried on staring at the glass. At what was in the glass. It was a gate. She could see it now. It was tiny. No more than the size of a pinhead. But as she looked at it, really looked at it, and as the room slid away from her perception, she saw.

It stretched away from her, its end point unknown, but a long way off. A very, very long way off. She knew this and marvelled at how she could know. The gate's structure was simple, elegant. And she knew, beyond all doubt, it would respond to her touch. Grow or shrink as she willed. Go where she willed.

~Touch it, Lottie. Reach for it. Take it. It is yours by right.

She closed her eyes, and the eel was there, swimming in her sight, turning over on itself, gliding in loops and coils. Grown solid, grown bold.

~I see myself through you. You call me eel. A slithering thing. A low thing. Is that your name for me?

Why did you say we're not safe here?

~Dorchadas will have us for his pets. He will have you. And me with you. Take up the glass.

"Lottie." It was Payge's voice, calling her back.

She mumbled something, moving with the treacle slowness of waking from a deep sleep. "What?" She turned, rubbing at her nose with the back of her hand, trying to focus. Payge and Dorchadas were watching her. Raven and Jackdaw were walking back from the far end of the room.

"We've reached an agreement." Payge indicated Dorchadas with an open hand, as if there might have been someone else that Lottie could have mistakenly thought he was reaching agreements with. "He has agreed to help us get back to Earth. Or stay here. But not back to Warth and Steals. I… uh… I told him everything you told me."

Lottie looked from Payge to Dorchadas. "What about Arkwright? What about our plan?"

Payge made a quick, sideways glance at Dorchadas. "We leave Arkwright be."

"If I might?" Dorchadas held up a finger to silence Payge, his attention fixed on Lottie. "I understand Mr Steals has done some quite remarkable work. But his reckless adventurism needs to be reined in. People cannot just be allowed to do what they want."

Lottie heard a log settle in the fire and the scratching of pen on parchment. "I'm not sure that's what we want."

Dorchadas waved his hand, the string of beads wrapped around his fingers swinging to and fro. "It's immaterial what you might want. And there is a further condition to our agreement."

Payge looked at him in surprise. A cold sliver of worry slid into Lottie's mind. Before Payge could speak, she asked her own question. "What condition?"

"You stay with me," Dorchadas said. His voice held a touch of regret. "I'm afraid you're too precious to trust with the likes of these…" He paused, as if searching for the right word. "These people."

Lottie looked around at her friends, saw Raven's features hardening and Jackdaw reaching a hand to his belt, saw Payge shake his head at them in emphatic negation. "What if I don't want to stay?" she said.

"You assume you have a choice." Dorchadas drew a weary breath. "Always the same with youth. The need to be taught. To be shown what they must do. You belong to me now. I've bought you for a fair price. Understand?"

~Now, Lottie.

It was a whisper in her head, a caress over her mind that brought an unexpected ripple of pleasure. Some noise escaped her lips, an inarticulate sound, a substitute for all the ways she couldn't express what she felt about what Dorchadas had just told her.

~Pick up the glass. It is heavy. I will help you.

The ripple of pleasure again. Up her spine and into the nape of her neck.

~Let me out. Free me. I'll share everything with you. Everything.

The knowledge of the elders cascaded into her mind. The gates: what they could do, what they could be, all of it flooded in. A cry of sweet release escaped her. The red, the scarlet, blazed in her inner vision, burning with light, spreading its wings. She called it by name.

Dragon.

It answered her.

~Dragon.

The tiny gate in the glass cube, still on its shelf, sparked brighter. She caught hold of that bright light, took the measure of its weight, found it was to her liking and threw it at Dorchadas.

A deafening whip-crack sound. Followed by a monstrous crash. All around, the noise of things falling, clattering and breaking, but she couldn't see what made the noise – she was on her hands and knees, retching up thin lines of bile and spit. Patches of vivid colour bloomed in her sight. She swayed, then caught herself. Spat on the floor to clear her mouth.

~Get up.

Do it again.

Dragon's voice. Her own voice. Speaking as one. A feral grin was plastered on her face as she raised her head and lifted herself up. One hand searched behind her to find a table for support, scattering what lay in its path. The other scrubbed at her lips. Over the top of it, she regarded Payge, Dorchadas and the ruined wall behind them.

Dorchadas was bleeding from a gash that ran for a

finger's length along the side of his head. He was staring at her in astonishment. Payge wasn't looking at her at all. He had turned to face the crater the glass cube had made in the wall behind him. Buckled and splintered shelving had ejected everything they held into the room, each object leaving its own trail of destruction where it had landed.

"Oops," Lottie said, still grinning. She could see the tiny gate flaring bright, buried in the wall, the glass cube surrounding it still intact. Wrapping her thoughts around it, she pulled it free. It hung in the air, rotating slowly on its own axis. At first weightless, but she could feel its mass piling up. She drew it towards her, and to her dark delight, it glided to her side. Dorchadas shook his head at her, raising a hand to ward her off. Her grip on the gate tightened. Relishing the look of fear that stole over his face, she got ready to throw it at him again.

Then it was gone. The connection was cut. The cube fell, clunked on the floor and was still. She tried to get it back, to re-make the connection but it was like grasping at smoke. Squeezing her eyes shut, she searched for Dragon, called to it by name. But there was no dragon. Vanished, along with her power to lift the gate. Opening her eyes, she cast round in despair.

The homunculus appeared above the rim of his pulpit. His dip pen had been replaced by a petite cross bow loaded with a barbed quarrel. Pointed at her.

"Hold," Dorchadas shouted. The homunculus lowered his weapon and muttered something unintelligible. Dorchadas waved it away. He stalked over to the glass cube, lifted it with his fingertips and inspected it. Satisfied with what he saw, he slipped it into a pocket. Then removed it and placed it with some care on the nearest table. When he spoke, it was to Payge. "I think we can now see why the girl stays with me."

Payge looked to Lottie, a thoughtful slant on his lips. "No. I don't think so."

"You don't think so?" Dorchadas said. "I do think so."

"We had an agreement. She wasn't offered as part of it."

"I'd propose a re-negotiation of some terms."

"I see," Payge said. He glanced at Lottie again. "Still no."

Lottie let the table behind her take her weight. Her stomach spasmed, threatening to make her vomit again. Spit flooded her mouth, and she swallowed down its acid taste. She let her head hang, feeling utterly spent.

~I am sorry. This is going to hurt.

She lifted her head. "What?"

~I will guide you. Reach beyond the glass. Reach for the gate.

She felt her mind lifted by a wave of force, roaring upwards on a vertigo-inducing trajectory, carried by wings the colour of rage. She focussed all her will on the tiny speck of light that was the gate.

Come to me.

Dorchadas signalled to his homunculus. It squeezed the trigger of the crossbow. The quarrel left the bow and flew towards Payge. Lottie thought they were all moving at a ridiculously slow pace.

The glass cube exploded, the gate blinked from a spark to a perfect sphere of translucent white, blocking the path of the quarrel that struck it, slowed, stopped and fell. Glass splinters pricked the skin of her face, and she watched Payge flinch at the expected strike of the quarrel.

Still the wave of force grew beneath her. With it came a wave of pain, racing faster, catching her. She steeled herself against it, but it still hurt, a searing, visceral hurt that threatened to steal away all reason.

~You have done so very well. Now finish it. Take us from here.

It was pushing her. Dragon. Making her move towards the gate. She fought back against it.

Not without them.

~Leave them.

No!

The pain was huge, swelling inside of her skull, putting knives behind her eyes as she tried to move the gate.

~You cannot do this. It will end us both.

Her jaw locked tight, pushing her teeth against their sockets.

Then let it end.

She could keep the hurt in no longer. It wailed out of her as she doubled over. She refused to let the wail become a scream.

Show me what I need, Dragon.

~Do this. Make this pattern.

She folded the gate just so. And thought it would end her. Her heart lurched in a thumping double beat before staggering back to a rapid tattoo of pit-pats. She clutched at her chest as she tipped over. She was falling. So very slowly. On her journey to the floor, she sent the gate out, spinning it like a coin flicked between fingers, sweeping it through the room, over Payge, over Raven, over Jackdaw. The gate spun back to her, over her. An instant of darkness and the floor changed in front of her eyes as she hit it.

The pain was gone. Her limbs wouldn't move. She was laid on her side, hunched in a foetal position, eyes staring, breath whistling between her teeth. No part of her body would respond to her call. She felt a thin trickle of urine escape between her legs, and her mind burnt with the shame of it.

The gate hung in the air in plain sight. Payge and Raven moved around it, coming towards her, looking at the gate with something between wonderment and dread. She heard their voices, the sound of them blurred and indistinct.

Have I killed us?

~No.

The gate. I have to close it. He'll send someone through it after us.

Reaching for the gate, she made the pattern in her head. A jagged spike of hurt shot through her. Lottie felt herself try to flinch. Her inability to move became terrifying. Warm tears tracked across the bridge of her nose and down the side of her head. The gate persisted, and she reached for it a second time.

Dragon swam into her vision, once more the curling red ribbon, but faded, trailing specks of light, sparks of its own being falling away from it.

~I cannot let you do that. You will die.

It stood in her way, blocked her thoughts, and she didn't have the strength to push it aside. Then it was in her thoughts, worming its way through all she knew and felt and treasured. It soothed and eased and mended some broken part of her. Her limbs unlocked, to flop on the floor. She blinked away tears and lifted her head a fraction. Still Dragon moved through her, penetrating her, finding what it needed.

~*This.*

It took a different pattern from her memory, pushed it to the front of her mind.

~*Do this.*

She saw what it wanted.

No.

~*Do it.*

No!

It made her do it. Against her will, it forced the pattern into place with what strength it still had over her. She sensed its exhaustion, its near dissipation. Its last, desperate act, as it held her mind in its own.

The gate folded and folded again. Became smaller. Moved towards her. A surge of pins and needles swept down her limbs. She lifted an arm, only for it to fall, her knuckles striking the floor. She tried again, and her body responded. Her limbs were lumpish, uncoordinated things, but she managed to sit up.

Payge, Raven, and Jackdaw were all rushing to her. The gate was the size of an apple. It was in front of her. She put out her hand, and the gate passed through it. It touched her chest, and she watched, horrified, as it sank into her.

It unfolded inside her, unpacking itself into a different pattern. Creeping through her, the feel of it making her brush at her skin, as she would brush away some crawling insect. Her motions became frantic. She crawled at her clothes, trying to get her hands to every part of herself, pushing with her legs, backing away from a threat that wasn't there. Dragon winding itself into the lattice of energy that was threading its way through her entire being. Dragon building its strength, feeding off her and the pattern growing within her. She moaned and scrubbed at her arms, scoring long scratches in her skin. Then Payge was kneeling beside her, cradling her. Raven was holding her hand, checking her face and eyes. Jackdaw holding her other hand, rubbing it gently, telling her she would be okay.

"It's in me." Pulling her hand away from Raven, she wiped the tears from her face. "Inside me. I can feel it. The gate and the dragon." With her hand pressed to her heart, she looked at each of them in turn, hoping for some understanding, some word of respite for her fears. "How do I get them out?" No one had an answer for her.

18

CLOSING TIME

"I must say, this is something of a surprise. Though a welcome one."

Lottie struggled to her feet, helped by Raven and Jackdaw, as Payge spun round at the sound of Steals's voice.

"Payge, a pleasure to see you again. And your thieving sidekick. The lady, I don't know, but I see you've brought Lottie back to me."

Payge took a step towards him, and Steals held up a warning hand. "Close enough for now." Beside him, Tawse lifted the barrel of his automatic rifle a fraction higher. Payge stopped but held his ground.

With a nod to Payge, Steals directed his gaze to Lottie. "I don't know how you did it, my dear. Getting yourself back here, I mean." He gestured round at his workshop. "I thought I'd lost you, and you've no idea how much that hurt me." He stopped for a moment, a pensive look on his face. Then his face brightened. He clapped his hands and rubbed them together. "But here you are. Appeared out of nowhere. I'd be fascinated to hear your story though I fear I need to deal with my old colleague, Payge, first. And his two friends, I'd imagine."

Lottie took a shaky step forward, not needing the support of Raven or Jackdaw but glad of their presence. The crawling feeling had faded from her skin; her body felt her own again. Dragon twisted away to some dark part of her mind she could not reach. Yet she felt the weight of it in her. Still there, watching, listening, thinking.

"There's a gate inside me," she said. "And I have this creature in my head. I think it got in there when I used the touchstone. I call it Dragon." She shrugged. "I know. That sounds pretty lame. It used me to get us here. Used me like…" She lifted a hand, then let it drop. "It used me." She looked to Steals, then at Payge. "You don't believe me, do you?"

Raven reached for her and took her hand.

"I believe you," Payge said.

"Me too," Jackdaw said. "I'd believe anything you told me after what you just did."

"I've never heard anything like it," Steals said. He looked away, pulling at his bottom lip. "There's a creature in your head? It talks to you, I assume?"

"Sort of. I thought I was losing my mind."

"Understandable. That must have been frightening for you."

"You do believe me?"

Steals looked surprised. "Of course. If that's your reality, I believe you. This creature, is it friendly towards you? Or hostile?"

"I don't know. It's been both. How it made me do what it wanted…" She felt Raven hold her hand that bit tighter. "What is it? How do I get rid of it?"

Steals shook his head. "I don't have any answers. Not yet anyway. But I'm sure we can find a solution."

Lottie nodded and looked to Payge. But he wasn't listening to either her or Steals. He was looking at Tawse, who was looking at the mechanical clock she remembered from her last visit. Its minute hand was approaching eleven. "Payge, what do you think?" she asked.

Payge said nothing as he looked around the workshop. His gaze fell on Steals's desk, where an open bottle of wine sat between two glasses. "I could use a drink," he said.

"Capital idea." Steals gave them all a grin. "Way better than us all fighting each other, isn't it?"

Again, Payge said nothing. He walked over to the desk and sat in Steals's chair. Reaching for the bottle, he filled the two glasses, picking up one for himself. Sitting back, he swung his feet on to the desk. They landed with a thump.

Steals's grin looked less friendly. "Make yourself at home," he said. "Please, Lottie, take a seat."

Lottie walked over with Raven at her side. They took the two seats in front of the desk.

"Ladies first, I suppose," Steals said. He ran a hand over his head while he looked around the workshop. "Tawse, bring some chairs over and see if you can find any more glasses. Anything will do."

Jackdaw hitched himself up on to the edge of the desk and sat, swinging his legs in the air. He scooped up the second glass and swigged it down. "Not a bad drop."

"What would you know about it?" Payge snapped.

Lottie saw the way Payge caught Jackdaw's eye before turning to look at the clock and nod at Tawse, who was hunting around the benches and tables in the workshop. Out of the corner of her eye, she could see Raven following the silent exchange. She wondered what any of them could do against Tawse, the only one in the room who held a gun. The clock ticked away to itself in its soft rhythm, the minute hand on eleven.

Steals snatched up the wine bottle before Jackdaw could reach for a refill. Stepping back from the desk, he moved to where Tawse had set down a small table and a chair. He placed a glass, a cup and two lab beakers on the table. "All I could find."

Steals seemed about to say something, then shrugged and began to pour.

"Nothing for me, boss," Tawse said. He stood behind and to one side of Steals's chair, his rifle slung on his shoulder.

From her place in front of the desk, Lottie watched Payge watching Tawse. The clock ticked on. The minute hand passed eleven and began its climb to twelve.

"Lottie?" Steals shook the bottle in her direction, the wine sloshing in it.

"Not for me, thanks."

"I'll have one of those," Raven said. She stood and walked over to Steals, holding her hand out for the bottle. Steals ignored it, picking up a glass and pouring for her. When she was seated again, Steals took a sip of his own drink and set his glass down.

"Now, what shall we talk about first? Perhaps the matter between us, Payge? It may be useful to all of us to get that dealt with immediately."

Payge swung his feet off the desk and stood in one swift movement. Tawse moved his hands to his weapon. The clock ticked on, the minute hand near vertical, ready to mark the hour.

Payge glowered at Tawse and stalked across to the table. Picking up the wine bottle, he sneered at Steals, then retreated to the desk, pouring what was left into his own glass, filling it near to the brim, draining every last drop.

Mellow chimes rang out as the clock struck the hour. Lottie opened her mouth to ask Steals again about Dragon. Tawse slipped his rifle off his shoulder. Payge picked up the empty wine bottle and threw it at him.

The bottle caught him on the forehead, breaking into shards and razor-edged splinters. Payge was moving, pushing himself up on to the desktop, driving off it, flying through the air to crash into Tawse.

Lottie was on her feet, Raven and Jackdaw pulling her away. A deep, percussive boom sounded, the room shook, glass tumbled and smashed. Steals was out of his seat. Payge and Tawse grappled and fought, Tawse now on top, one hand on Payge's throat, the other raised in a fist that swung down on Payge's face. Payge blocked the fist with his free hand, grasping the wrist, holding back Tawse's strike. The two of them stayed locked together, limbs trembling with effort, Tawse's greater strength winning out.

Jackdaw ran to the hearth, snatched up a fire iron and slung it to Raven. She snatched it out of the air as she ran towards Tawse, then swung it in a wide arc at the back of his head. The iron whistled through the air, hitting with the solid thump of metal on bone. Raven drew it back and swung a second time. Blood flew from the impact point. Tawse fell sideways and lay still.

Payge pulled himself free, lifting Tawse's fallen rifle. Checking the safety, he pointed it at Tawse and kicked his head. Satisfied with the result, he turned the weapon on Steals.

The older man sat back down, a fearful expression on his face. "This will be it then, Payge. Your moment?"

Lottie heard gunfire. "What's going on? Shouldn't we do something?"

"We will," Payge said. His gaze never left Steals. He directed the gun's barrel at Tawse. "Your man here worked for Arkwright. He was about to kill you. Kill all of us. Except Lottie." He glanced up at her before turning his attention back to Steals.

"Now you're going to do the same," Steals said.

More gunfire. To Lottie, it sounded like it was right outside the workshop door. "What's happening out there?"

"Arkwright's people," Payge said. "She's making her move. Besides Tawse here, I don't know how many of Steals's people she has turned. By the sound of it, enough to give the main force a chance to blow the gate and get inside."

"Payge," Raven said, "we have to go."

Jackdaw called from the workshop door. "Clear here."

"Do what you have to do, Payge." Steals's words were bitter, his eyes downcast.

Payge brought his weapon to bear on the seated figure. Lottie stepped in front of him. He motioned her to one side with the barrel. "Get out of the way."

"No."

Payge side-stepped to get a clear line on Steals, and Lottie followed, matching him step for step. She stared past the gun barrel into his eyes. "I need him. To help me with this thing inside me. He's maybe the only one who can. I won't let you do this."

Payge settled the rifle into his shoulder, adjusting it to get a better position. Lottie reached up and pushed the barrel out of the way. "Please. Let him live."

He hesitated a moment before lowering the gun.

"Thank you," Lottie said. "I can only guess how you feel about doing that."

Payge grunted at her, then sighed and drew a breath, wiping a hand across his mouth. "Maybe not what you think. There's only so much you can carry with you before you're worn out." He gave her a weak smile. "We should get out of here before they find us."

"Can we bring him with us?"

"Steals?"

"Yes." She fiddled with the hem of her jerkin, not looking at him. "I know it's a lot to ask."

"It is."

She glanced up. "You didn't need to agree with me that quickly."

"It's not my call." He turned away from her. "Jackdaw, Raven. Lottie wants to bring Steals with us. How do you feel about that?"

"More of us to shoot at," Jackdaw said. "Less chance it's me they might hit."

"Raven?" Payge said.

A look of distaste crossed her features. "If it helps Lottie."

Payge turned back to Steals. "You. Up."

"Wait," Lottie said. "Can't we use your gate? Get out that way?"

Steals shook his head. "I doubt we have the time I'd need to set it up."

"Then we do it the old-fashioned way," Payge said. He stooped to search Tawse, coming up empty-handed. "Doesn't anyone ever carry any spare magazines with them? Jackdaw, take point. Raven, at the rear. You pair behind me." He strode over to the door. "Ready?"

Jackdaw slipped into the corridor outside the workshop, and they followed behind him in single file. He passed a stair leading upwards, checked it, then carried on. Gunfire sounded but it was distant, muffled by walls. Another two steps and he froze when a woman stepped round the corner at the corridor's end. A woman with olive-coloured skin and oval buttons of jet black for eyes.

"Dirna?" Jackdaw said.

The woman lowered her assault rifle. "Jackdaw?"

She raised it again when Payge lifted his weapon and called to her. "On the floor. Now."

Dirna stood her ground. "You planning on shooting your own kin, Payge? It's just Steals that Arkwright wants. You leave him with me, and I didn't see you." She shifted her head to one side, away from her rifle. "Damn. That's the girl, isn't it? Arkwright wants her too. Alright. We could work something out here. You come with me, and we deliver them together. This could work for all of us."

"Put the gun down, Dirna. I'll think about it."

Dirna shifted her grip and changed her stance a fraction. "Okay," she called. "Okay." Lifting one hand off her weapon, she held it up and lowered herself to a kneeling position. As she laid her rifle on the ground, a second person stepped round the corner, followed by a third.

Payge opened fire. The sound was deafening in the enclosed space. Lottie back-stepped, Raven dragging her away from the shooting. She had a brief glimpse of one of the people tumbling to the ground, the other ducking behind the corner and Dirna scuttling backwards on her hands and knees.

Jackdaw retreated past Payge, shoving Steals as he went, shouting at them all to get to the stairway. Raven bundled Lottie up the first few stairs. She poked her head out as Jackdaw and Steals climbed up beside her. "Cover," she called to Payge.

There was a moment of silence then another burst of fire. Cartridges tinkled on the ground. Payge slid round the corner and joined them on the stairs. "Up," he said. He caught Steals by the arm. "Where does this lead? Is there a way out?"

Steals nodded. "My private rooms are up here. There's a way to get to the other side of the building and stairs that will get us out."

"Go then," Payge said.

They climbed the stairs, Payge going halfway up, before turning to cover their retreat. More gunfire sounded. A cry echoed up the stairwell, a drawn-out wail that broke up into a jumble of sobbing and cursing. Payge walked up the stairs backwards, covering their retreat. When he reached the top, he nodded down the long hallway that stretched away from the stairway. "Go check along there."

Raven and Jackdaw started off, then doubled back. "More of them," Jackdaw called. "No way out along there."

Payge waved Lottie and Steals out of the way and fired at the group coming towards them along the hallway. Shouts came from below. Payge swivelled round and fired downwards, three shots, then his rifle clicked empty. He swore, but it was a quiet, passionless sound.

"In here." Raven held the nearest door open for them. She shepherded them all through, closed the door and turned the key in the lock.

"What now?" Jackdaw said.

Lottie looked round at the room they were in. A study of sorts. Bookshelves, a desk, a map table. No other way in or out.

Payge crossed to the French windows that made up one wall of the room. Lottie came over to squeeze in beside him as he opened one for a look out. Three storeys below, she saw a walled compound with a shattered gate, bodies strewn in the space between the gate and the main entrance to the house they were in. Payge pushed her back inside, none too gently. "Too high to drop from. Maybe I could." He looked at her. "Not you. Jackdaw, Raven, they could climb down…"

The door to the study creaked. The handle rattled as

it was tried from the outside. The thump of a shoulder thrown against the wood.

"That won't hold them for long," Raven said. "We should leave Steals. We can maybe get Lottie to the ground between us by passing her down."

Payge looked out the window again, checking the drop. He said something but Lottie didn't hear it. She touched her hand to her chest. *I moved a gate before. I can do it again. Just wasn't inside me last time.* She closed her eyes. There was nothing. No hint of the gate.

Dragon.

She called to it, searched for it. Caught a flicker of scarlet, far away in the depths and chased after it.

I need you. Come to me.

Closer now. Catching up to it.

Dragon—

Being shaken. She was being shaken. Opened her eyes, blinking up at Payge, who was talking to her. His lips formed words that took her brain a second to translate into meaning. Everything seemed so slow.

"What are you doing?" Payge said.

She pressed her hand to her chest again. Or her hand had never moved since she had placed it there a moment ago. She wasn't sure. The world around her had taken on a viscous feel, as though submerged in a body of thick liquid. "The gate inside me. It's maybe our way out. I tried to find it, but I can't."

"Try harder."

She bit at her lip. "It's stopping me. It doesn't want me to do it."

"What's stopping you?"

"Dragon. The thing inside me."

Gunfire from outside the study door. Splinters flew away from the lock. The door was kicked open. Payge lifted his empty weapon, aiming at the doorway. Dirna stepped through into the room. She stood for a second. Arkwright walked in behind her, looking over at Payge. "Nice try," she said. "You could throw it at me I suppose."

Payge dropped the rifle to the floor. The thump of its landing made Lottie start. "Try harder," he said.

Lottie closed her eyes. The scarlet ribbon twisted and swam before her, grown thick and strong.

Dragon.

~Yes, Lottie?

Help me.

~No.

Her anger flared hot and pure, making her grab at Dragon, as she had reached for the lines of the gates. And caught it. Shock at the feel of it. Like laying her hand on the casing of a machine spinning at incredible speed, the vibrations from it sending a burning feeling into her skin. She felt Dragon's own surprise, its outrage at its vulnerability. And behind it, she saw its desire.

Arkwright. You want Arkwright, not Steals. To take you back home.

~You see me. How can you see me?

The petulance in its voice gave Lottie a warm glow. She opened her eyes. "It wants to be with Arkwright," she said. "That's why it's keeping the gate from me."

Arkwright fixed her gaze on Lottie. "No idea what

you're talking about. And while this has been fun, it's way past time we tidied things up." She waved one of her people forward. "Shoot them all except the girl. She comes with me."

Payge turned to Lottie, sadness etched on his face. "Sorry," he said. "You deserve better than this." Then he pushed her out of the window.

19

THE GRAVITY
OF THE SITUATION

His hand thumped into her sternum. Falling backwards, reaching out to grab at something, at anything, she lost her balance and gravity took her. The awful realisation there was nothing under her but open air. The window, and Payge standing in it, shrinking with terrifying speed.

~Lottie, we do not have very much time left.

Part of her was screaming, the primitive part of her brain, screaming out in terror at her imminent death.

~Lottie, you need to listen to me.

The window was small now. Yet she still tried to reach for it. The last safe haven she had known. Her own scream sounded far away. She felt calm, detached from the flailing, fear-stricken animal that was falling. She remembered a dark time, not long past. The medicine her carers had given her then made her feel exactly like this. Numb. The feeling of feeling nothing at all.

How can you do this? I should have hit the ground by now.

~And you will. Very soon. We both will. I have opened a space inside you. Created a place where we can think faster. But we are still falling.

When I die, you die with me. You wouldn't do this unless there was something you could offer.

~The gates are just one manifestation of the pattern. They can do so much more.

Can it make us fly? Because I can't see any other way it can help.

~Not flying in the strictest sense of the word.

What do you want from me?

~To let me use you.

How?

~I will release the gate. I need you to be the crucible for it. I will use it to free us from our enemies.

How do I know I can trust you? You'll take me back to Arkwright. I'll be her prisoner. Forever.

~Lottie, we will hit the ground in a quarter of a second. Do you want to die?

Wait. Payge said Arkwright had a backer amongst the makers. I'm sure he did.

~Lottie.

Dorchadas said Arkwright was to be left alone. I remember. Maybe Arkwright works for Dorchadas. You said we weren't safe around Dorchadas. Do you want to risk going back to him?

~Arkwright. Dorchadas. I see. Now will you let me in?

Tell me what you are first.

~We do not have time for this.

Then you'd better talk fast.

~I am the one they left behind.

You're one of the elder race?

~The last one.

Why did they leave you?

~They were pitiless in their pursuit of the godhead. Every flaw had to be erased. Every weakness. But someone had to be left behind to carry out the final act. Who else but the last one who was flawed?

They abandoned you?

~They did.

What do I need to do?

~Nothing. Open yourself to me. That is all.

I don't know how.

~Like this.

Dragon swam into her vision and showed her the way, the technique she needed to use. And like a key fitting into a lock, her mind opened to the gate. It built up inside her, spread through her, pinned her in a structure of force.

Awareness came back, the feel of air rushing past her ears, her hair streaming around her face, the window now impossibly distant. Dragon filling her inner vision, a vast wave of scarlet bearing down on her.

What will you do now?

~I will free us from our enemies, from those who would use us.

How?

~I will kill them all.

Everyone up there?

~Everyone on this world, Lottie. I see what you are now. What you really are. It is best not to take any chances. After this world, every world where you have ever been. Now I'm warning you, this might hurt a little.

Dragon reached and manipulated the gate, folding it so it flipped into another pattern. She saw this with the detached part of her mind, even as that detached part fragmented, and she screamed in agony as her body felt skewered and burnt by driving spikes of white-hot metal.

The pain passed as quickly as it came. She was panting for air, not falling, her hair strung across her face, then dropping down to hang normally, as she was lifted into a standing position. She goggled down at her own feet, hanging inches above the ground.

I'm floating.

Around her, lines of light sprang up, curving inwards in glimmering arcs, looping round her, intersecting to form a cage that enclosed her. Then she was moving upwards, propelled through the air, up towards the window.

I'm flying. I'm really flying.

~Yes. Is it not wonderful? This is the least part of what we can do together.

The lines of light thickened and drew together, becoming a flat ring that centred on her body. She felt the ring's growing potential, the gathering of mass she had experienced before. Energy was flowing through her, flowing out of her, Dragon channelling it from the pattern he had made inside her, using her as a conduit, drawing it from some source she could barely see and found she did not want to look at.

339

STEPHEN DG FRAME

Dragon weaving through her mind. So very close to her.

~*The gates, Lottie. They can be made to emit many things. Heat. Light. Radiation of all kinds. You can warm your hands by them. Or burn a world.*

The ring around her had become fat and gravid. Its lethal potential baked off it, like heat from a kiln-fired brick.

~*Think what it would be like to be at the very centre of such an event. Would that not be a fine thing?*

She was level with the open window now, drifting through it, past the spot where Payge had pushed her from. Where Payge still stood. He stepped back, a calculating look in his eyes.

~*Payge. Who nearly killed us. One of our enemies.*

People shuffled back as she alighted in the middle of the room, their expressions ranging from disbelief to awe. The ring was a plump torus, its skin stretched thin. Barely containing the need it held in check. The need to be released.

~*It is time.*

No.

She fought against it. Against Dragon and against the split that appeared in the torus. Energy was leaking from it, making it glow, bringing it into plain sight, a brilliant white halo around her. She tried to hold back the torrent of energy Dragon kept pouring into the ring, but it was like trying to hold back a waterfall with her bare hands. She fought harder against the flow and despaired at how little difference she had made.

340

Why are you doing this?

~To save you. What you are doing is remarkable.

The people in the room were shuffling away from her, driven back by the heat and the light. Only Payge remained close, holding his hands up to shield his eyes. She saw Arkwright raise a handgun and fire at her. Yellow pops of light showed where the bullets vaporised as they crossed the halo around her.

Dragon twisted all around her, enclosing her mind in its scarlet folds. This close to it, intimately close, she could feel the grain of its thoughts rubbing against her own, the prickle of its madness, the heat of its fury. She could see how old and tired it was, how broken and mended and re-broken from all the long years of its imprisonment.

~Look at what you have done. Look at what you are. I could never have done so much on my own.

It showed her. The vast potential now locked in the torus, teetering on the edge of release. A burst of radiation that would spread around this world. Killing everything.

~Dragon. A good name for us. It is time to breathe fire.

Payge was walking towards her, walking into the light, walking into the fire. She wanted to call to him, to tell him not to, that he would die. She shook her head at him in silent negation. He went on walking, hunched over, as if against a driving wind. Now he turned to Raven, urging her forward. Pointing to Steals, calling to Jackdaw. "Bring him." She saw realisation dawning on Arkwright's face, saw her take a hesitant step forward.

I won't let them die.

~You can't stop it.

She could feel how tired it was. Spent from its exertions. Weak. Vulnerable. But she had no strength left herself. Every scrap of effort she could muster was holding back the lethal energy in the torus. And it was slipping from her grasp.

Don't be a victim. Payge told me that. Feels like a lifetime ago.

Payge. Who was still walking towards her. Towards his death. Along with the only people in the room she cared about.

There's always another way. The gate is out here. It needs to be inside.

The trick Dragon had done to fold the gate inside her. The technique. She could see it. It lay in her mind, along with all the other knowledge from the elder world.

Dragon's too weak to shield it from me. It's over-reached itself. It's made a mistake.

She thought to look, to find something in all that knowledge she could use.

No time. Use the weapon to hand.

She began to fold the ring in on itself. It took no effort. The pattern changed, self-replicating her first fold, squeezing the energy inside it, releasing blinding white light.

~What have you done?

She didn't answer. Her focus was on the pattern, following it, fixing it where the pressure of the energy contained within threatened to rupture it. The ring shrank and shrank, closing in on her. She could feel a matching pressure in her skull; blood was dripping from her nose. Sounds became muffled and distorted. Her sinuses ached, then hurt, then spiked with pain. She squeezed her eyes shut, tears leaking from the corners. Dragon batted at her mind in helpless rage.

The ring grew smaller and smaller still, the pattern endlessly folding in on itself, beyond her ability to stop it. Mad thoughts ran in her head, of endless lines of marching brooms with arms and hands made of sticks and twigs, carrying buckets of water. Blood cascaded down her lips and chin. The world seemed very far away. The ring became a speck of light lodged inside her. Payge was by her side, holding her up. Her arms and legs felt like they were floating away from her.

The speck of light shivered and wobbled.

It's not happy. Not happy at all. I know how it feels.

Lottie looked down at herself. Someone had poured a pint of red ink down her front. It dripped from the hem of her jerkin on to her feet.

That stain's never coming out.

The speck of light swelled within her, pulsed once, threw off a corona of light and shrank to nothing.

Here it comes. So tired. Need to do something. Lottie needs to do something.

Raven was holding on to her. Speaking to her. She couldn't hear. She tried to smile back at her friend to tell her she was fine. Her lips twitched up, showing teeth sheened with blood. She saw Raven flinch.

Lottie needs to do something, Raven. Payge, Jackdaw, Mr Steals. Lottie needs to…

The corona of light was racing upwards from her core, accelerating outwards.

Something gave out, you see. Couldn't hold it all in. And now it's coming to gobble us all up. Need to tell you…

༄

"What's she trying to say?" Steals said.

Payge shook his question away and leant in closer to Lottie. Jackdaw moved up beside his sister. All of them huddled around her.

Arkwright watched for a moment, then waved to one of her men to pass over his assault rifle. She snatched it from his hand and lifted it, aiming it at the group around Lottie, selected full automatic fire.

"Tell Jackdaw," Lottie whispered. Her tongue was sticky with her own blood.

"I'm here," he said, taking her hand.

"Tell him there really are dragons."

The light inside her grew and grew, gathering a terrible momentum as it flew outwards. She tried to hold it tight, tried so desperately to bind its searing energy within herself. It burst through her and still she held it, felt its burning touch as it blew through her skin and travelled onwards, towards her companions, towards those who hunted her, towards the world of innocents outside the walls that surrounded her.

It became heat and fire as it roared away from her, the bodies in its path igniting like oil-soaked kindling. Growing into a wavefront that filled the room, passing through walls, cracking brickwork, charring wood, roasting flesh, it carried on into the town beyond.

20

THURSDAY'S CHILD

"How many?" Lottie asked.

Payge paused from wiping her face with a cloth. Dunking the cloth in a bowl of water, he wrung it out. The water that ran from it was tainted red. "Hold still," he said. Gently, he wiped around her nose and mouth.

"How many?"

"Knowing won't do you any good."

"How many?" She bobbed her head away, trying to avoid the cloth.

Payge sat back on his heels and dropped the cloth into the bowl. "I don't know. Arkwright. All her people. All Steals's people."

"And in the town?" Lottie shifted, sitting up straighter against the wall at her back.

Payge shook his head. "We haven't found anyone alive yet."

345

Lottie felt she should cry but there was nothing left inside her to cry with. "How many lived here, do you think?"

Payge followed her gaze, past the ruined gates of Steals's compound to the homes beyond, where thick smoke rose from fires and where no living thing moved.

Payge drew a breath. "Some thousands, perhaps."

"I tried, Payge. I really tried."

"I know." He picked up the cloth, looked at it, then set it down again. Sitting down beside her, he clasped her hand in his. "You saved us."

"I held it back as long as I could. Once it was outside of me there was no way. I saw it hit you. You, Raven, Jackdaw, Steals. You were all close to me. Those other people… Payge, they just burnt. They caught fire and burnt."

His voice was harsh. "Don't do this to yourself. It was not your fault."

"What about Dirna? She didn't deserve—" Lottie's hand shot to her mouth. "Payge. Your people. They were all in there, weren't they?"

He sighed. "Some were. I don't know how many."

A hollow sadness filled her. Still no tears. She thought perhaps they had all been wrung out of her. They sat in silence for a while before Payge spoke again.

"This thing inside you, Dragon, you called it, is it still there?"

Lottie nodded her head. "I can feel it. It's hiding itself. It's weak right now." She licked at her lips.

"Go on," Payge said.

"The gate inside me as well. I thought it had gone. It hasn't. It's growing again. It's tiny but it's there. Dragon…"

"Say what's on your mind, Lottie."

"Dragon is feeding on it. I'm sure." She swallowed on a dry throat. "It's feeding on whatever the gate is giving off. And I'm scared. Scared of what's in my own body. Scared of what I might become. Scared that what the gate is giving off might be killing me. Scared Dragon might come back and this time it'll be stronger than I am." Her fingers knotted themselves together in her lap. "It bound me. Held me against my will. Made me act out its will. And I think it's still doing it. I can't reach the gate inside me, can't call up any of the knowledge from the elder world. What might it do when it's strong again?"

Payge shook his head. "I don't know but I'd guess nothing good. Like Steals says, we need to get you back to where it came from. The elder world. See if we can find a way of getting it out of you."

"I was right to save him, wasn't I? I know what you think of him, but it was the right thing to do, wasn't it?"

"It was your decision. You don't need me to tell you it was right or wrong." He scuffed his boot on the ground, driving up a ridge of dirt in front of it. "But if you do need me to tell you, then yes, it was the right decision. If we need him to help you, definitely the right decision."

Smoke drifted through the gate, chased on a breeze that carried with it the crackle of burning wood.

"How will we get back to the elder world with Steals's place a wreck?" Lottie said.

"Just another thing we don't know yet. Maybe we can dig our way into his gate." Payge stared off at nothing, worrying away at his fingernails.

Lottie glanced at him. "There's something you're not telling me, isn't there?"

"Yes."

"So tell me."

"Maybe now isn't the time."

She cuffed him on the shoulder. "You pushed me out a window, mister. Don't think I haven't forgotten about that. You owe me."

"It worked out, didn't it? Pushing you out the window."

"You couldn't have known at the time."

"I had an idea."

"How could you possibly have had an idea?"

He gave her a wan smile. "I spent a lot of time in a bookshop. What else was I going to do but read and study?"

"Fibber."

She grabbed his sleeve and gave him a shake. His smile grew brighter, then faded away. "I'd rather have seen you dead than as Arkwright's pet. It was a selfish thing for me to do. Speaking as someone who's lived a life of being owned and bound by others."

She shifted sideways towards him until she could rest her head on his shoulder, and he had put his arm around her. "I forgive you. Just don't go doing it again, you hear?"

"I hear."

"Now answer the question."

"Dorchadas."

"What about him?"

"He's interested in what Steals has done. He'll want to know what happened here. I suspect he was Arkwright's patron. Or at least, was supporting her."

"I thought so too."

"You did?"

"Yeah." She shifted her head to a more comfortable position. "I used it against Dragon."

"Good for you. That was a smart move."

"I nearly killed you all. You're saying Dorchadas will come after me?"

"That's what I'm saying."

"Payge, wherever we go next, will you come with me?"

He drew a breath before answering. "If you'll have me. I think my days of being a bookkeeper are behind me now."

"We're still in a lot of trouble, aren't we?"

"Yes, Lottie, we are."

Jackdaw wandered up and threw a pile of gear at their feet. "This is as much as I could find. Raven's off to fill the water bottles."

Payge looked up at him, shielding his eyes against the sun. "Where's Steals?"

"Wandering around his yard like a lost soul, looking for a way in. Doubt he'll find one. The whole place looks about ready to collapse."

Raven walked up and set five water bottles on top of the pile of gear before squatting down beside Lottie. "How are you feeling?"

"A bit washed out but okay."

"Think you can walk?"

"Sure."

Raven held out a hand for her and Payge gave her a boost up. On her feet, she swayed a little. Hands reached to steady her. "I'm fine." She let a big breath out. "Really, I'm fine."

"Jackdaw," Payge said. "Go find Steals. Bring him here. Drag him if you need to."

"He's coming with us?" Raven's voice was cautious.

"Lottie thinks he's the only one who can help her. I'm inclined to agree."

"Seems fair enough."

Lottie watched as they split the pile of guns, knives, bottles and backpacks between them. "Where are we going now?" she asked.

"To my home," Raven said. "We can rest up there a while, figure out what to do next. Any objections to that?"

"There's some hostile territory to get through on the way," Jackdaw said.

"Payge?" Raven said.

Payge looked at Lottie.

Lottie nodded. "That's where we go. Where is it, anyway? And how do we get there?"

THE END